LETHAL CHAOS

I face the stuff of raw nightmare:

Nightmare—The gray sky had developed a crack. On the far horizon a metal city sprang up from nowhere. Out of the darkness came rows of mechs carrying cages. Cages with humans in them . . . .

Nightmare—Slimy octopus things were squirming through hatches, slithering across the ground. They were moving fast—and coming toward us . . . .

Nightmare—I felt a rush of wind, heard a popping sound. Something loomed before me; it looked familiar. **It was me** . . . .

———

And a disembodied voice shouted through the portholes: THIS TOO IS TEMPORARY. ALREADY I CAN FEEL THE FIRST TREMORS OF CHANGE. SOON I SHALL, NO DOUBT, APPEAR SOMEWHERE. BE PATIENT. I AM WORTH WAITING FOR.

"Electric—staccato—exciting: reading Haiblum is like hitchhiking on a runaway meteor!"
—Lin Carter

The Latest in Science Fiction from
Dell Books

INTERWORLD

ISIDORE HAIBLUM

A DELL BOOK

Published by
Dell Publishing Co., Inc.
1 Dag Hammarskjold Plaza
New York, New York 10017

A portion of this work
first appeared in *Swank* Magazine.

Dell ® TM 681510, Dell Publishing Co., Inc.

ISBN: 0-440-12285-6

Printed in the United States of America

First printing—April 1977

PART ONE
HAPPY CITY

CHAPTER ONE

HELP! DISORIENTATION HAS SET IN. I MUST GET MY BEARINGS. HERE THERE IS NOTHING. I TURN OFF ALL MY SENSES. NOW I AM NOTHING TOO. I WAIT.

I'd been driving close to an hour when my headlights caught the sign: Cozy Rest Home. Swinging left, I followed the crooked arrow onto a narrow, twisting gravel road.

All hell was busy pelting the car. Trees on either side of the roadway strained against their roots as if trying to take off for friendlier climes; wind wailed and the rain lashed out like some mad, lost thing caught in a trap. A hateful scene if ever there was one.

I rounded a bend, came to a clearing. The gravel underneath turned to soft, soupy mud. I peered into the darkness like a drunk hunting a light switch. Lightning crackled and flared; in the sudden glare, I saw an old, weather-beaten mansion—a four-story job of wood and shingles, looking as chummy as the corner mortuary. The sight was gone in a roar of thunder.

Parking my heap in a large, disorderly puddle, I got out, started for the house. A rowboat would've helped plenty.

Three stone steps took me up to the front door. I banged on it. Nothing happened.

I did some more pounding. There should've been a bell somewhere, only I couldn't find it. All this racket was murder on the knuckles, but if I stayed out here much longer I'd need a life belt.

Sounds finally from inside. Bolts were being undone. *Bolts? In a rest home?*

The door slid open.

A startled-faced lady—somewhere in her mid-thirties—stood there, dressed in a nurse's starched white uniform; she stared at me as if one of the trees had hobbled over to ask for shelter. I took that for an invite—the only one I was apt to get—and brushed past her into the house. "Yes?" she asked coldly. Her lips, I saw, were bright with lipstick, arched eyebrows were penciled in. She looked as trim and spiffy as a dimestore dummy.

"I'd like to see Joe Rankin," I told her. "Tom Dunjer's the name; I'm his brother-in-law." I lowered my voice, "It's a family matter."

"Wait here," the nurse told me and hurried away.

I was in a large hallway. Lumpy yellow wallpaper crawled up the walls, a maroon carpet stretched itself along the floor. Any second I expected the black window drapes to slither over and fang me. At the hall's end, stairs—tame and ordinary by comparison—led to the second floor. The only sound was the rain outside.

A door squeaked down hall; the nurse was back, a large, stout, brown-jacketed party in tow. Cocking a bushy eyebrow my way, he waddled over with outstretched hand like a huge seal. Head bald, shiny. Lips, large and pouting. Three chins danced as he walked. He wore the perfect smile of a man whose teeth came from the dimestore.

"My name, sir," he said, "is Dr. Spelville."

"Dunjer," I told him.

The sweetheart in nurse's uniform shot us both a look of dark disapproval and went away. Spelville pumped my hand as though trying to dredge up water from a very deep well, led me into his office, folded himself into a wide chair behind a cluttered mahogany desk and gave me a bright smile. "A visitor on a night such as this—a delightful surprise, I assure you. How may I be of service?"

I told him. I explained I wanted a brief chat with my in-law, who was—reportedly—taking the cure here. It seemed a simple matter.

"So—" Spelville sighed, as if he'd just learned I'd towed a small mountain to his doorstep and expected him to climb it. "I fear I can be of little help," he sighed again. "Your brother-in-law is gone."

"Gone?" I said. "Where to?"

The doctor shrugged, shook his head, pulled on an earlobe with a fat thumb and forefinger. He didn't get up and tango, but that was probably next on the agenda. "The things that happen, sir—you have no idea. Mr. Rankin packed his bag and departed this afternoon. I believe a car picked him up at our door. A sick man, sir." The doctor wiggled a finger at me. "A very sick man. Certainly in need of rest. High-strung, nervous—" his voice became confidential, "possibly deranged. But what could I do? What indeed? Mr. Rankin was a free agent, so to speak." The doctor spread his palms as if he were going to sing a very long and complicated aria. "Perhaps you would like to see his room?"

It was my turn to shrug.

"Splendid," Spelville said. He pressed a button on his desk. A door to my left opened soundlessly. An attendant or something came shuffling through. He was a short, broad gent with stooped shoulders, long, dangling arms and a face that looked like a rock pile. I'd figured this day couldn't get much worse, but I was wrong.

"Waldorf," Dr. Spelville said, "take this gentleman to the room Mr. Rankin used to occupy." Waldorf nodded at me, led the way. I followed him down a series of white-walled deserted corridors, smelling disinfectant, floor wax, the odors of damp wood. We took a lot of turns, came to an elevator, got in and rode up to the second floor. Waldorf hadn't said a word yet. Maybe he didn't know how.

Rankin's room, when I finally got there, was as empty as a railbird's wallet.

We went back the way we'd come, a bland, uneventful trip. What I'd learned couldn't exactly be called a windfall. The doctor hadn't moved an inch from behind his desk, as if he'd become fixed in an invisible block of ice during my short jaunt. The ice thawed. "Satisfied, Mr. Dunjer?" I wagged my head. Not quite the word I'd've chosen, but any one would do now. We traded our goodbyes solemnly. The fat man remained seated.

The sourpuss nurse let me back into the rain.

I waded to the car, climbed in, started the motor, splashed through a number of puddles, hit a bend in the gravel road and pulled over. Getting a flash and gun from the glove compartment, I put up my coat collar, slid into the wet. In an instant the car was swallowed by the dark. I was running back through the rain toward the Cozy Rest Home. If Rankin was holed-up in that place, I aimed to flush him out. Twenty years of sleuthing should've stood me in good stead for this kind of workout. But three years as head of Security Plus had got me out of practice. I hoped I still remembered what to do.

I HAVE NO NAME. AS YET I AM MERELY A VOICE. THERE ARE WORLDS AND WORLDS. NOTHING IS AS IT SEEMS. BE VIGILANT. WATCH FOR SUBTLE SHIFTS, GRADATIONS. EVEN MIRROR IMAGES MUST ULTIMATELY DIVERGE. THIS IS, OF COURSE, NOTHING MORE THAN A HINT, AN IDLE DIGRESSION, BUT ONE WHICH HELPS TO PASS THE TIME. YET, WHERE I AM THERE IS NO TIME—ONLY EMPTINESS. THIS TOO IS TEMPORARY. ALREADY I CAN FEEL THE FIRST TREMORS OF CHANGE. SOON I SHALL, NO DOUBT, APPEAR SOMEWHERE. BE PATIENT. I AM WORTH WAITING FOR.

CHAPTER TWO

The house was dark and still. No light escaped from the shuttered windows. It was an old, ugly mansion and it reeked of decay.

This time I circled the joint, and came up behind it, slipping in the mud. Moss grew up the walls, along with a couple of dozen parasites I couldn't name. A great spot for a weed garden, if the weeds could stand it.

I flicked the beam of my flash up the back wall. No windows on the first floor—they'd been cemented over; those on the second floor were shuttered tight. I'd've needed a ladder to get up there anyway, or a pair of wings. No other door that I could see. A swell set-up—you couldn't get in or out without using the front entrance. That wouldn't do at all. I tried the sides of the building. Not a crack. Retracing my steps, I kept the light pinned to the ground. About halfway around the joint I found it: the coal chute.

I went down on hands and knees. The two sides of the chute were padlocked tight. My gun was out. I waited for the lightning. It came a long moment later. Thunder followed it, went off around my head like a Tri-D aspirin commercial. Before the sound had faded, I'd blasted off the lock, was sliding into the basement.

The stone cellar was as dank and dismal as a leaking bathtub. I shined my feeble light against walls covered with cobwebs, dirt and grime. Too bad I wasn't hunting spiders; I could've had my pick.

Finding steps, I started up in a hurry. Inching the door open on top, I peered out. Another door faced me, the one I'd come through earlier that night. The ground floor was lit up like the old Happy City fun-house, but not a soul in sight having fun. I wasn't about to complain. I left my hiding place. No one stopped me. The corridor was all mine. I listened for voices. There weren't any. The rest home had taken a mickey; the sour-faced nurse had done in the doctor and orderly; they'd all murdered each other. It was fine with me; I had my own problems.

The stairs leading to the second floor were on the right. I took 'em two at a time. Opening the door at the top, I stepped through into darkness.

I didn't want to bother anyone with a lot of light. Getting my flash out, I started turning doorknobs softly.

Five minutes of that and I'd tiptoed through a dozen empty rooms, all like the one I'd seen earlier, and come up with precisely nothing. This floor was as bare as a nudie in a girly show, but not half as entertaining. That left the third and fourth stories. Having gotten this far, I decided to go the whole hog. Returning to my stairway, I climbed to the next landing. Another door greeted me. I stopped, opened it slowly.

The beam of my light criss-crossed the walls as I started down the corridor. I felt the sound rather than heard it. I threw myself to the side.

Something went smack against my right shoulder. An instant ago my head would've been there. I dropped the flash and the light died.

Movement in the dark. I went down on the floor as something swished past my right ear.

I kicked out, was answered by a deep grunt. I pushed myself in that direction, grabbed feet, got kicked in the ribs for my trouble.

I yanked at the feet, put my weight behind the effort. The feet toppled over. A body came with them, cursing and snarling. A quiet chat between opposing factions didn't seem called for. I drove my fist into something—a face. I did it again. The face didn't like that. Hands, large and powerful, caught me by the neck, began squeezing me like a lemon. The dark seemed to light up with all kinds of winking and dancing specks like a circus of fireflies. I took hold of what I hoped were two little fingers and began to twist them. The hands—suddenly—let go. I could breathe again. I put my foot into a stomach and felt it fall away from me. I rolled over out of harm's way and fumbled for my gun. I was up on one knee, like an aspiring torch singer, when I heard it: a high-pitched scream—a woman's voice—somewhere in this very hallway.

The lights snapped on.

Waldorf, the orderly, stood by the light switch, his face blood-smeared from our tussle. He wasn't looking my way. I couldn't blame him.

The biggest and ugliest thing I ever saw was standing there. He was the stuff of raw nightmare, what strait jackets and padded cells were all about. He must've been over seven feet tall, all muscle and bone. I blinked my eyes, but he didn't go away. They rarely do.

In his arms, dangling like a toy, he held what was left of the hard-case nurse. She'd stopped screaming. Her neck projected at a funny angle as she hung there like a torn rag doll. He'd done it to her with his hands.

Waldorf let out a moan, made for the creature. What he should've done was head for the nearest exit. The orderly was a powerful man, but next to this thing he was a midget. The monster let go of the nurse with one hand and took hold of Waldorf's arm with the other. I heard the arm snap. My stomach started to crawl up my windpipe.

Waldorf screamed—once.

The thing jerked him up lightly and threw him against the wall as though playing with a rubber ball. It caught him easily on the rebound. It lifted Waldorf and held him high over its head, nearly touching the ceiling. Then it brought his body down on one raised knee. The sound was like the cracking of a chicken bone. Waldorf's days were done. It tossed him aside like an empty cigarette pack and turned its attention to me. Just what I needed!

I was sitting with one knee on the floor, as though I'd been nailed to it and my mouth hung open like the gateway to a large, useless tunnel. I was damp with sweat, as if the rain had especially sought me out here in the inner confines of the rest home. I hadn't moved a muscle since the light had gone on. I was paralyzed.

The thing looked at me dully. It looked at me as though I was an annoying fly that perplexed it, an insect it wasn't exactly sure how to swat. Something resembling a light appeared in its eyes.

Its large jaws began to work. The thing could speak. Its lips moved. It said two words: "Lugo fix."

I had no doubt what it intended to fix.

It came straight at me.

My hands were shaking so I could hardly hold the gun. I sent five slugs into the thing's belly, squeezing the trigger slowly each time. I held the gun with both hands. The thing kept coming, hands at its sides, fingers working spasmodically, eyes fixed on me, its face expressionless. It didn't slacken its pace. It didn't even blink.

I started to laugh. I was shaking and laughing. You couldn't kill it. Bullets couldn't stop it. Bombs and cannons would be mere irritants. I couldn't see straight because the sweat was dripping into my eyes. Both hands were palsied. The gun was so heavy I could hardly raise the muzzle.

The thing was almost on me. I could hear its breathing, see it needed a shave.

I raised the gun one last time and fired.

A large round hole appeared where its left eye had been.

It gazed at me reproachfully with its one remaining eye. It stood there looking down at me as though carefully considering what its next move ought to be.

Then it toppled over.

I barely got out of the way in time.

It lay there, a wide puddle of blood beginning to

spread under it, a sight that didn't darken my mood at all.

Slowly I got up on feet that felt like rubber stilts and started walking. After what seemed a long time, I reached the head of the stairs. I was about to go down them and hopefully far, far away when something caught the corner of my eye. The door to one of the rooms was half ajar. A foot and ankle stuck out into the hallway.

I stumbled over for a look-see.

Sprawled on the floor was a small skinny bird in a blue and white striped shirt and black trousers. I knew he was somewhere in his mid-forties. He had sandy hair and still wore a pair of rimless eyeglasses. They'd do him no good. Part of his head had been bashed in like a very soft boiled potato. I'd found Joe Rankin and this time he was really gone.

REMEMBER THIS: FIRST APPEARANCES MAY BE TOTALLY DECEPTIVE. ANALOGUES ABOUND. ANACHRONISMS ARE RAMPANT. YET FROM AN ALTERNATE VIEWPOINT, ALL IS PRECISELY AS IT SHOULD BE. FORTUNATELY, HERE WHERE I AM, THERE ARE NO WORLDS AND I MAY SAFELY IGNORE SUCH CONTINGENCIES. THE QUESTION IS: FOR HOW LONG? I ADJUST MY SENSES TO MEDIUM ALERTNESS. NOTHINGNESS, I SEE, STILL PREVAILS.

CHAPTER THREE

I leaned against a wall and slid down to the floor, wondering which way to turn. The house was still again. Even the downpour outside had become muted, as if in reverence for the dead. The dead, namely Joe, was lying there, his face half-turned to the wall, offering neither advice nor company. Just as well; another shock might've done me in.

I glanced over the remains with a calm, professional eye—the first calm thing I'd managed since sighting Lugo. Aside from the crease in his bonnet, Joe seemed mostly intact. No dangling arms or chewed-off legs disfigured his cadaver. That scratched Lugo, all right; here was work of a subtler kind.

But whose and—in heaven's name—*why,* eh?

Joe Rankin had been a worthless deadbeat all his life, an idler from the word go; he hardly rated this much attention. A lot of blood under him, I saw; he'd probably bought it here on the spot. I turned him over. A round, red hole punctured his back; the work of a projectile weapon, not a laser. Both were a dime a dozen in town.

I combed through his pockets:

Some keys. A wallet. A few credit cards. Six bucks in folding money. I kept the keys, put back the other stuff.

Getting to my feet, I left Joe with no reluctance at all, and slowly made my way downstairs.

Spelville wasn't in his office; his desk held no papers now, his closet no clothing. Walking through a number of empty rooms gave me only exercise. With the exception of a small potted palm I seemed to be the only living thing left in the joint. The palm wouldn't mind if I went away. I did so in a hurry.

Rain hammered the windshield like an apprentice carpenter showing off his new skills. I sat hunched over the wheel, woozy and bleary-eyed. I had plenty to think about, none of it nice.

If I called the constables, filled them in on the night's doings, there'd be hours of endless red tape and lots of trouble. As chief of Security Plus, the last thing I needed was lots of trouble. I wasn't too keen on endless red tape either. But if I failed to report this matter and they tied me to it, things'd be worse. Worse was something I could do without.

One thing at least seemed more or less clear, if not perfectly: in all this I was merely a bit player, a hapless walk-on who'd accidentally stumbled over someone else's rotten mess. . . . Or was I?

The not perfectly part worried me.

Security Plus had made lots of enemies through the years. Right now I was its all-too-visible factotum. Maybe somebody didn't like me? Maybe all this was somehow staged for my benefit?

All at once, what I needed most in life was a quiet chat with a friendly office appliance. I was lucky. At this hour I'd have the place to myself. I swung the car in that direction, wondering how I'd suddenly become lucky.

Happy City twinkled and tumbled around me in a wash of rain. Multilevel traffic and pedestrian strips curved and spiraled between looming glass structures. Neon posters flashed: Support Your Constables, You Need Them; Secure Your Home With an Auto-Mech Watchman; Buy at Eat-Sharp, Gain an Extra Vote on Poll Day; Play Safe, Insure Your Spouse Against Debts at We-Care.

There it was, I thought bitterly. My sister Linda

hadn't insured her spouse—Joe Rankin—and now she'd have to pay through the nose. Of course, the premiums would've cost more than the debts. But then what could you expect in Happy City . . . ? Still, it was a darn sight better than some of those other city-states. In some of those other city-states, you didn't hardly stand a chance at all.

Strangleberg, Fearsville, Deep-Hate Junction, now those were *really* tough towns, made Happy City look like a picnic by comparison. Most citizens used to work for the old Federal Government—long ago—and when it went broke *everyone* went broke. Very demoralizing. Caused a lot of bad feeling, of course. Bad Feeling village was, in fact, founded that very year. Served as a model for later city-states. Put up a lot of no-trespassing signs, along with walls, moats, drawbridges. The truth is, Loveberg, Smilesville and Friendship Haven aren't much better. But then what is?

The mech doorman glanced at my pass, let me into the darkened building. I took the speed lift to my floor, used a key on the office door and went down a dark hallway to my private domain. Turning on the desk lamp, I hung my wet coat on a peg, sat down, reached for the recorder and jabbed playback.

The voice was flat, nasal, like some pug's who'd taken one too many in the beezer, and spoke in a whisper.

"Dunjer?"

"Uh-huh," my voice had told the phone. Over the line I could hear some woman warbling a torch song, a tiny band playing along. Dishes rattled. Voices murmured.

"You lookin' for Joe Rankin?" the whisper asked above the racket.

Rankin? I'd sat there gripping the phone as if it might crawl away. I hadn't even told my lawyer about Rankin. "Who is this?"

"Never mind, chum, just listen. Rankin's stashed hisself at the Cozy Rest Home. That's at the edge of town. It's in the directory, see? Maybe he got tired, right? Only how long he stays tired is somethin' else. You get me?"

I'd got him. The line went click and I was alone again. Just great, I'd thought. The Cozy Rest Home, of all places. And on a night like this. . . .

But why the Cozy Rest Home?

It was still a good question.

I thumbed stop, then rewind, got up, plugged the recorder into the wall socket which fed into the computer system, and was about to ask for a trace on the voice, its location, the Cozy Rest Home, Dr. Spelville, Lugo and anything else I could dredge up, when the alarm board went "Geek!"

Geek?

What kind of alarm was *that?* I'd never heard *geek* before.

My hand rose automatically, tightened around a switch, activated the board's response system. I said, "Something's wrong?"

The board said nothing.

A small light had gone on over numeral 487, was glowing a lackluster, meaningless gray.

I knew the number by heart, one of Security Plus's most important charges: the safety vault in the World's Emporium.

Impregnable, of course.

So why the gray light and nitwit syllable?

Stepping over to my ninety-first-floor window, I looked down. Diagonally across and below me the outer shell of the Emporium shone a dim, milky blue in the darkness and rain.

Nothing doing out there. And hardly news. Trouble outside would've meant gongs, bells, whistles and sirens. Trouble like that wouldn't just come sneaking up on a man. The vault itself—my headache—was inside the Emporium structure, deep in the subbasement, encased in a couple tons of unyielding alloy. Good old unyielding alloy had a way of taking care of itself. At least, that's what the manufacturers had claimed.

Returning to my desk, I used the communo, punched out the necessary co-ords. Now we'd see a thing or two. Or would we?

"XX21?" I said, addressing the mech guard on duty.

Dull static sounded back in my ear. XX21, apparently, wasn't talking either. Only for a mech that was impossible. Mechs responded on cue or what good were they? No good at all, a small voice seemed to whisper in my ear, while another one bawled:

MALFUNCTION!

I flipped on the viewer fast. It showed me the vault area from a number of angles. XX21 was nowhere in sight, but everything else was in its proper place as neat and orderly as a pickled fetus.

I sat back in my swivel chair, gave a swivel, and let out a sigh, thankful for the dumb providence that'd brought me back here. Ordinary malfunctions were bad enough, but one in the general vicinity of the safety vault was pure murder. If the news ever leaked out, stockholders, board of directors and customers would be very irate, not to mention boiling with rage. They'd know just who to blame too. *Me, that's who.* There was no one else.

I looked up at the alarm board. "Go on," I said, "say it again."

The board remained silent.

"Not feeling well?" I asked.

"I am in fine fettle," the board replied.

"You remember saying 'geek,' of course?"

"That word is not known to me."

"Uh-huh. And why is your light gray?"

"I wouldn't know, sir."

"Neither would I, 1A. And if they ever want to feed you to the slag heap, they can certainly count on me."

"Thank you, sir," the board said gravely.

There was nothing left to do, it looked like, but get

up; I did so, went to the closet, dug out a small, black utility bag—hoping the repairmen's union wouldn't hear of it—took it and myself to the interoffice wall chute, punched out the co-ords, stepped in and shot down ninety-three levels to the heart of the World's Emporium.

Trouble, here I come.

LISTEN. JUST AS NO PAIR OF TREES GROW ALIKE, SO NEITHER DO THE WORLDS ON ANY GIVEN TIME TRACK. NATURALLY, THERE WILL BE BROAD SIMILARITIES. BUT MANY SPECIFICS ARE SURE TO BE UTTERLY DIVERSE. THIS NEED NOT, NECESSARILY, LEAD TO CONFUSION. ALTHOUGH IT CERTAINLY CAN.

CHAPTER FOUR

The chute let me off in the subbasement, a longish haul from my destination, but as close as I could get by conveyance. Interoffice chutes were open to too much chance traffic; it wouldn't do for just anyone to come popping in to the vault. Not before our mechs could size 'em up. These mechs each had an eagle eye and cost only a third as much as humans. Up until now that'd seemed like a real bargain.

I started hiking. My footsteps making small, discouraged sounds on the polished floor; the utility bag— usually restricted to union personnel—jangling accusingly by my side. The overhead lights kept reminding me of the inquisition sure to follow if the public ever got wind of an alarm failure. You couldn't blame 'em. They paid through the nose for the safety vault; they expected safety, maybe even deserved it.

When I came to the side door marked Keep Out This Means You, I hurried through. Here sights had turned to narrow corridors, bare thrifty floors. The place had been redecorated only last year, in the spring of 1978. Someone had made a pretty penny on this section, I figured, stepping around an unpainted wooden column that looked like it held up the ceiling. I didn't bump it. Idly I wondered if they'd jailed the contractor. Probably not. The constables—who passed for law in these parts—were no whizzes. I wished 'em well. A little more on the ball and private outfits like mine would've folded long ago. I turned a corner.

A wide metal door blocked my way. This was getting worse by the minute. The secondary defense system, it seemed, had sealed off the vault area.

Quickly I got the master control cube out of my utility bag. When standard tuning got me nowhere, I switched to override. The door slid up into the ceiling.

XX20—twin of XX21—was seated on the floor facing me. Behind the mech a gleaming metal corridor stretched into the distance.

"What're you doing?" I asked in some wonder.

"Sitting down. A breather, that's all. Rest and recreation," the mech tittered. "Soon I shall sing a ditty perhaps. Surely you do not begrudge me that? A mechanical must get off his feet sometimes."

"Why?"

"Because," the mech hesitated, "his feet . . . hurt?"

I asked, "You wouldn't mind telling me what's going on, would you?"

"We mechanicals," the mech explained, "are not as dumb as some humans expect. Then again, we're not all that bright either."

I turned him off.

Just great; the malfunction was all over the joint.

I reached a quick decision: this was no time to start fooling around with old XX20. The important thing now was to find out the extent of the damage, see how far it'd spread. Then maybe I could sic the utility bag on the whole mess at Computer-Central. Doctoring a loopy mech wasn't in my line. By now I was beginning to wonder what was.

I started my trek again. Metal gleamed on all sides of me: up, down and sideways. Four Dunjer reflections kept pace. I was glad of the company. There was something about the tall, friendly figures that I admired. Their high foreheads, dark piercing eyes, aquiline noses, neatly combed and parted black hair. They certainly inspired confidence. Hardly the type of faces you'd expect to find smeared across the *Daily Tattler*, staring out at the scandal-crazed denizens of Happy City under the caption: Security Ace Trumped. Or were they?

Coming to the large, double-domed, engraved bronzed doors I had another surprise.

Vaults climbed the walls on the other side of those doors; countless traders who peddled their wares topside at the Emporium stored their valuables here. The safety vault—the inner sanctum of strongholds—was at the far end. The bronzed doors, one of ten pairs leading into the area, were ornamental and didn't even lock.

The pair I faced was locked. How about that?

I ran my eyes over the doors' unbroken surface hunting for a keyhole or something; something new they'd put on and neglected to tell me about. Only "they" were me, and I knew damn well I hadn't ordered any locks for these doors.

Snapping open my utility bag I started taking inventory. I wasn't sure what I was after. Maybe a thermometer to see if I was running a temperature. My hand came to rest on an inspection cube. Not bad. If there was one thing this mess could stand, it was a keen-witted inspection by an impartial third party. And nothing was more impartial than a stupid inspection cube. I got it out and beamed it in the right direction. Two tiny words sprang up on the cube's readout screen: magnetic field.

For all the sense that made, it could've spelled out boiled onions and cabbage. Magnetic fields? There weren't any within miles of the vault. Maybe the inspection cube had gone rotten too?

I was just about ready to start hunting for a crowbar when I remembered the master control cube. It sure couldn't hurt. I fished it out, expertly thumbed the override button. The doors seemed to quiver. That was all. I touched one with a toe. It swung in lazily. I could go through now, having overriden the magnetic field or whatever it was. Twenty years of sleuthing and I had to fall back on a mindless cube. I went in.

A bellowing voice screamed:

"MASTER! MASTER! IT COMES!"

LANGUAGE, ON ANY GIVEN TIME TRACK, PRE-
SENTS NO GREAT PROBLEM. IDIOMS, SLANG AND
COLLOQUIALISMS MIGHT VARY, BUT THE LAN-
GUAGE ITSELF, BASICALLY, WOULD REMAIN THE
SAME. A REAL BOON FOR TOURISTS, IN THEORY.
IN PRACTICE, OF COURSE, THERE ARE NO TOUR-
ISTS.

CHAPTER FIVE

I almost dropped the bag and my pants too.

My eyeballs did headstands over doors, walls and hallways.

No one.

I was as alone as a worm on a fishhook, but not half as comfortable. Not even a rug for anyone to hide under.

But a miniature vocal cord and spotter eye could be planted anywhere.

So much for massive malfunction. What I was facing here made massive malfunction look like a real treat by comparison. Someone, apparently, was in the process of knocking over the safety vault!

Impossible, of course. So why were they doing it, and why was I sweating?

My options were suddenly all shot to hell, reduced to absolute zero. All I could do now was ring in the help, call for the constables.

The siren switch was next to the door. I put up a hand and yanked it.

Dead silence. As though the gizmo's innards had packed up and hitched a ride out of town.

I used the cube on override. For all the good that did me I might have used a jump rope and yo-yo. Someone had done a small but thorough job on the siren.

I stood very still and listened hard, hoping to hear what Master might sound like. And how many of him there were.

Nothing. As if some overzealous charwoman had vacuumed up all sound and corked it in a bottle.

Five metal corridors faced me, led off at different angles. I got my legs moving, went nine paces to my left, fingered part of the wall. The wall, at least, still operating, slid back. I was glad to see it; the opposition hadn't run off with all the tricks.

I removed the laser handgun from its hidden cubicle, felt its comforting weight in my palm. Things were now a little better, better being a very relative term.

I set off down the center corridor at a fast trot, the shortest route to the safety vault. Safety was the last thing I was likely to find there. What I should've done was head back to the office and put in for a quick vacation. One beginning yesterday. Still, if it turned out I was bucking an army or something, I could always go away. Provided they let me.

Along the way facts began turning up like ground glass in a custard pie: mechanicals lined the aisles, lay motionless on the shiny floors. Thumbing my control cube didn't disturb them in the least. They were as inert now as their blood brothers, screws, bolts and thumbtacks.

But XX20 had still been functioning more or less before I'd turned him off. That gave me an idea. I pressed a button, turning him on again via remote. The double-X squad were superior mechs set to handle any and all emergencies. I used a final button on the master control—the red one—under the S-V designation. Whatever double-X mechs were still awake would now walk, stumble or crawl to the safety vault. What they'd do there was anyone's guess. The one I'd spoken to had seemed a bit under the weather. His appearance, though, might surprise Master. I wouldn't mind.

The safety vault was a huge silver sphere. A door in its side that was usually locked let people in and out. Now the door was wide open. Fifty yards of empty space separated me from it. Lying flat on my stomach at corridor's end I took in the vast, domed hall that held the vault and the dozen or so little figures who were very busy looting it. No sign of XX21 or his buddies. Whatever was going to be done here would be done by me—alone.

No one, so far, had even noticed me. With all that Master commotion a while ago, they should've been ready and waiting. Well, if they couldn't take a hint, it was fine with me. I wasn't about to stand up and wave a flag at 'em.

Slowly I raised my laser, took aim at one of the busy little persons and pressed the trigger, just like it said in the training manual. If I killed a few, the rest might go away.

Blue light exploded, congealed around me, swayed and wavered. The beam I'd sent slicing down the hall had burst into fragments like a Roman candle. Colored sparks danced and shimmered in the blue air, lost themselves in clouds of smoke. The training manual had said nothing about this.

The figures were gone. Along with the sphere, hall and corridors.

I was in a darkening whirlpool.

A voice spoke out of the whirlpool, a booming one: "WHO DARES DISTURB MASTER?"

A good question. I could see why Master might want to know. It was Master's job to know, wasn't it? I felt just like any other eight-year-old in grade school. I wanted to please Master. I raised my hand, hoping he would call on me. I noticed the laser and pulled the trigger. Pretty sparks lit up the whirlpool.

"DOWN, INFIDEL!" Master's voice roared.

I wondered vaguely whom he meant. Not me. Master and I were thick as two peas in a pod. Was someone else in here too? I wouldn't like that. I wanted Master all to myself. I held my breath. He'd be sorry now, sorry he hadn't called on me. Yes, I'd hold my breath and, for that matter, I wouldn't eat my spinach either.

A very large, hefty sledge hammer came up out of the darkness and conked me right on the noodle.

TECHNOLOGY FLUCTUATES GREATLY ON ANY GIVEN TIME TRACK. MATTER-TRANSMITTER WORLDS OFTEN RUB SHOULDERS WITH THOSE OF THE HORSE-AND-BUGGY ERA. THIS, ORDINARILY, WOULD CAUSE FEW PROBLEMS. UNLESS, OF COURSE, THERE WERE CROSSOVERS.

CHAPTER SIX

I woke up slowly, sedately, as if I were coming up after a dive into a very deep, polluted lake.

"Come on, boss," a voice said with all the charm of an electric can opener.

"Go away," I mumbled.

Something hard, cold and metallic prodded me ungently in the ribs, something that seemed to be a cross between a shoehorn and a coat hanger. It was very annoying.

A voice said, "Up and at 'em, chief," sounding as cheery as a rusty nail being extracted from a coffin; mine probably.

I asked myself what I wanted most in life. I had no trouble answering that question. I wanted these voices to stop. I had a feeling that if I did what they asked, I'd regret it. I had done nothing at all so far and I was regretting it already.

With a lot of effort I pried open an eyelid. I was lying on a metal floor. Light glanced off the metal, sent stabbing beams into my eyeball. I groaned as cold fingers grasped me by arms and elbows, lifting me to my feet. I opened my mouth to complain. My mouth felt as if it had been stuffed with sawdust.

I opened my other eye. The door of the safety vault was still hanging ajar but the looters were gone. I was surrounded by four of my trusty mechs, XX20 to XX24. A bit late on the scene, but here nonetheless.

"What happened?" I rasped.

Four pairs of metal shoulders shrugged in unison.

Running a shaky hand across my forehead, I said, "You guys don't remember?"

XX21 became spokesman. "Not a thing, skipper." A note of sudden anxiety crept into his voice. "Nothing *bad*'s happened, has it?"

"Heaven forbid," I managed to squeak. "Go inspect the vault." They went, pronto. I remained standing where I was. If I didn't move, maybe it wouldn't hurt. The inspection was short, if not very sweet, and told me next to nothing. The vault was a mess. If something were missing, it didn't catch the eye cell, right off. "You fellas up to taking inventory?" I asked them.

"Certainly."

"Okay," I said, "why don't you."

Back in my office the alarm board greeted me with familiar words, too familiar:

"I hope nothing bad's happened," the alarm board said.

"You don't know either?"

"Know what?"

I flipped on the viewer, saw the safety vault; a flawless silver sphere, its door closed. An inside view was even more impressive. No clumsy mechs traipsed around going over the damage. Why should they? There was no damage. Everything was as neat and immobile as a painted landscape. Photo stills usually are.

"You've been sabotaged," I told the alarm board.

"Are you certain?" it asked. "I've just checked my circuits and they're all 1A. Actually, I feel quite spry."

"Quite spry, eh?"

The communo let out a bleep.

"Well?" I said.

"Hello, skipper," XX21 said. "We have completed inventory."

"And?"

"Everything's accounted for. With one minor exception."

"The billion dollars in gold? The uranium deposits?"

"No, boss."

"*No?*"

"This is a very tiny thing that's missing."

"Don't tell me," I said.

"It's the Linzeteum."

"Linzeteum, eh?"

"That's it, chief."

"They took some, eh?"

"They took it all."

"All, eh?"

"Right, skipper, down to the last droplet."

"No money. No jewels. No uranium. No stocks and bonds even?"

"Nary a one, boss."

"They usually go for those stocks and bonds, you know."

"Not this time, they didn't."

"Just the Linzeteum?"

"That's the size of it."

"H-m-m-m-m," I said. "What's Linzeteum?"

"You don't know?"

I had to admit it.

"Neither do we," four mechs chorused.

"Okay, guys," I said, "stand by."

I rang off, sat back in my chair and did some mental calisthenics.

Someone had jury-rigged just about everything in sight—unlikely as that seemed—and cracked the safety vault. But instead of doing the sane and obvious thing, like running off with a king's ransom, they'd helped themselves to this Linzeteum. So before I wrote out my resignation or slit my wrists, the thing to do was find out what made this stuff so hot.

That shouldn't be so hard. Making it the first thing this night that wasn't. I reached for the bound green and gold office ledger and started thumbing pages. After a while I had what I wanted. Almost. Almost, the way things were going, wasn't half bad, but it wasn't all good either.

The entry told me that a case of Linzeteum was

being held in the Emporium vaults only until the Terra-North Lab could pick it up. The date on the top left-hand corner told me we'd had it only a couple of days. The blank space below told me we had no more information.

Terra-North, the giant lab complex. Big money. Big research. Open for business bright and early next morning.

The lack of data—if nothing else—was understandable. This Linzeteum had merely been passing through, wasn't slated for long-term storage.

Easy come, easy go, I thought bitterly. *And that went for my job too.*

Only getting it hadn't been easy. And losing it would be murder. I'd end up back on my knees peeping through keyholes for a living. At my age I'd never stand the eyestrain. My one chance, I knew, was keeping the lid on, finding the Linzeteum before word dribbled out that I'd lost it.

A cinch maybe in some city-states. But not in Happy City. Here half the population was busy bugging the other half. It gave 'em something to do.

I took care of the formalities, put the mechs to work on the alarm and defense systems, put the systems to work on themselves, punched out the co-ords on the interoffice chute that'd take me to the public conveyance, stepped in and was taken.

Cheery Village:

I got off at Dainty Row, walked up the stairs past the slot machines and hoofed it the rest of the way to Placid Towers. It had stopped raining.

Up above me five lit walks rose into the darkness, blotted out the sky like man-made retribution. Late-hour crowds streamed along like wind-up dolls with cranky springs, bumping, twisting, turning. Sounds of traffic rattled, jangled, wheezed—all but mooed and meowed.

Beyond the walks and traffic ramps, five solid miles

of Cheery Village poked its domes, chimneys and speed-lift shafts through the clouds. Here human and mech shopping centers hustled for customers and came up with new gadgets each month—mostly old gadgets in different boxes. The box people were getting rich; at least, *someone* was living the good life. Produce marts juggled prices like circus pros. It didn't matter; all that synthetic foodstuff still tasted the same. Entertainment Tri-D tapes rented dirt cheap, did a boom business. Happy City, surrounded on all sides by competing city-states, had made Tri-D jamming into an art, was so good at it, in fact, that they loused up their own transmissions too. At least with rerun tapes you got a picture. . . . If you wanted one. Some didn't any more. They'd lost heart.

Craning my neck I gazed up at a fifty-story aluminum structure, one of the smaller items noted for its homey atmosphere. Thirty-two flights up and four windows over was Linda's digs.

I took the lobby speed-lift to the thirty-second floor.

Standing in the green-carpeted hallway, I stared at the door bearing the bright, golden 32G and had a thought: *I could still go away.*

As thoughts went it was satisfying enough but left something to be desired. If I didn't give Linda the scoop on Joe's demise, someone else might, someone less lovable and considerate, like the constables. A wrong word from my sister, a hint that I'd been tracking the departed, and they'd be all over me.

I couldn't afford a wrong word; I had to see her now, tell her what's what before my other troubles caught up with me and carted me off.

I pressed the buzzer, heard it buzz reassuringly.

I was hoping she wouldn't become hysterical. You can never tell with these women. If she became hysterical, *I* might become hysterical.

After a while, when nothing more happened, I used my knuckles, then dug out Joe's keys. *Linda had said she'd be home.*

I unlocked the door, pushed it open and looked inside. Inside looked back at me. It was some mess. Chairs, tables, stands, rugs and doodads were scattered every which way. A quick look in the other room showed me more of the same. All that was missing, in fact, was blood. Uusually when a joint looks like this, there's a lot of blood.

Old Linda was pretty high-strung. Maybe she'd gone berserk and busted up the furniture. Then again, maybe she hadn't.

The speed-lift let me off in the basement. I seemed to be alone; how long that condition might last was another matter. I'd never jimmied a security bug-chest before, and the firm didn't handle this building. But if you could put 'em together, it stood to reason, you could take 'em apart. I put my trust in reason.

I found the chest near the west wall by the oil pipes. Unfortunately, it had company. An old party in a wrinkled blue uniform was sitting on a stool, his back to the large metal door. "Hold it, bub," the old party told me.

I looked around for the mech guard. The oldster chuckled, "We done away with the mechs, bub; obsolete, you know. You got to do business with me. Yessir-ree-do-dee, Don't you see the OG on my cap?"

"It means og?" I asked.

"It means Official Geezer," the granddaddy said. "That's me, son."

"The mechs," I said with some reluctance, "are, eh, obsolete, and *you're* replacing 'em . . . ?"

"Yep," the OG beamed.

"Well . . ." This was a new one on me, the first time I'd run into a watch*man* holding down a bug-chest. It complicated things.

"Don't be bashful, sonny," the OG said. "You need a tape, right? That's what I'm here for."

"You are?"

"Sure thing. Them mechs, now, they wouldn't help a body no-how. 'The book says this, the book says that.' No leeway. No human understandin'. Now us OG's got lots o' understandin'. We can sympathize with a body. Which one you want, boy?"

"Er, the Rankins, 32G."

"That official or unofficial?"

"There's a difference?"

"Official I got to see your security clearance, got to register you. Three buck fee, sonny; ain't hardly worth the bother. An' some folks don't have no clearance a-tall."

"Yeah," I said, "and unofficial?"

The oldster grinned. "Ten bucks, buddy. It's a bargain. Slip it to me quick, before some busybody comes along."

I slipped it to him quick; it *was* a bargain.

"Mechs," the oldster said, "didn't have no initiative. Couldn't reason with 'em. Be surprised how that used to burn folks up. Some folks, that is."

"Nothing," I said, "will ever surprise me again."

The old-timer cackled. "Enlightened management, sonny; it always finds a way." Rising, he took out a large brass key ring from an inside jacket pocket, opened the bug-chest. Thousands of tiny monitor spools, maybe a third slowly rotating. The bugs were voice-activated.

"32G?" the OG asked.

"Uh-huh."

Putting out a wrinkled hand, he removed one of the spools, held it between thumb and forefinger. The spool went into the copier, a slim boxlike dingus welded to the inside of the metal door. The copy clicked through a slot, went from my hand to my wallet. The original went back on its spindle.

"Much obliged," the oldie called after me, locking up. "OG's got heart, sonny, don't you forget it."

I wasn't apt to. I'd been all set to turn off the mech

guard with my master control cube, which was a felony. What I'd just done, I hoped, was a lesser crime. At least it'd be harder to prove.

"Yes, madam," the male voice said. "A pitiful situation. He calls for you constantly in his delirium."

"He does?" Linda's voice said.

"Assuredly. It would melt a stone to hear it. We must go to him at once."

"Listen, mister," Linda's voice said, "if Joe's callin' for me, it's the first time in five years. Who are you, buster, and what's the pitch?"

"Madam, I implore you, there is no time to waste."

"So go take a flying leap," my sister said.

"Frank! Max!" the male voice called, sounding very stern.

"Come on, sugar," another voice, a gruff one purred, "be nice." Frank or Max.

"Is that so?" Linda said.

The gruff voice let out a bellow. Something went crash. Frank or Max probably, landing on the floor. All kinds of other noises followed. Like kicking, hitting, the breaking of furniture. Someone had forgotten to tell these birds that Linda knew judo and karate. By now, they'd probably figured it out for themselves.

After a while the racket stopped. Sounds of feet shuffling across the floor. Someone cursed. A door opened and closed. They were gone. And old Linda with them. She'd known judo and karate, all right. Too bad it'd only been a passing acquaintance.

A new sound on the tape recorder. Someone entering the flat, halting by the door, then going through the two cubicles. That would be me. I turned off the machine, sighed. A missing sister and hijacked goods. Either one should've been enough. Both together hardly seemed sporting.

Nothing to do about the latter till morning. Making sure, I ran "Linzeteum" through the computer. The computer told me to look in the safety vault. Only the stuff wasn't there anymore. So much for making sure.

That left Linda. I was afraid it might.

Well, I'd already pegged that other voice without much hardship; to miss it would've been tougher. Dr. Spelville. But when you knew that, just what did you know?

Why would he—or anyone—want to snatch my sharp-tongued sister? Unless they were looking for a good dressing down. . . .

I fed the computer Spelville's name. The computer sent back an address: the Cozy Rest Home. Nothing more was known about the rotund medic—at least under the Spelville moniker.

I tried on Cozy Rest Home for size. The computer fed me four words: Institution for the demented.

Uh-huh. I punched out: *Owner?*

Dr. Cyrus Spelville.

Great. We were running in circles.

Previous owner?

Forman & Mason, Real Estate.

Dead end. Forman and Mason were as open and aboveboard as the Happy City charter. If they conned you, there'd be a law somewhere saying it was legal . . . and for your own good.

This kidnap tape was no font of knowledge. But I still had a card: the other spool, the one with the flat, nasal pug who'd tipped me to Spelville in the first place. I'd been about to slip it to the computer when the heist got in the way. Now was as good a time as any. What did I have to lose that I hadn't lost already except maybe a good night's sleep?

Along with everything else, Security Plus kept tabs on a whole slew of night spots. Whisper voice, with the torch-song accompaniment, band, dishes, and murmurs, obviously hadn't been calling from a phone booth. Maybe what I'd heard was a Tri-D in someone's kitchen. The computer would know. It'd fiddle with audio dimensions, come up with the joint's size; check out female wobblers stored in its memory bank, give me a name; the rattle of dishes would mean something, so would the crowd. I expected a long list of eateries, one that might take days to run down. What I got was a small slip of paper with three printed words on it: the Swell Pillow.

I looked at the slot. There was nothing else. I resisted the impulse to press the talkie button. Mechanicals gave me the willies. I pocketed the whisperer's spool along with a miniature playback. Rummaging in my war chest, I passed up a laser for a plain old .38. I figured the temptation to make holes in someone might be too much for me; laser holes are apt to be permanent.

I rode down the speed-lift, picked up my car at the fifth-level basement garage and took a drive to the Swell Pillow.

CROSSOVERS, THANKFULLY, ARE HIGHLY UN-COMMON. OTHERWISE THERE ACTUALLY MIGHT BE CHAOS RATHER THAN THE FIRM, SATISFYING ORDER TO WHICH WE HAVE ALL GROWN SO AC-CUSTOMED. AT LEAST, MOST OF US.

CHAPTER SEVEN

Happy City was under me as I chose the elevated highway. Windows were dull smudges of light in tall buildings. Fog buried 'em. I had the high-drive to myself. Downtown Happy City, a sleek collection of multishaped structures, dropped away. I punched the accelerator. High drive joined mid drive, soon became ground drive. Happy City looked mostly like it'd been hatched by a band of cross-eyed loonies. No such luck. Even loonies would've done a neater job. The damn thing had evolved on its own. No two parts of town were alike. A scattered jigsaw puzzle had more togetherness. Wet, gray concrete unrolled under my headlights like a soiled strip of gauze. Short three- and four-story wood shingle houses squatted like frogs in the mist. The Swell Pillow wasn't landed gentry, that was for sure.

My heap pulled up near a dingy row of dark, sullen-looking buildings, tenements whose gaudy, multicolored aluminum fire escapes almost lent the section an ounce of gaiety. Refuse and trash cans elbowed each other for pavement space. Dim red neon lights on the corner said Swell Pillow. I got out of my jalopy and went there.

A middle-aged doorman with a bulldog jaw, the build of a gorilla and a row of shiny brass buttons stood under the awning, gave me the once-over. When he didn't club me, I went past him into the joint.

Cigar and cigarette smoke had turned the air a solid gray. The stink of cut-rate whisky filled the room. I was sorry I hadn't brought along my oxygen mask. The men and women who lined the bar and sat at the small square tables jawing at each other looked as though they'd been chiseled out of cheap gray rock. We ops hate to mingle with the suspects and this place looked loaded with 'em. I shook down my memory, tried to dredge up the right approach, the right lingo. It'd been a long time. I went to a corner table, sat down, ordered a tall glass of hootch from a short gent in a dirty white apron and kicked at the sawdust on the floor. After a while I motioned to him again. Shorty waddled over.

"Yeah?" he said, eyeing my still unfinished drink. Already he looked suspicious.

"Got a second?" I asked, waving him toward the empty chair at my elbow.

The waiter shrugged, sat down. Small, hazel eyes squinted through the smoke out of a white, sagging face. His sparse bluish hair was pasted straight back, parted in the middle. His thin lips made two unfriendly lines.

I said, "I want you to hear something."

My companion said nothing. Around us the merriment was going on full tilt. I dug the playback out of a pocket, inserted the spool. Shorty's face remained impassive as he listened to the tape. When it was done, he shifted his gaze to my left shoulder and said, "So?"

I said, "Who is he, the guy with the whisper?"

Shorty blinked, looked at my right shoulder. "Search me, mac. You someone?"

I took a swig of my joy juice, sat back, folded my arms, said, "Not the law."

"No, huh?"

"Uh-uh. This is private."

"Yeah? How private?"

I got out my wallet, put a ten on the table.

The waiter's eyes went from the ten spot to my face. "That's only semiprivate, mac. Don't you know nothin'?"

A fiver joined the ten.

"Uh-huh," he said, "now it's private."

"Well?" I said.

His hand crept toward the money; he said, "Listen, mac; I gotta know more——"

I shook my head. "Private is private, buddy. Watch those fingers."

"Look, I make this Joe—only he's a regular." The hand had reached the dough; it lay there like a dead fish. The eyes had wandered back to my left shoulder, a bad sign. The waiter licked his lips. "Trouble'd screw me, mac; trouble ain't worth no fifteen smackers."

"How much's it worth?"

"Twenty?" Shorty asked hopefully.

I shook my head. "Uh-uh. Fifteen's tops."

"Big spender!" the waiter sneered.

"Snap it up, buddy; it's that or the vice squad."

"Vice squad?"

"Yeah. And those guy's can turn up vices a fella don't even know he has."

"Who are you, mac?"

"A private citizen."

The waiter sighed. "It must be your winnin' personality, mac; you convinced me."

The fifteen clams went into his apron pocket, his eyes went back to my face. "Aces Tommy. He camps two, three blocks from here." Shorty gave me an address. "You never seen me, right, mac?"

"You're a stranger to me, buddy," I assured him, getting to my feet. Someone had fed the juke a nickel. The lady torch singer I'd heard as background began exercising her tonsils. She crooned after me as I went back into the night.

I walked the damp streets. Mist swirled around dented lampposts. Five-story tenement houses tilted at peculiar angles as if adversity had brought them to their knees. I passed an empty, boarded-up brewery, a dark field of scraggly weeds, a faded yellow-brick garage, a vacant supermarket. These blocks were as

spent and empty as a wino on a fourth-time cure. I
came to the building.

Aces Tommy holed up on the third floor. I climbed
a crooked staircase. Greenish oil cloth covered each
step. A small single bulb glowed weakly on every landing. The walls were smeared; gas jets from the horse
and buggy era protruded from them. Gray metal gas
and electric meters stuck out near the ceiling at both
ends of the hallway. I felt my way along. Two doors
faced me. I lit a match. 3C was on the right. My hand
moved toward the knob, turned it quietly. I leaned on
the door, felt it slide ajar. That was something. I put
an eye to the opening, saw darkness, which told me
nothing. It didn't matter. Here was an opportunity I
couldn't pass up. Easing the door open another notch,
I stepped through.

I felt a rush of wind, heard a popping sound. Something loomed up before me. It seemed familiar. I didn't
know who or what it was.

Then I did. It was still dark but somehow I could
see. It was me. But *what* a me! It/me was transparent
. . . behind it I seemed to glimpse an entire building—
a different one—also as see-through as a peek-a-boo
blouse. And behind that, transparent pavements, vehi-
cles, small jerky figures. An opaque shape—a man?—
wavered near the right elbow of the transparent me. I
was about to say something when the other me raised
a leg, suddenly as hefty and real as a baseball bat, and
sent me spilling. The room seemed to twist, and I was
down on the floor, the thing gone.

Guns shrieked from two directions. Orange-red flame
erupted in the dark. Bullets hammered the walls, splintered the door frame where my head should have been,
but wasn't.

I waited, hugging the floor like an expectant lover.

These gun-happy wise guys, whoever they were,
would have to figure their job done, their mission ac-
complished. Soon it would be time to inspect the
handiwork. And my turn.

The .38 was in my hand when the lights snapped on. The young blond guy with the beaklike nose got off one blast that nicked door frame and wall before my bullet found his leg, sent him spilling like loose timber caught in a tidal wave.

The other—a balding, husky, round-faced man in a green leather jacket—took one look at what was happening, grew round-eyed and plunged through an open door to the next room. I admired his reasoning. It didn't keep me from going after him.

A window leading to the fire escape in the room—a large kitchen—was open.

Five steps took me to the window. I looked out.

Above, the burly man made for the roof.

Something moved in his hand. Bullets whined off metal rungs.

Pulling back, I waited a while, then crawled out on the fire escape.

No one was there now.

I climbed up, wet rungs slippery under my shoes. Dark clouds hid the sky. Darkness was everywhere here, covering buildings, roofs and metal ladder. I used my left hand to climb, my right held the gun.

I scrambled over the edge onto the roof, lay still for an instant, flat against the wet tar, searching in the dark.

Sounds of traffic came from far off. I could hear the faint rumble of thunder.

Ahead, something seemed to flutter. Then, nothing.

I crouched lower to watch for more. Large square chimneys jutted from the roof—chimneys behind which a man might hide. I couldn't wait any longer. This game of tag was all wrong. Too much desk work had put a crimp in my thinking, made me forget basics. While I hunted up here, the blond kid might slip away —and this one was hardly in the bag. Slowly I inched forward, crawled through a number of puddles, ended up by one of the chimneys. I gave my ears a workout.

Soft sounds of movement came from the left, behind a large square stack.

I eased to the right. A bug couldn't've made less noise.

Not six feet away, his back to me, a figure huddled. Stepping forward, I growled, "Reach, buddy."

He whirled, the gun still in his fist. Didn't this punk know English?

My rod slammed down on his hand, sent his clattering to the roof. My fist drove into his face. He stumbled back, his foot catching on a pipe. He twisted sideways. His lips opened to yell. The edge of the roof came up to meet him. There was nothing to grab.

I dived, threw myself after him, my fingers closing on empty air.

The guy in the leather jacket was gone; his scream, like a wild bird's, cut short by the pavement six stories below.

I looked down over the side, saw nothing. There wouldn't be much left to see anyway. I shuddered, shook my head and staggered away.

The rooftops connected one with the other. I went over them. No time to pick up on the blond kid; he'd have to fend for himself. My best bet lay in making tracks, fading out while I still had some anonymity left to preserve. Eight houses down I found an unlocked door. The hoarse sounds of sirens could be heard outside as I wound my way down the empty stairs.

The constables were just starting to run up the steps of Aces Tommy's tenement when I turned a corner— in the opposite direction.

I was alone. I didn't mind. Wet pavement and dilapidated buildings hid themselves in night and mist. Street lamps shone yellow in layers of fog, sent a tired glow into the darkness. The blocks stretched before me like a beggar's crippled hand. Sirens behind me still shrieked and moaned—more constables on the prowl. Here, where I was, only my footsteps kept me company. I

ambled along taking the long—and I hoped, private—
way back to my buggy.

Odds had it no bug chest had lent an ear to the
goings-on in the flophouse I'd just vacated. Bugs were
for respectable folks, namely those who couldn't afford
the latest model jammers. Whatever business Aces
Tommy had with Rankin, Spelville or me wasn't apt to
show on someone's tape. That was good. If anything
else was good, it didn't exactly spring to mind. I was
more tangled in this mess than ever and if it didn't
cook my goose, there was always the Linzeteum heist
waiting in the wings, a sure thing if ever there was
one. I wondered idly what had sent me tripping just
when the fireworks began. Did I owe it money or a
prayer? Maybe it was some sort of ESP, a warning
going off in my own noggin. There were lots of cases
like that, only most of 'em were in nut houses. The
truth was, I didn't have the faintest notion. Thinking
about it only gave me the willies. I decided, fast, to file
this question with all the rest, turned a corner—my
final one—and was back at the Swell Pillow. I didn't
linger. I crossed over to my car, got in and drove
away. Sweet and simple. Or was it?

A voice from the back seat whispered, "Keep
drivin'." I didn't quite jump out of my skin. I followed
orders, put my foot on the pedal and swung onto the
high drive.

The whisperer spoke: "That's me they was gunnin'
for," it said bitterly.

Glancing at my dashboard mirror, I saw a long-
faced guy with a flat nose, heavy lids and short-cut,
gray hair. He'd been crouching on the floor, now he
leaned over the seat, glared at me, his left hand was
wound around a laser; casually he put it away.

I said, "Aces Tommy?"

"Uh-huh," Aces Tommy said; his face—the left
side—doing a number: eye winked, lips twisted, cheeks
twitched in time to the eye. I watched this performance
with some interest, then said:

"Thanks."

"Uh-huh. For what?"

"Joe Rankin."

"You found him, huh?"

"Uh-huh."

"The creep. He spill his guts, huh?"

"Uh-uh."

"Uh-uh? Waddya mean uh-uh?"

"He was croaked."

Aces Tommy whistled. "Like that, huh?"

"Like that." I gave my attention to the high drive. The fog and my car had it all to themselves. Tommy said:

"An' Spelville?"

"Powdered out."

Aces Tommy cursed. "You let him?"

"He didn't exactly ask my permission," I explained.

"How come you want me, chum?" Tommy asked.

"My sister's been snatched."

Tommy's face did its number again. "You don't say? Know who turned the trick?"

"Sure. Your pal, Spelville."

Tommy spat. "No more, he ain't. That was his boys back there—the Mugger gang."

I raised an eyebrow. This Mugger gang was a cheap bunch of hoods and grifters, led by one Louie Mugger. Strictly small-time. A two-bit outfit. I couldn't see them putting the grab on Linda. I said as much.

Tommy shrugged. "Search me, chum. I'm an ex-Mugger, see? I'm in on this knockover, see? Only they rook me, don't come through with my end, see?"

I saw. I'd've been blind not to. "So?"

"I switch dodges. No more strong-arm, no more hustle; now I'm a stoolie."

I wished him luck.

"Don't knock it, chum," Aces Tommy said. "It can maybe steer you to the missin' person."

"My sister?"

"Uh-huh. Like I know their stash. How much you spendin'?"

"For that and what else?"

"Just that. Rankin was in with Spelville, sure, only me, I ain't got the what or where."

I asked, "You gimmick your flat?"

"I *what*?"

"Rig it against trouble?"

Aces Tommy shrugged. "What for? I'm dustin' out, chum; I just stuck around long enough to make a buck, maybe."

"Sure, twenty bucks," I said earnestly.

"Well," Aces Tommy said, "it ain't no bundle, is it? But what the hell—a ghee in my racket can't be too choosy. The dough's crap, but there's lotsa laughs, huh?"

I gave him the money. He gave me an address. "You can drop me anywhere, chum."

I let him off.

CHAOS—WERE IT TO MANIFEST ITSELF—MIGHT ASSUME NUMEROUS FORMS. ALL, HOWEVER, WOULD ALMOST CERTAINLY PROVE THOROUGHLY DISGUSTING.

when they go mad, it's time to stir

CHAPTER EIGHT

It was a three-story brownstone far on the edge of town. I parked down the block. Not the nicest section, but still livable. Scraggly trees and dim lamplights lined the street. Parched, neglected lawns—standouts even in the dark—spoke of better days the area'd never see again. Some of the houses were boarded up, candidates for the demolition squad.

I decided my visit should be a surprise.

Using my pass keys, I got the front door open, tiptoed in. This would be fast and sweet—a classic rescue job, done by the book.

An empty hallway took me into a dim living room. Pale light came from one small lamp on a corner end table. Floor, walls, ceilings and furniture were shadowed. At first I saw no one. Then something moved in the semidarkness—a small, ratty man in blue pants and white undershirt ran toward me on the balls of his feet. Pointy white teeth flashed; yellowish eyes gleamed. His hand clutched a poker.

I had the .38 in my fist, obscured by a flap of my jacket. I was ready for bear, elephant, eagle and anything else that moved. I was ready to take on armies—almost. But I didn't want to put a hole in this bird. Noise might waken the establishment.

The little man grinned, swung his poker. I went to the side. The poker went past my shoulder, took a thick slice out of the air. I stepped in close, drove the .38 into his face, snapping back his head. He fell down. I kicked him a couple of times. He stopped moving. When they do that, it's time to stop kicking. I stopped, feeling moderately satisfied. The feeling didn't last long.

All this horseplay had taken less than thirty seconds, but the house was already springing to life as if my presence had broken a spell. I'd hoped for privacy—I wasn't going to get it. Ahead, a staircase to the floor above: sounds of doors slamming and feet running. To the right, a hallway leading further into the house: more racket—only less of it.

I was rousing the dead; soon I'd have more company than a man could stand. It was no time for idling. I moved.

The hall was as good a direction as any. I went that way.

A large, half-dressed man loomed up before me, snarling. My gun swung down in a whistling arc. Head and gun connected.

I stepped over the wreckage and kept going, taking a look-see into a couple of empty rooms as I ran. No sign of Linda.

Behind me the action had risen to a circus roar. Falling chairs, flying doors, pounding feet and raised voices joined in chorus.

I turned a corner and found I'd run out of corridor. A large door blocked my progress—one that wouldn't open. Any locked room in this joint claimed my interest. I couldn't see going back anyway; they'd have a cannon set up by now.

I used my .38; the door moved as the lock fell away. Gunfire burned at me.

I went down, rolling sideways into the room. One lone, squinting guy handled all the gun there was; it shook in his hand like a malted-milk mixer.

I'd come in too fast and low to give him a good target. Thank goodness for the Detective's Handbook; it diagrams all the right moves.

I blasted the guy from where I sat. The bullet hit him in the arm, sent him back against the wall.

Feet pounded in the corridor behind me—racing, scrambling feet.

I took in the room at a glance: four walls and one door—the one I'd come through—a narrow high window in the far wall; a table, some chairs and a dirty red couch. That was all. It would have to do.

A single light bulb glowed in the ceiling; my bullet ruined it.

Darkness came as the first one sprang through the door. At his heels a swell of bodies surged forward. That was fine with me! These characters hadn't counted on darkness. Now their momentum sent them spilling, piling one on top of the other.

I heaved the table at the melee, threw a chair in for good measure. I crouched, my back to the wall—out of line with the partly lighted doorway. I emptied my gun into the ceiling, then crawled behind the couch for safety.

Pure, blind panic had seized the man-made bottleneck that jammed the doorway and filled half the room. Arms and legs groped, scratched and tore. Mouths cursed and growled. The damned in hell would have a long way to go before they could equal this!

I chucked another chair at the high window. Glass shattered and tinkled. Moist air rushed in.

I got out of there as a swarm of heavies spilled over in that direction. I moved straight for the door. No one asked to see my ticket.

I was in the hallway. I kept going. I was glad of the chance.

All this was too much row for me. I was having trouble holding up my end. The thing to do now was go away while I had the chance. Let the constables save my sister; better ruined than dead.

The living room was empty when I reached it; the front door just ahead.

A sound drew my attention, made me look toward the staircase.

The smooth, round shape of Dr. Spelville towered high above me, leaned far over the banister. His face

was solemn. One dark, round eye narrowed to a slit.
The eye winked at me. His hand went over his head
like a pitcher winding up for a slow-motion throw. A
dull gray object—caught in a gleam of silvery light—
came twirling down.

Spelville was gone.

I flung myself under the alcove beneath the stairs and
tried to crawl into the woodwork. Behind me the floor
gave way, exploded into tiny bits of wood and small
splinters.

Flame worked over floor and staircase, sent red
fingers up the wall. I gathered myself up on legs that
seemed to be held together by small, tired pieces of
string and moved toward the door, smoke dusting my
heels.

Outside nothing had changed. The neighbors were
still catching their forty winks. Some neighbors.

A sound reached me—an idling engine. It came
from the back of the house—the alley. I ran that way,
digging the gun out of my coat pocket again, as if it
and I had finally merged, become one. A less-than-
sane grin split my face. Suddenly all I could see was
blood—red, ripe and dripping. This certainly wasn't
part of the Detective's Handbook. I'd become a devia-
tionist.

A fence got in my way. I went over it. I made the
back trotters, looked around for something to shoot.
Two taillights were busy disappearing down the alley.
I aimed my .38 at them, squeezed the trigger. The gun
clicked emptily.

I stood there, as alone as the office water cooler five
minutes after quitting time. The car was gone.

Another sound came to me—a woman's voice
screaming, somewhere inside the house.

Screaming fit my mood perfectly.

Safe to go back, I figured, what more could happen?
The brownstone residents had just taken a very quick,
guilt-ridden powder.

I returned to the now-empty house, followed the complaining voice up a flight of charred stairs—small rivulets of fire still smoldering—let myself into a bedroom and found my sister on a hard-backed wooden chair trussed up with a length of rope like a prize package about to be sent through the mail.

"Hello there," I said.

"I've been kidnapped," she told me bitterly.

"Yeah," I said, "so I see."

I used my pocket knife to cut her loose.

"What's it all about?" I asked her. "Eh?"

"You've got me, big brother."

"Uh-huh. Just what I've always wanted."

Sending Sis out to wait in what would—hopefully—be the safety of my car, I began giving the joint a good going-over. I came up with a lot of empty desk drawers, dusty closets and a large beat-up trunk that held nothing.

A thin wail, like the sound of some tormented beast, came from a long way off, grew louder, more urgent. Sirens. I went to a window, peered out.

A squad car was pulling in at the curb in front of the house, its red spotlight, like a giant inflamed glass eye, sweeping the streets. The constables on the scene. A bit late to protect me from vicious attackers, but just in time to get me in Dutch. They piled out onto the sidewalk. Six of 'em—big, hefty, red-faced fellas. Two were already trotting up the walk.

I beat it out the back way, on the double.

I was in the alley. Dark sky overhead, puddled asphalt underfoot. I moved cautiously toward the street, flattened myself against a wall, looked out.

Two constables lingered by the front door, the rest had gone in. Across the street, where my car should have been, a large empty space seemed to wink derisively.

I stepped farther back into the shadows.

Headlights appeared down the block, grew brighter, wheeled over the damp street, heading my way.

I recognized my heap. Just in case I didn't, its horn began making loud, discordant noises. The two joes at the door turned their heads, stared at the disturbance.

I trotted out into the street. I didn't have much choice.

The jalopy swerved, a door popped open; I got a foot up on the running board, grabbed hold, almost had arms, shoulders and head yanked off. Skidding onto the sidewalk, we missed a tree and a trash can by inches, rode through the gutter, cut into the center of the street, screeched over wet pavement, and shot down the road in a wild spray.

I climbed behind the wheel as Linda slid over.

The constables we had left behind were piling back into their car in a frenzy of activity. They shrank in size as we pulled away, vanished from sight as we turned a corner.

I turned some more corners, wound my way through a maze of back streets, burned up a lot of rubber, saw we had the road to ourselves and hit the mid drive back toward the center of town.

I said, "Listen, the horn; never honk it. Not on a rescue mission. *Always* maintain silence on a rescue mission."

"Who cares about stupid old horns?" Linda said. "Imagine; kidnapped from my very own domicile. How humiliating."

"What isn't these days? Did they give you some reason, a hint maybe?"

"They were *very* uncommunicative kidnappers."

"No doubt. Why did you move the car?"

"The constables were coming. And you said this was hush-hush."

"So I did. Next time, sit tight, eh?"

"Next time? *What* next time?"

"With my luck," I said, "there's bound to be a next time."

"So why hush-hush, brother dear?"

"Because of Joe."

"You found Joe?"

"Yeah. He is no longer among the living."

She turned to squint at me. Linda was a small-boned lady with pert features, short black hair, striking green eyes; she had on an orange blouse, pleated green skirt, high-heeled shoes. She said, "He's *dead,* you mean?"

I nodded. "That's what I mean. Sometimes emotion makes me tongue-tied and people don't know what I mean, but that's what I mean. Look, what was he doing these last few weeks? He must've said *something.*"

Linda sighed. "Joe, brother dear, never did anything. He was a very tight-lipped, creepy little person."

"I can believe it."

"At least," Linda said, "it'll save me all those divorce fees."

"It'll cost," I said, "in other ways."

"*Still?*"

"You're in Happy City," I reminded her.

"Well, I am quite certain of one thing: no matter what, brother dear, *you* will hold up *beautifully.*"

"Don't bet on it."

I'd found Joe, all right, but too late to do much good. Under city law, a man's wife was liable for all his debts. So was his widow, and Joe owed the bookies a bundle. That left Linda in hock for the whole bit. She might actually become a *terrible* burden to her family, and I was the only family she had.

Switching from mid-drive to low, I gave Linda the low-down on the Spelville doings, how I'd found her errant spouse. I brought in some of my office woes, just for a touch of local color. "Whatever happens," I said, "act surprised. You don't know anything. I can't afford to show in this."

"Funny," Linda said, "but a couple of times last

month, I could have sworn Joe had gotten a steady job. . . ."

"Grief has affected your mind," I told her simply.

SOME FORMS OF CHAOS. HOWEVER, WOULD DOUBTLESS PROVE MORE DISGUSTING THAN OTHERS—NOT TO MENTION LETHAL.

CHAPTER NINE

The alarm clock woke me. It sure as hell wasn't the phone—I'd disconnected it last night. Eight-thirty. So why did I feel so lousy? I seemed to ache all over. Suddenly I remembered. And started to feel even worse.

I yawned, managed to shave, shower and get dressed. These minor accomplishments cheered me. Now if I could only make it out the front door. . . .

"Good morning, Mr. Dunjer."

"No, Miss Follsom," I said with a shake of my head, "it isn't. If it stood any chance at all of being a good or even fair day, I'd be the first to say it. We must face facts, Miss Follsom."

"If you say so, boss."

Miss Follsom was our chief junior exec (whatever that was), a languorous, buxom blonde with long flowing hair and trim black suit. Usually I spent a lot of time looking at her. Today I had other things on my mind.

"Tell me, Miss Follsom, just between us, who's servicing our alarm and defense systems these days? Still Grange and Morton?"

Miss Follsom shrugged a trim shoulder. "I could look it up."

"Why don't you?"

I went into my office, sat down at the desk. When that didn't make me feel better, I reached for the phone, dialed the Terra-North Labs, set up an appointment with Director Conklin. I still didn't feel any better. Maybe I never would.

Miss Follsom came into my office. "It's Underwood and Snow, boss."

"What is?"

"Our new servicers."

"Oh, *no!*"

"Oh, yes. As of two months ago. It says so right here in black and white." She waved a file at me.

"How . . ." I asked feebly, "how did this happen?"

"Wendell Goodyear. He switched us from Grange and Morton to Underwood and Snow. They cost less, it says here."

"I'll kill him," I said.

"Too late, Mr. Dunjer; it was his last official act. He quit five weeks ago. Mr. Goodyear is with Money, Inc. now."

"Money, Inc? Sounds promising. Why wasn't I told of all this?"

"You didn't ask."

That made sense. "Bounce 'em, Miss Follsom; get rid of Underwood and Snow. There's got to be some loophole; our contracts are full of 'em!"

"Yes, sir."

"Get hold of Grange and Morton, have 'em go over all our systems. Personally. I want a complete report. I might as well tell you now, Miss Follsom, we may all be in the soup. Last night the safety vault was breached—cracked open like a rotten egg. All the thieves took was something called Linzeteum. As soon as I find out what that is, I'll know how much trouble we're in. Meanwhile, we've got to keep the lid clamped. Tell Grange and Morton, but no one else. If anyone asks, deny all and everything. My sister might call. Speak to her yourself. No tapes, no notes. Commit everything to memory. I'm off to Terra-North now. I'll phone. Got all that? Don't answer. I'm not up to repeating it."

"Yes," Director Conklin said, "Linzeteum. I heard you."

Conklin was a large, red-faced man, seated behind a wide, imposing desk. Outside, the Terra-North Lab complex made smooth, important patterns against the morning sky. We were on the ninetieth floor of the Admin building, as high as you could get, administratively speaking.

I looked at Conklin.

"Certainly I'm acquainted with the term," he said. "What is it?" I asked.

The director shrugged. "Don't you know?"

I said I didn't.

"That makes two of us. So what's the problem?"

I took a deep breath. "It's simply this, Mr. Director: the term 'Linzeteum' tells us what we've got, but not what it is or what it's worth. Usually, if we've got the crown jewels or something, it says so on the package and we know how to handle it."

"How *do* you handle it?"

"We put it in the safety vault and forget about it."

"But this Linzeteum?"

"Precisely," I said. "Crown jewels, you see, don't leak, don't smear and never blow up. Not of their own accord, at least. But your product, Mr. Director, what does it do?"

Through the wide windows I heard the sound of cars, copters, cycles, the rumble of motors small and large. Happy City on the go. A paradise for all kinds of engines.

The director spoke:

"What you say, my dear Dunjer, is true enough. Unfortunately, our product isn't our product. Tell me, Dunjer, all is in order at the Emporium, I trust?"

"What could be wrong?" I shrugged, glad to note lightning wasn't striking me down.

"Well," the director said, "whoever thinks up your forms then is plainly in error. If the product blows up —you don't think it's going to blow up, do you, Dunjer?—no one could hold us responsible."

"I don't see how," I said.

"Neither do I. Your form should have had a blow-up clause in it. Glad to have this settled, Dunjer. Is there anything else I can do for you?"

"Yes," I said.

"There is?" the director looked disappointed.

"You can tell me what the hell you know about this product."

"Damned little, Dunjer. As I've said, it's not our product."

"Whose is it, then?"

"Dr. Sass."

"Humperdinck Sass?"

"It seems unlikely there would be any other around," Conklin pointed out, "with a name like that. You know him?"

"By reputation. The scientist."

"Well put," the director said. "And that also sums up the extent of our knowledge. Linzeteum is his creation. An invention pure and simple. It does something or other. When his facilities proved inadequate, he rented ours. For more tests, you see. Terra-North Labs prides itself on its facilities. Sass is to take over an entire floor and continue doing whatever he has been doing with this product. As soon as the proper conditions are created, of course."

"Of course. And what would they be?"

"Why, security conditions, Dunjer, security conditions. They must be foolproof. Dr. Sass was most adamant on that score. Absolutely foolproof. That's why we chose the safety vault, you see. Couldn't afford any slip-ups. Sass's product was shipped directly from his laboratory to your Emporium. Safety first, you know. And when we have completed our own security measures—when Dr. Sass has convinced himself of their adequacy—we shall remove this product and bring it, under the heaviest guard, you understand, here to Terra-North. Linzeteum, whatever it is, Dunjer, must be priceless. Or at least Sass seems to think so. I wouldn't know, of course. Why, my dear Dunjer, you look absolutely ill. Is something wrong? A breath of air, perhaps? Here, let me open a window."

H-M-M-M-M. . . . DO I ACTUALLY BEGIN TO DE-TECT SOME CHANGE? IS SOMETHING ABOUT TO HAPPEN OUT HERE? I DO BELIEVE IT IS. . . .

CHAPTER TEN

I used a pay phone down in the lobby of the Admin building, dialed my office, my fingers feeling like bananas, my clothing like the wet sheet they wrap patients in at the loony bin; my voice, when I spoke, sounded like a frog with laryngitis. "Miss Follsom?"

"Is that you, Mr. Dunjer?"

I told her it was.

"You have your head in a pail of water?"

"I just sound that way, Miss Follsom. For kicks. We still in business?"

"I don't know about you, boss, but I have an iron-clad contract. Things around here have been pretty quiet. Grange and Morton are on the job. The damage to the systems was pretty extensive, but correctable. Grange and Morton are busy correcting it now. The systems are correcting each other. The mechs are giving themselves medicals. The vaults are closed to the public for the time being. Otherwise, Mr. Dunjer, it's business as usual. The chairman of the board hasn't called, neither has the press, or anyone else. What's our line on inquiries?"

"There shouldn't be any. My sister call?"

"Yes. Her husband's body was found, along with a lot of others. An investigation's in progress."

"What's one investigation more or less, eh, Miss Follsom?"

"Eh yourself, Mr. Dunjer."

"Right you are. I'm hopping a chute back to the office. Sit tight."

* * *

"Dunjer, baby!" Grange said. He was a middle-sized gent of thirty-five or so, sporting an oval face, smooth features and thinning black hair with a center part. He wore a pin-striped business suit and a wide checkered yellow and red tie. His cuff links were gold and monogrammed.

"How's it going?" I asked.

"What can you expect?" He looked gloomy. "Dropped us cold, you did. Without a so-long, even. Now everything's stinko. It figures, right?"

"An administrative mix-up," I explained. "I didn't even know about it."

"I thought you knew everything."

"You've got me confused with the *Daily Tattler,* Grange. Anyway, you've got your old job back, so quit squawking. What's the verdict?"

I looked around. Here I was back at the safety vault—scene of last night's skulduggery—its huge silver sphere spotless but somehow violated. Empty space glittered neatly around it. No one could tell at a glance that trouble had hit the chamber and knocked it for a loop. It just went to show how appearances lied —along with everyone else, including me. I just hoped I was doing a good job of it.

Morton stepped out of the safety vault's interior, a tool box in hand.

"Hello, Dunjer," he said.

Morton was a small, wide individual in his late fifties with graying, longish hair, a number of rings on his ample fingers, and a pointed, long nose. He wore the latest two-tone green and orange tunic and cream-colored sandals.

"Hello, Morton," I said.

"Dunjer, do you wish to know about the blue smoke?" he yelled. Morton always yelled.

I said I wished.

"An hallucinogenic. Gas, Dunjer; you were gassed. While what you saw, felt and heard were all fictions of the mind, the laser fragmentation was real enough. It was extraordinary."

"Extraordinary *what?*"

"Expensive," Morton told me. "You grasp the implications? The laser diffusion process is exceedingly costly and highly classified."

"So how do you know about it?"

"Because *I* am exceedingly costly and highly classified."

"I almost forgot."

"Never forget that, Dunjer. How could you drop us after all our years of faithful service?"

"It was only three years. And, come to think of it, you *are* exceedingly costly. Anyway, it was all a mistake. I've already explained to Grange."

"Some explanation," Grange said.

"I said I was sorry. Give me more on those implications, eh?"

"One," Morton said, "we are dealing with a kind-hearted rapscallion. Laser diffusion means laser immunity. Nobody gets hurt. Very thoughtful. Two, we are dealing with a wealthy rapscallion. Reasons already given. Three, we are dealing with an exceedingly influential rapscallion. To obtain the laser diffusion process is no mean trick."

"Neither was the rest of it," I said.

Morton went back to the vault. Grange put his hands in his pockets, smiled at me and said, "Here's the scoop on your systems, pal. Persons unknown rewired them, substituted all kinds of parts so they wouldn't respond, or respond only partially, or incorrectly. Like saying 'geek' instead of 'help.' Very professional. Your mechs were—it looks like—electronically spooked. What happened to them is what happens to humans when they get falling-down drunk. I'll take your word about the magnetic field. No can check."

Grange told me that repairs would take another couple of hours and followed his partner into the vault. I went back to my office and used my phone.

"Dr. Sass's residence," a cool, feminine voice answered on the first ring.

"Sass, please," I said. "This is Dunjer of Security Plus."

No, the voice was adamant, the doctor couldn't be disturbed. Perhaps the voice could help?

It couldn't. I explained who and what I was. The voice went away, was presently replaced by another, a man's.

"Sass," it said.

That almost made sense.

"Dunjer," I said. "I've got to see you, doctor."

"Impossible," Sass said. "Is that all?"

It wasn't.

"Security Plus," I tried again. "I'm the guy from Security Plus!"

"Of course you are," Sass told me. "Now may I go?"

I gripped the phone by the neck and started to squeeze. "Emporium," I said through clenched teeth.

"What about Emporium?"

"Security Plus guards the Emporium safety vault!"

The voice was quarrelsome. "Is that so? And how should I have known *that?* I am a physicist, not a busybody. What in blazes do you want?"

I lowered my voice. "To tell you that I've got to see you—in person. Now."

"That tone will get you nowhere. I am engaged in serious research, sir. More than can be said for some persons. I do not wish to seem abrupt, but if you do not state your business within, say, the next twenty seconds, I will end this unprofitable conversation permanently. Do you understand?"

I understood. "Linzeteum," I said.

"Ah! So that's it? No, my dear sir, I have no statement to make about my product. It is still, so to speak, under wraps. Except to state that we are—I am, that is—seriously considering changing its name to Sassite. Has a more respectable ring, wouldn't you say?"

"No."

"What's that?" Sass said. "You reject Sassite?"

"The no was for the sentence before that. The one about under wraps. It isn't."

"Isn't?"

"Under wraps. That's what I'm calling about, Dr. Sass; that's why I've got to see you. It's not under wraps any more."

"What did you say your name was?"

"Dunjer."

"Look here, Dunjer, come to the point, can't you?"

I sighed. My office had now taken on all the aspects of the friendly neighborhood gas chamber. This fool was going to make me spill the beans over the public lines, yet.

I said, "You want me to tell you over the phone?"

"If it is not too much trouble." The doctor was all ice.

"Okay," I said. "You're sure?"

"Don't be an imbecile, Mr. Dunjer."

"I'm trying not to, doctor. It's not under wraps because it's gone."

"Gone? And what does that mean?"

"It's been stolen."

"Ha-ha," Sass said weakly. "The safety vault is impregnable. It says so in the brochure."

"Listen," I said. "Last night someone swiped your product, Doc, ran off with it. That's what I was going to whisper to you, person to person, so no one'd know. Now, maybe, they know. Well, don't panic yet, Doc. We can mount an operation, try to get it back. I've got the mechs lined up; ready at the word go. Sharp, shining mechs, man-hunters; the best wires and insulation that money can buy. We can ring in the human angle, too: gumshoes, sleuths, shamuses and dicks, not to mention ops. We can unleash an army. We're covered by insurance, and it says we can put an army in the field if it don't cost more than the maximum allotment. H-m-m-m. That'd be about eight and a half men, I figure. Plus mechs. Although, it seems, our mechs can be gotten to with the right electronics. Anyway, it's the trained op that counts in all this, Dr. Sass. But it'll take teamwork between the pair of us, complete confidence, dedication and aboveboardness. No more beating around the bush. Now all this I've said, I was going to say on the q.t. But maybe this is better. Maybe I couldn't've said it so good face-to-face, because shyness would've made me tongue-tied or stupid. And maybe—who knows—this line isn't even tapped. So it's still just between us and the bad guys. We'll probably find out soon enough, eh, Doc? But the thing now is to get together. Pow-wow, chit-chat, and generally talk it up. That's the old ticket now. So you warm up your tonsils, Doc, and I'll scoot on over by and by and we'll both give this Linzeteum caper a whirl, eh?"

A cool feminine voice replied:

"It's Jake with me, Jack, only the doc here passed out cold five minutes ago. Damned if I dug a word you said, Mac; but the doc don't pass out every day. Maybe you better mosey over like you said."

"Maybe I'd better. Give me an hour, eh?"

"For my dough you can take two."

AH-HA! YES, DEFINITELY! ORDER, I THINK, IS ABOUT TO REASSERT ITSELF. I SNAP ON MY SENSES TO FULL POTENTIAL, TAKE STOCK. THERE HAVE BEEN CHANGES.

CHAPTER ELEVEN

Charlie Underwood sat at his desk looking my way from under a pair of black, bushy eyebrows. Dark lines ringed his eyes. His head was bald, his skin tanned on a tall, hefty, fiftyish frame. He hadn't risen to shake hands. Behind me the door opened and Sonny Snow joined us. A small, round-faced man of fifty-five with thinning gray hair and rimless spectacles. He pulled up a chair to Underwood's right and sat in it, not even glancing at me. The door opened again and red-headed Ed Morgan, the firm's counsel, entered. "He goes," I said.

Snow shrugged, Underwood nodded and Morgan went.

Snow glared at me. "You took our contract away from us," he said. "You crazy person you."

Underwood shook a finger at me. "Are there no laws to protect the innocent? No justice for avenging the wronged? Think, Dunjer. Are we pushovers? Are we neophytes? What are we?"

"Crooks," I said.

"Businessmen, Dunjer. And what you've done is bad for business."

"You'll be punished," Snow said.

"You can't just break a contract," Underwood said. "That's anarchy, Dunjer. This goes to court."

"And you fellas go to jail," I said.

"Talk sense, Dunjer," Underwood said. "Pretend you're grown up."

"Sense?" I said. "Well, if you want me to talk sense, I've go to do a few things first."

"O-ooo, I hate him so much," Snow said.

"Go right ahead," Underwood said. "Pretend you know what you're doing."

I got the inspection cube out of my pocket, flashed it around the room. Underwood and Snow watched placidly as one readout appeared after another on the small screen:

Electric lights, intercom, recording device, telephone, electric typewriter, recording device, electric stovelet, blue-movie projector, dictaphone, recording device, listening tube.

I put the cube away.

"Don't you trust us?" Underwood asked.

"You're such a suspicious person, Mr. Dunjer," Snow said.

"I don't mind the blue-movie projector," I said, "but the recording devices will have to go. And stuff up that listening tube, will you? If I'd wanted Morgan in on this, I'd've said so."

"Snow's right," Morgan said through the listening tube. "You *are* crazy."

"Mind your own business, Morgan," I said.

"This *is* my business," Morgan said.

"Let's humor him," Underwood said. "Disconnect the devices, Snow."

"What do I look like," Snow asked, "the janitor?"

"Morgan," Underwood said, "come in here and disconnect the devices."

"I'll send in the switchboard girl," Morgan said.

"All right," Underwood said, after the switchboard girl had come and gone, "now have your say, Dunjer."

I had it. "Tell me, gents, what does this great product do that's worth all this trouble, eh?"

"Nothing's worth all this trouble," Underwood said. "What product? For this you had us disconnect the recording devices?"

"And exclude poor Mr. Morgan from this grueling ordeal?" Snow asked.

"All right, guys," I said, "you want to be cagey? Be cagey. Let me give you my side of it."

"Who's been stopping you?" Underwood asked.

"Is he going to talk sense now?" Snow asked.

"The safety vault," I said, "was knocked over last night. Only do me a favor. Don't go making faces now. No shrugging of shoulders, no creasing of brows. No yelling or screaming or hair-tearing. The recorders are off, remember? So this is just between us insiders."

"I'm not yelling," Snow said. "Do you see me yelling, Mr. Dunjer?"

"I'm certainly not tearing my hair," Underwood said calmly, "now am I? I couldn't, even if I wanted to, now could I? Knocked over, huh?"

"Why should you yell, why should you tear hair, fellow insiders? Yeah! Knocked over like a crumbly statue in Deadbeat Park."

"I'd rather not belong to this insiders' club," Snow said.

"Cleaned you out, huh?" Underwood said.

"Just took the product, gentlemen—the Linzeteum."

"Some product that must be," Underwood said.

"So what is it?" I asked.

"You're asking *me?*" Underwood said. "Do you know, Snow?"

"Don't be inane," Snow said.

"Cagey bastards," I said. "Well, it doesn't matter what it is, really. The important thing is to get it back."

"We certainly wish you luck," Underwood said.

"We have not always been close, Mr. Dunjer," Snow said, "not always seen eye-to-eye, but it would be ungentlemanly not to wish you success in this undertaking. Allow me to wish you success."

"Thanks, pal."

"It was good of you to take the trouble, in this trying hour, to tell us," Underwood said. "But we're still going to sue for breach of contract."

"Uh-huh," I said. "Two months on the job for old Underwood and Snow and the safety vault goes under. How? Why, everything, but everything, gets rewired, so that nothing works. The mechs go to sleep; the viewer shows phony pictures; the systems mumble meaningless words and make stupid jokes. We've got the evidence, fellas: rewired from the inside. Welcome to the insiders' club, pals. But how did you figure to beat the rap? I mean, even if you were completely innocent, you still couldn't beat the rap, it's so air-tight. Only you boys had the keys to the systems, only you could've serviced the systems to sleep. So what does it get you? Maybe thirty years in the hoosegow, maybe life. Congratulations. I hope you enjoy the product—whatever it is—when you get out. *If* you get out. But that's not very likely, is it? Only one minor problem connected with your imminent decline bothers me. Not that Underwood and Snow will close its doors and a lot of needy employees will have to hunt up a new racket; your stooges aren't exactly babes in the woods. Nor that your wives and sweethearts will miss you. I figure they'll dig up some other patsies soon enough. And not even the loathsome prospect that you birds'll have to hob-nob with low-lifes, social inferiors and maybe even criminals, in the calaboose. Uh-uh. That ain't it. It's that I'll be ruined too, along with you. I confess I find that rather disturbing. I find it, in fact, appalling. So hear this, guys: it's not too late, yet. You can still save yourselves—and me too, while you're at it. Let's make a deal, fellow charter members of the insider's club. Give back the Linzeteum and we'll call it square. No one need ever know. Fork over the goods and we'll squash the squawks, wipe the slate clean. What could be fairer than that? What could be more noble, truthful and self-serving? It's either that or the jug. Think it over—what's it gonna be? You've got maybe a half-second to make up your so-called minds. Don't rush now, boys; we club members gotta stick together, right?"

Underwood looked at me. Snow looked at me.

Behind me a voice said:

"Don't be a dodo, Dunjer, they didn't do it." Ed Morgan stepped into the room.

"I thought the listening tube was off?" I complained.

"It was. I listened at the keyhole," Ed Morgan groaned, clutching his back. "Damn keyhole's built for a midget."

Morgan pulled a chair up beside Snow.

"Tell him we didn't do it," Snow said.

"Yes, for God's sake," Underwood said. "Tell him we didn't do it."

"I already have," Morgan said. "Use your head, Dunjer. Look at my two clients. What are they?"

"Crooks," I said.

"Precisely," Morgan said. "Anyone can see that even at a glance. Now what kind of crooks, Dunjer?"

"Old crooks," I said.

"Ah, there you are. Old crooks. Of course they are. Why, I could easily list the various underhanded, dishonest, ignominious schemes that this crooked pair has perpetrated in their long, dismal career devoted solely, it seems, to wrongdoing, bilking the public, robbing the kitty and fleecing the soft touch."

"There's a soft touch born every two minutes, it's been calculated," Underwood said.

"And we fleece him," Snow said. "If not us, someone else would."

"Someone less deserving," Underwood said.

"You see," Morgan said, "they boast of their criminal acts. Oh, I could list them, all right, only it would take too long; hours, if not actually days. You'll take my word that they're no good?"

"Yes," I said, "I'll do that."

"Yet, Dunjer," Morgan said, "here they sit, the two of them."

"Here we have always sat," Snow said.

"Scot-free," Morgan said. "Why, Dunjer? Ask yourself why?"

"Someone forgot to turn them in?" I wondered.

Underwood tapped his forehead. "Because we're smart," he said.

"That's why, Mr. Dunjer," Snow said. "Smart."

"Old crooks; experienced crooks; smart crooks," Morgan said. "Too smart to pull a dumb stunt like this. Listen, Dunjer, these two wouldn't throw out the baby with the bath water, wouldn't place themselves in a position where they were the only, sole and singular suspects. Not unless they had hardening of the criminal instincts, they wouldn't."

"We're not that old," Underwood said.

"A scandal, Mr. Dunjer," Snow said, "would hurt us as much as you. We'd both be out of business."

"Our front would be gone. However," Underwood said, reaching for a ledger, "you must be at least partially right. Who else but one of our employees could have done this stupid thing?"

"Some imbecile employee," Snow said, "with no sense of loyalty, with no moral fitness."

"My clients," Morgan said, "will help you catch this dummy."

"Dummy?" I said. "The ghees who pulled this were pros, not dummies."

"But somewhere," Underwood said, "a dummy's involved. That would be their weak link. Here." He handed me a yellow sheet. "The names of our servicers who worked the vault."

It was a long list. Most of the names were just names. One wasn't. Suddenly I got it, understood perfectly why Linda'd been snatched. Here it was, that one little —very trivial—item she might've known that could've tipped me to the heist, put me on guard. And the opposition, not sure whether she knew it or not, hadn't taken any chances.

"Since when has Joe Rankin been a servicer?" I heard myself ask.

"Since he took lessons," Snow said.

"Very ambitious lad," Underwood nodded.

"He *asked* to be put on the vault area," Snow said.

Underwood spread his hands as if to show how clean they were. "How could we refuse? Your brother-in-law, after all?"

How indeed?

NOTHINGNESS HAS TURNED TO BLACK, I SEE—A DEFINITE IMPROVEMENT OF SORTS. I HAVE ALWAYS WELCOMED IMPROVEMENTS; IT IS MY NATURE.

CHAPTER TWELVE

A mech ushered me into the Sass abode, swept an eye cell over my apparel. "Are you perhaps the undertaker, sir?" it asked. "Dr. Sass said he was about ready for one."

Before I could think up a smart answer, a long-legged, black-haired woman in a red and gold skirt and jacket stepped out from behind a curtain, batted an eyelash at me. "Dunjer?"

"Uh-huh," I said.

"This way," she said.

"I spoke to you on the phone, didn't I?" I asked, following her down a long, polished hallway past small end tables, vases, plastic flowers, a wilderness of man-made doodads.

"Yeah, Jack, and it was Jake with me."

"Uh-huh. You have a name?"

Her name, it turned out, was Miss Norwick and she was the doctor's assistant. "You want my rank and serial number too?"

"Forget it," I said magnanimously.

We were slowly working our way to the back of the house. It was some long house, this house. The science business must've been doing okay, only my mind wasn't on it. I kept thinking about my poor old in-law. With Rankin front and center in the safety vault heist, the law was bound to reach me no matter what, start a rumpus that'd turn Security Plus on its ear—and me out to pasture. *If* this Linzeteum was really something. Maybe it wouldn't be something.

"Up those stairs and through that door," Miss Norwick pointed. "You're on your own now, big boy. Good luck."

I went up the stairs, through a door. The girl went away somewhere.

I was in a wide, sunlit study. Three ivory walls were lined with leather-bound books, the fourth was made of glass and overlooked a garden. I'd hiked clear through the whole joint. There was a red couch over by the right wall and a little man in white toga and yellow sandals was on it.

This, no doubt, was Dr. Sass. He blinked at me out of wide gray eyes and sat up. His head was round, bald except for two tufts of white hair that sprouted behind each ear; a short white Vandyke beard decorated his chin. His cherubic features were, at the moment, turned down in a frown. He spoke:

"You are Dunjer?"

I admitted it.

The small man sighed. "Perhaps," he said, "you had best, for a starter, tell me exactly what happened?"

"I suppose so," I said, sitting down, "but I'll hate every second of it." I told him. Lord knows it didn't take long.

"And . . . ?" Sass asked when I was done.

I spread my hands. "That's it, all I've got. Now what in heaven's name is this Linzeteum?"

The small man looked at me, spoke five words:

"The key to the universe."

In the silence that followed, I heard myself say, "Uh-huh. Now if you could just tell me what that means—"

"The universe," the little person said, jumping up. "What is wrong with you, Dunjer?"

"Shock," I said. "I'm suffering from terrible shock. Why not humor me and spell it out?"

"Very well, Mr. Dunjer, I will tell you all there is to know about Linzeteum. I seem to have no choice in the matter. You know, I presume, what a key is? It is to open doors. Picture the universe if you will. . . ."

The little person was pacing now. "The universe has doors, many doors. Would you accept that?"

"Try me," I said earnestly. There seemed to be a note of pleading in my voice, one I could get to hate pretty quick.

"Doors," Dr. Sass said, "which separate one universe from the other. Or, more precisely, one continuum from another."

"What's a continuum?"

Dr. Sass glared at me, shook his head, sighed again, shrugged. "I don't know. The whole procedure is, ah, somewhat untested. We have sent monkeys through and retrieved them—in fine health, I might mention—but they have told us nothing."

"Won't talk, eh?"

"Can't. Monkeys, you know. . . . We have sent cameras through and have gotten back snapshots, developed them, and found worlds that are in some respects very much like our own. We think."

"Think?"

"How can we be sure? Our research is still in its infancy."

"Worlds?"

"More or less."

"*We?*"

"Me."

"No partners?"

"Hardly. I choose to work alone."

There was a something about the little man's tone through all this meandering that rang a bell, a something we ops know all about because we use it so often. It was only a hint, but I can take a hint as well as the next op. In my mind neon lights seemed to blink on and off, were spelling out *Liar*.

The last thing I needed now was neon lights on the brain.

"Tell me, Sass. You had this stuff insured?"

The doctor worked a smile. "Oh, yes. I am not a complete ninny."

"That's nice. How much?"

"In the vicinity of ten million, I'd say, give or take a million."

"Give or take. That's private insurance?"

"Of course."

"Which leaves our standard safety vault policy."

"So it does. Add another ten."

"A cool twenty million," I said, stunned.

"Yes, in the middle of my preparations to hang myself because of this terrible loss I had suffered, it suddenly occurred to me that I was a millionaire. What a boon for research, Mr. Dunjer."

"But you've lost your Linzeteum, Sass, haven't you? Your work's ruined."

"Work? What work? Why, I'm rich, man, rich." The doctor chuckled. "Just a whimsy on my part, sir, pay it no mind. You are quite right, of course, a terrible tragedy. The waste. The lost years. You understand, Mr. Dunjer, I was very upset. Horrified, you might say."

"You don't *sound* horrified."

"Oh, not anymore. I remembered something, you see; that a man of my vast wealth could surely buy all the Linzeteum he needed."

"This Linzeteum is spread all over the map? All you need is dough?"

"Nonsense, young man. Quite the contrary. On the entire globe—and for all I know, in the universe—the only other supply of Linzeteum is Crossworlds in the Firegold stronghold."

"Crossworlds? That's hundreds of miles of hostile, deadly terrain."

"Yes, yes," Dr. Sass smiled absently, seating himself. "A small cache of Linzeteum. Just lying there, you know. Research-abandoned years ago. Why, that fool, Dr. Minkle, had no idea of its true worth, its incredible properties. Not an inkling. I will certainly be able to purchase some."

"So all this desperation on your part, Sass, was just a bluff, an act?"

"Genuine, Mr. Dunjer. Hardly an act, I assure you. I was shaken, uncertain. At first it seemed as if doom had descended on my little project; but fortunately logic prevailed. Bit by bit, I saw my way through to the next contingency. A scientist can do that, you know. I was wealthy, now; I could purchase more of the product and still carry on. Better than before, in fact. Yes, Mr. Dunjer, at first I was truly distraught. Who wouldn't be? Then it occurred to me that if you found me prancing about for sheer joy at what was ostensibly so melancholy a moment, it might, er, confuse the issue, might point the finger of suspicion at *me*."

"Heaven forbid," I said, sinking back further into my chair like a rock going down under a very high wave.

"Perhaps I overdid it," he said. "Still, not a bad job of thinking on one's toes, ah?"

"Maybe," I said, "but you blew it. Everything you said has to go into my report, there'll be at least ten copies of the damn thing making the rounds; everyone will want to get into the act. Count on it, Doc: the insurance companies, the city constables, the Science Commission, the Chamber of Commerce. That's the whole truth, Doc; you'll be investigated from top to bottom, put through a fine sieve, bounced like a ping-pong ball and twirled like a yo-yo. You won't like it."

"It will tie up my insurance claim?"

I allowed myself a bitter chuckle. "Personally, Doc, I'm prepared to buy your little yarn; everything you said sounds just stupid enough to be true. But take it from me, pal, it'll be years before you collect on this deal; maybe centuries."

The doctor turned a pale green. "Centuries is too long."

I nodded. "There's more to thinking on your toes than meets the eye. You've been living in a dream world, Sass; all this wealth is nothing but a pipe dream."

"But then I really *am* ruined," the doctor wailed.

"Uh-huh. You, me and everyone else connected with this oozing mess."

ANY MOMENT NOW I SHALL PROBABLY START TO MOVE. IT IS TOO SOON TO EQUATE MOTION WITH PROGRESS. HOWEVER, I HAVE HIGH HOPES.

CHAPTER THIRTEEN

We went back along the hallway I'd traveled earlier, the doctor talking all the while.

"It is a senseless theft. Linzeteum is merely the fuel. To breach the continuums, an activator is necessary, and I possess the only three there are."

"Yeah," I mumbled, "senseless. What about this terrible danger you mentioned?"

"Unspecified danger, untested danger."

"But danger."

"Theoretically," Sass shrugged. "This way." We turned into a short corridor, then a darkened room. Long drapes covered the windows. Going to one, I pushed it aside. Bars. A mech stood motionless by the right wall. I looked at it; it looked at me. A picture hung on the wall: trees, flowers, a setting sun.

"My stronghold," the doctor said. "When an activator passes through the doors of the universe, Mr. Dunjer, something happens; I was hoping to find out what. It is, I think, a matter of duration, of how long the activator is in use, of how long the transferred objects or personnel remain in their new continuum. What I think happens is everything blows up."

"*That*'s what you think happens?"

"It's a thought. I have others."

"You want me to guess?"

"Immaterial, now. Purely academic. I fear it will be many a long, futile day before we power another activator."

"Tell me anyway."

"Some things blow up. Some worlds. The universes. Both. Or a combination of the two. A continuum that might be termed Interworld. Something along those lines. Perhaps."

The doctor was removing the painting from the wall. Behind it a large wall safe glistened. Holding up a thumb, he pressed it against the safe, registered a print. Something went click. The door popped up into a crevice like a curtain rising on a stage.

Two objects lay in the otherwise empty safe. Both were identical, looked like small transistor radios. They lay side by side as though in a dime store display window. There was room for a third thingumajig, but someone had obviously bought it. All that was left was a clear, shiny space on the smooth metal.

I turned to the doctor. The little man promptly keeled over, stretched himself out on the floor. I put out a hand, shook the mech by the shoulder. The mech fell face down, next to the doc.

"Miss Norwick!" I bellowed.

"Should we allow it?" Miss Norwick asked me.

"Why not?"

We were back in the book-lined study, back with the wall window, couch and little supine person. It was beginning to feel natural, this merry-go-round, a sure sign of no progress.

"Okay, peerless leader," Miss Norwick said, "so sit up." She extended a slim hand which the doctor grasped, heaved himself to a sitting position.

"See, my dear," he told Miss Norwick, "I am sitting up and nothing bad has happened."

"That's because it's already happened," I explained, drawing up a chair and seating myself. Miss Norwick perched on the armrest. I told the doctor:

"Straight talk, eh?"

"I am prepared to swear on the Bible, if you have brought one along."

"Unnecessary. Suddenly you sound honest as all get-out. Tell me, that stuff about doom and disaster—on the level?"

The doctor nodded glumly.

"The blowup's for real, eh?"

The doctor shrugged. "Who can tell? It would seem so, at this stage of our research. Blowup or something equally unpleasant. And final."

"This, er, final thing," I said, "is going to happen to *us?*"

The doctor looked at me. "Who else?"

"What kind of crummy commission lets dangerous experiments like this go on?!" I roared.

"Dangerous? Who said anything about dangerous? The Scientific Commission has backed me fully on this project. Only in the unlikely event of gross negligence does Linzeteum pose a threat."

"Unlikely?"

"Well, *I* wasn't planning to use it negligently."

"Don't worry, others will make up for your omission."

"It does rather look that way, doesn't it?"

"What about Miss Norwick?" I said, pointing a thumb.

"What about her?"

"She works with you, doesn't she?"

"In a manner of speaking, yes."

"And I earn every miserable penny of it," Miss Norwick said.

"No one doubts that, my dear," Dr. Sass said.

"And the mechs?" I said.

"My dear sir, are you suggesting I collaborate with mechanicals?"

"They've got the run of the place, no? They'll have to be checked; Miss Norwick will have to be checked; *everything*'ll have to be checked. If there's one thing I can't stand, it's the thought of that final thing happening to *me*."

AH, YES. HERE WE GO.

CHAPTER FOURTEEN

Back at the office I gave Miss Follsom my names: Norwick and Sass. "Shoot these down to the master computer to check out for friends, acquaintances and casual hangers-on. I want to know who Norwick and Sass pal with and who the pals buddy with; I want a detailed report on everyone. Send the mechs out on the street if you have to. Follow-ups by persons when called for. Reports on my desk by this afternoon. If anyone from the *Daily Tattler* shows up between now and then, tell 'em I've got stomach cramps. On the double, Miss Follsom, the universe may be at stake. Let's shake it for the universe, Miss Follsom; there won't be any universe to kick around if we slip up on this one. It's one universe to a customer-r-r-r. . . ."

Miss Follsom left. I decided to put off being hysterical for a while longer and went out for lunch.

Miss Follsom stuck her blond head through the interoffice doorway. "Gulach Grample, boss," she shouted.

"What was that?" I said, sitting down. "Have a nice lunch?"

"A name, boss. I didn't bother with lunch."

"A name? Sounded like baked fish or something. You on a diet, Miss Follsom?"

"I couldn't resist, boss. I had to find out what's cooking. It's Gulach Grample!"

"Yeah," I said. "So what did the computers come up with?"

The alarm board cut in. "What Miss Follsom is

attempting to explain," the alarm board explained, "is that your case is solved."

"Solved?"

"Honest, boss, you're saved," Miss Follsom said.

"Saved?"

The alarm board intoned, "Due to the extreme alertness of the master computer, the wrongdoer has been speedily and thoroughly unmasked."

"Unmasked?" I said, "so soon?"

"That's right, boss. Gulach Grample!"

That's the culprit, the wrongdoer? This Gulach Grample?" I asked.

"Gulach Grample," Miss Follsom said, making me think of anchovy paste. "Look on your desk, boss."

I looked. It only took a glance through the stacked pile of readouts to get the picture. It was all Grample. He turned up and tied in no less than 216 times, it said in the summation. I went through the material. It took a while.

Miss Norwick was currently dating one Morgan La-Suer, who held down a foreman's post at a canned goods outfit owned by Gulach Grample—a relationship that plainly showed how Grample might've got wind of Sass's invention. Joe Rankin, my departed in-law, owed a bundle to a bookie who was bankrolled by Grample through Money, Inc. Wendell Goodyear—once our employee, but now a Money, Inc. exec—had put Underwood and Snow on our payroll before quitting, and they'd promptly installed Rankin as our servicer. Dr. Sass's safe had been bought from Feel-Safe, which was owned by a Grample holding company. The truckers who had hauled the Linzeteum from Sass's house to the Emporium safety vault were controlled by a Grample subsidiary: Truckers United. The union boss of TU was married to a Grample vice-president in the big Grample complex: Business Anomalies. I'd heard of that one, who hadn't? But the name associated with BA was Morris Wangdangle, a nice normal name by comparison to this Grample creep.

So why had I never heard of Gulach Grample?

A second look at what I was reading gave me part of the answer:

Our culprit was half-owner of the *Daily Tattler,* chief dirt-digger in Happy City; if they didn't tattle, who would?

"See, boss?" Miss Follsom said. "It's in the bag, isn't it?"

"Maybe. Why haven't I come across this peculiar name before?" I asked the alarm board. "It sounds like some kind of spaghetti and the guy seems to own the whole town."

"That's why," the alarm board said. "He owns the whole town. The master computer had to go on override to release his name. It did so—exercising the wisdom one has come to associate with the noble mechanical—only due to the urgency and gravity of the problem, declassifying the Red-Alert data."

"Red-Alert? That's municipal security stuff. Does this cracker think he *really* owns the town?"

"He *is* the town," the alarm board said.

I sat back in my chair and fixed Miss Follsom with a tired eye. "What did you say was in the bag?"

"Our early retirement; excuse me while I go type up the forms."

"A bit premature, Miss Follsom; better put it off till tomorrow."

"Tomorrow? What happens today, you call the constables?"

"I wouldn't mind. Only they're crooked as hell and this Grample bird probably owns them too."

"There's another course?"

"Yeah, me; that's the other course. I upset the apple cart, get judicial clearance for an unspecified raid, use company mechs and humans, go up against this Grample in force, see what's what and where and try to justify it all afterward."

"Risky, boss, isn't it?"

"Maybe, if this guy's all the computer says he is. But

that's what lawyers are for and we've got dozens; let 'em earn their keep. We've got this Gulach Grample dead to rights, an open and shut case. Everything points to him. Damned if I can figure out why he didn't cover up. Anyway, as soon as I wangle a raid order, we knock over this guy's estate, heh-heh, if we can find it. He's got to live somewhere, right?"

"Dr. Sass, incidentally, called during lunch, Mr. Dunjer. He said it was urgent."

"Not now, Miss Follsom. I've got to see a judge first—about a raid order."

BLACKNESS GIVES WAY TO GRAY. I PICK UP SPEED.

CHAPTER FIFTEEN

The estate was in a valley.

Trees, gates, fences and walls hid it from the surrounding populace. Happy City stretches a long way and Grample Village was almost at its borders. It wasn't called Grample Village, of course. Morris Wangdangle was down as the property's owner, just as he was, supposedly, top dog at Business Anomalies.

"If the world only knew," I said to Hennessy, as our copter, one of thirty-eight, zeroed in on the complex.

Hennessy, one of the nine human ops along for the ride, turned to me. "It wouldn't care," he told me.

I looked at the diminutive, dark-haired sleuth. He had a point.

We landed—on the button, wheels cutting sharp lines into the green lawn.

I punched battle stations on the pocket controller, leaped out of the copter, Hennessy at my side. Water splashed underfoot, wet grass slushed unpleasantly. Yesterday's rain was all over the place.

"We shoot them?" Hennessy yelled.

"We show 'em the raid order first," I yelled, *"then* we shoot 'em. After they start resisting. Remember, we want this strictly legal."

"How come we're yelling?" Hennessy yelled.

"Damned if I know," I said.

Turning up our coat collars against the wind, the pair of us headed for the main building.

Up ahead we could see the mechs manning their posts—or, more properly speaking, meching their posts —stationing themselves at windows, doorways, on rooftops and generally making a nuisance of themselves; they were leaving wet, dirty footprints everywhere. An occasional human op could be seen too, trying to get out of the way of possible fire. Possible fire was probably the human op's greatest hazard on this kind of mission, and all the human op's ingenuity went into keeping out of its way; like lagging behind mechs or crouching near copters or running in the opposite direction.

"Let's stay behind this tree," I said, pointing to a tree, "until the fireworks are over."

A voice boomed over the grounds:

"Welcome, Dunjer!"

"Forget the tree," I told Hennessy. "They hardly ever say that if they mean to put up a fight."

"They know your name," Hennessy exclaimed.

"Why not? They seem to know everything else."

I punched out stand-by orders for my mech crew, and we marched up to the triple-decker mansion. A tall, graying individual in a tuxedo met us at the front door.

Hennessy whispered at my elbow, "A human butler."

Classy, all right, and as hard to find as a friendly mammoth.

Suddenly I wondered if my tie was on straight, if my pants hadn't lost their crease in this foul weather.

"This way, gentlemen," the butler said, leading us down a purple-carpeted hallway, past displays of chain mail, armored suits, stuffed game and brilliantly painted pinball machines.

"Maybe we should freshen up first in the men's room?" I whispered to Hennessy.

The butler had led us into a huge, plush sitting room.

"What do we do now?" Hennessy whispered back.

"Sit down. There're enough chairs, Lord knows."

We sat, leaving twenty chairs still vacant. Plants and potted trees shared the room with these chairs. An Oriental rug of intricate design absorbed the water that leaked from my shoes. The butler, instead of going away like he should've, took an easy chair across from us.

"It's Mr. Grample we've come to see," I said.

"Yes," the butler smiled, adjusting his tux, "he said you would be calling, sir."

"Oh."

"He left word that I should entertain you in his absence."

"You?"

"Yes sir, I."

"Entertain? You do tricks?"

"Not quite. Perhaps I had best introduce myself. I am Morris Wangdangle."

"You, Morris Wangdangle, a butler?" I heard myself gasp.

The butler nodded. "Only part-time, of course. The rest of the time I am president of Business Anomalies."

"But how's that possible?" Hennessy blurted out.

"He bought me," the butler said.

"Tea?" a dainty maid entered carrying a tray.

"My God!" Hennessy shouted, beside himself. "Dina Good-dish, the famous Tri-D star!"

"He bought her too," Morris Wangdangle said.

When we were alone again, the butler explained the situation. "You see, Mr. Grample has bought almost everything. Scads of it."

"He hasn't bought me," I told him.

"That is true, sir."

I thought it over. "Eh, you wouldn't know . . . if maybe—"

"I *am* sorry, sir, but in Mr. Grample's absence I am afraid that would be quite out of the question."

I sighed. "Absence, eh?"

"Oh, yes. He is away, sir."

"Run out of things to buy around here, eh?"

"He does not take me into his confidence, sir."

"Of course. You said something about entertain."

"Yes indeed, sir. Mr. Grample said I should play this for you, sir."

The butler touched a tape cube on an end table with a long finger; the cube explained:

"This is Gulach Grample speaking. Time is money, so I'll be quick. I'm elsewhere, Dunjer. Out of your reach. Somewhere you'll never find me. Not that it matters, Dunjer. I could always buy you. Take as much time as you want looking through this joint. I'm not here. Some joke on you, ha, Dunjer?"

In the embarrassed silence that followed I asked, "That's it?"

"That is it, sir."

"I didn't find that very entertaining," I said.

"But it *was* quick, sir, as he promised."

I admitted it.

"Mr. Grample, sir, no doubt found it entertaining."

"No doubt."

"Would you care to search the premises, sir?"

I shrugged. "What for? If he's here, he'll just buy me, right?"

"Quite right, sir."

"I didn't find that joke of his very funny either."

"I doubt that you were meant to."

"I guess not. Coming, Hennessy?"

"I'm mesmerized, boss."

"It's the tea, sir. Mr. Grample insists on very brisk tea."

"You *like* this Grample creep, Wangdangle?" I asked, rising.

"He is a very robust character, sir. I was one of his first purchases, you know. Quite a bargain. But *everything* was less costly in those days, wouldn't you say?"

"Listen, Dunjer," Dr. Sass ran up to me as I entered his study. "Thank God you've come. I know where he's gone . . . I know . . . I tried to reach you earlier . . . why didn't you call me? . . . you must find him . . . bring him back . . . I charge you with this awesome task, Mr. Dunjer. The universe, sir, what would we do without it? My monitor shows activity, Mr. Dunjer; that fool Grample is using the Linzeteum—"

"In the activator?"

"Certainly. Where else would he use it?"

"I was just asking."

"Bring him back, Mr. Dunjer."

"Yeah, I know; you already said that. How do I manage it though, with a net or fishing tackle?"

"The Firegold stronghold, use your head, man. They have a cache of Linzeteum. For pity's sake, Mr. Dunjer, there isn't a moment to waste. I will lend you my test-o-meter. You must find and bring back that product!"

"What's a test-o-meter?"

"It shows Linzeteum activity. Dr. Minkle is the one you want; he'll have the product. Ask for the lab building."

"Ask?"

"At the stronghold."

"A stronghold, yet, and on the other side of the world. You couldn't've picked a *nicer* place?"

"The Happy City jet?" Mayor Strapper said. "Are you crazy, Dunjer?"

"Actually," I said, "I'd rather not go into that just now. Show him the form, Morgan."

Red-topped Ed Morgan showed him the form.

"What's this?" the mayor demanded, glancing at the paper.

"Public requisition notice," Morgan said.

We were on the four hundredth floor of the Happy City City Hall, in the mayor's gilt-edged office. The venetian blinds were rolled up, offering a fine view of the clouds for anyone who cared to see 'em at eye level. Strapper was a medium-sized, paunchy individual with round glasses, white hair and a gray mustache. "Since when does Morgan work for you, Dunjer?"

"Since I borrowed him from Underwood and Snow."

The mayor leaned back in his chair, eyed us with curiosity. "Run out of your own counsels, Dunjer? The last time I looked, your firm seemed to have thousands of them."

"Uh-uh. That's just for the rubes. We have maybe thirty lawyers."

"Thirty? That's still a lot."

"One for each of the bad things that can happen to us. We tallied it up."

"So why him?" the mayor waved a thumb at Morgan.

"The thirty-first thing finally happened."

Strapper took off his glasses, sighed. "I'll sign this thing, but you must be crazy, Dunjer. If you don't bring the Happy City jet back in one piece, it'll cost you a fortune. Where do you plan to fly it anyway— in circles over the city? An advertising stunt, perhaps? That's illegal, you know. And if you fly it over those foreign cities, they'll shoot you down. They're mean, those foreign cities; they're not nice like us."

"We'll have to take our chances," I said.

"Good grief," the mayor gasped. "You *are* thinking of pulling some crazy stunt, aren't you?"

"As is specified by public requisition form 2AB6—" Morgan began.

"I'll have to take it to court," Mayor Strapper said, "if you boys won't tell me the score. It's mandatory under the Happy City charter."

"Go ahead," Morgan said, "it'll be a good long case."

"Long enough for you to do whatever you have in mind, ah?" the mayor asked shrewdly.

"We certainly hope so," Morgan said.

I said, "How many Happy City jets you got?"

"Ten."

"Prepare for nine."

The mayor wiped his brow. "It'll cost you a fortune, Dunjer."

"Not if it's a public service, it won't."

"Try and prove that!"

"What do you think we've got those thirty counsels for?"

AT THIS RATE I SHALL CERTAINLY FIND MYSELF AT THE TIME TRACKS IN JIG TIME. AND ONCE THERE—THE VOID AND THE MANY WORLDS.

CHAPTER SIXTEEN

"Easy does it," I said.

"We know our business, Dunjer," Underwood said.

"You are such a disagreeable person," Snow said, squinting through his glasses.

"I wasn't talking to you," I said. "I was talking to it."

"We mechs know our business," the mech said, "you disagreeable person, you."

The mech, at last, got the Ringer machine out of the panel truck and began lugging it across the Happy City airfield to the Happy City jet. I watched it, feeling rotten. If there was one thing I hated even more than that *final thing* which might happen to *everyone,* it was the idea of that final thing happening *only to me.* I really couldn't stand that idea. And here I was putting my neck right in the sling, just asking for something heroic and final to get me—the only me there was, the one I'd grown accustomed to and loved. For the hundredth time I thought of sending a mech on the mission. I could sit back at the office and try to figure things out —maybe I'd use algebra or geometry or something along those lines—while the mechs saved my hide. For the hundredth time I had to reject this very sensible solution. Not that the mech union would balk at the prospect of one of its tin cans going off on a suicide jaunt. The proposed union had folded after two days of staunch mech wrangling. Those things couldn't see eyecell to eyecell on what polish to rub on each other, let alone come up with a workable union charter. No, the mech union wouldn't care because there wasn't any. But *I* might care. That was it, plain and simple. No mech had ever been sent this far beyond the city boundaries on its own. No way to guess what'd come up along the route, what kind of woe the intervening cities might pitch at a solo expedition violating their air space. I just couldn't afford another foul-up. There had to be a man on the scene. And volunteers didn't seem too likely.

The mech and Ringer, meanwhile, had disappeared into the jet.

"What do you call him?" I asked, indicating the mech with a nod.

"Old Butterfingers," Underwood said cheerfully.

"Is he the mech tech you're sending with me?" I asked.

"This one installs them," Underwood said.

"Another one programs them," Snow said.

"Another one?" I said like some stupid recording.

"Oh, yes. He'll be along shortly," Snow said. "A technical type, Mr. Dunjer, his mind works like a slide rule."

"His mind *is* a slide rule," Underwood said.

"*He*'s my mech tech?" I asked.

"No indeed, Mr. Dunjer," Snow said, "we have a third one drilled in that discipline."

"You guys always take turns in talking?" I asked.

"Every now and then," Underwood said, adjusting his tunic, "when the mood takes us."

"We're in the mood now," Snow said.

"Keep checking," I said.

"If you don't trust them," Grange said, "why do you use them?"

"I trust 'em. It's mechs I don't trust. Anyway, Underwood and Snow's mechs haven't won any efficiency awards lately."

"Neither have I, Dunjer, baby," Grange said.

"At least you're human," I said. "How does the machine look?"

"For a Ringer it looks fine."

"Will it work?"

"How should I know? Who ever tests a Ringer? I mean, where would you test one?"

"That's the best advice you can give me?"

"The best advice I can give you, baby, is to forget this screwball scheme."

"It's my back," Hennessy said. "See, I have the medical report right here, boss. It's a damn shame; with a back like mine there's no chance I could go along on this little trip of yours."

"No chance," I said.

"No matter how much I'd like to."

"Uh-huh," I said.

"And I really would like to if it weren't for this terrible back that came upon me all of a sudden, as the medical report will verify."

"Verify," I said.

"It better," Hennessy said. "It cost a bundle."

"Bundle," I said.

"Otherwise, I'd actually go right along with you. After all, why should you be the only one killed?"

"Why?" I asked.

"I like the way you're taking this," Hennessy said, leaving, "and good luck, you crazy, mixed-up kid you."

Miss Follsom came into the office.

"Why are you all doubled up in your chair that way, Mr. Dunjer, sir?"

"My stomach hurts."

"It must be something going around. Just look at this," she waved a sheaf of papers at me. "Eighteen sick-leave notices in the last hour, boss; who could believe it?"

"I could."

"Why, there won't be a human operative left to see you off if this continues."

"It'll continue."

"An epidemic," Miss Follsom said.

"Don't worry," I said. "You're immune."

"I am?"

"I wasn't thinking of asking you to come along, Miss Follsom. Except maybe for company. A man going off by himself—as I am, apparently—could become very lonesome."

"Oh, Mr. Dunjer, suddenly I feel this terrible pain in my Weltschmerz, sir."

"That's where they all feel it," I said. "Very well, I will go alone, Miss Follsom."

"You don't have to go either, boss. They can't *make* you. There's nothing in your contract that says you've got to get yourself killed."

"If you knew what was at stake, Miss Follsom, you'd *want* me to go."

"Never, Mr. Dunjer, sir. What's at stake?"

"Continued life on this planet, maybe."

"So, go already."

"As your trusty alarm board, I wish only to remark that I would gladly accompany you on this mission fraught with danger . . . as you know, however, we alarm boards are totally immobile . . . therefore, it is quite impossible—"

"I didn't ask you!" I yelled.

OBSERVING THE WORLDS ON ANY GIVEN TIME TRACK IS SIMPLE ENOUGH. THERE ARE PORTHOLES IN THE FABRIC OF THE UNIVERSE WHICH ALLOW A SPLENDID VIEW OF ALL THE WORLDS. ONE NEED BUT GO FROM ONE PORTHOLE TO THE NEXT TO EXAMINE EACH SUCCESSIVE WORLD. THE LESS STABLE ONES, THOSE TWINED WITH THE FABRIC ITSELF, MAY BE INSPECTED ON THE SPOT, INTERNALLY, AS IT WERE. ONLY WHO WOULD WANT TO?

CHAPTER SEVENTEEN

I had taken a seat up front.

There was something about being alone with sixty mechs, alone with 120 probing eyecells in sixty metal headpieces all containing cogs, wheels, wires and current, and that something was plain lousy.

We were above the clouds, the Happy City jet engine purring like a cat high on sour cream. Every once in a while I aimed an eye at a convenient window just to make sure things were still moving along. They were.

Outside the forty-nine Dead Ringers kept us company. Those Dead Ringers made quite a sight, one that inspired me with a certain tiny amount of confidence, if not overwhelming enthusiasm. For all intents and purposes, a squadron of fifty planes had taken to the skies. Radar, telescopes, the naked eye and any other whatsis the opposition below might fix on us would reveal nothing less. Not a jot. Or I'd get my money back, provided I was still around and had paid money in the first place.

Most cities—Happy City included—couldn't afford this much useless flying equipment. Land grabs were as slack as the suspenders on the dieting champ of the year. What with limited trade and research coming up with new items all the time, intercity rough and tumble was as rare as a bearded lady in a beauty contest. So how come I was about to unload a parcel of grief on unsuspecting, innocent foreign turf? First, the Firegold strongholders weren't all that innocent; second, I figured I could get away with it; third, I seemed to have no choice in the matter. Reasons enough, eh? I had, however, thoughtfully painted out the Happy City insignia on the side of our jet, adding, I hoped, that certain touch of mystery.

The gamble was a simple and chancy one: the Ringer produced ringers—phantoms that couldn't be distinguished from the real McCoy. Any number. Any kind. I'd settled on forty-nine ringers plus the original. Too many to shoot at since—who knows?—we might shoot back, or maybe drop things that exploded; yet not so many as to seem ridiculous. If someone got the right idea, started throwing ack-ack our way, the *real* Happy City jet might get hit. Against *that* there was only prayer, and with a cargo of sixty mechs, who could we pray to, the God of the smelt works?

Down below the small cities looked like pieces of a child's game. Valleys, hills, walled and unwalled cities, but a vast scramble of architecture all laid out differently, no two cities alike. I was glad they were down there and I was up here. It gave me that added bit of perspective, not to mention a lot of safety.

"We are now over Knock-Out City," a mech reported.

I left my seat to join the pilot at his controls. "Knock-Out City?" I said. "They won't try to knock us out, will they?" There were so many cities around, I'd never heard of half of 'em.

The mech pilot was reassuring. "It's not that kind of knock-out."

"You mean it's a beautiful place?"

"Not that either."

"So why do they call it Knock-Out City?"

"It's the populace. They're all knocked out. The dope center of the eastern seaboard, you know."

"No kidding?"

"They die young."

"Who runs the town?"

"Mechs. Mechs run everything. Mechs wouldn't bother to shoot us down. Mechs are peaceable, friendly and loving. Also they don't give a hoot."

"It takes all kinds."

"Next we hit Ambush City."

"Ambush? That sounds bad, doesn't it?"

"Not to worry, they only ambush the weak and helpless."

It was a relief to hear it and I said so.

"Fist City is after that," the Mech said. "We had best fly around it. Frankly, I don't care for the name."

"Frankly, I don't blame you. Is Peaceful Valley around here?"

"A couple of hundred miles."

"Let's fly over it. Peaceful Valley is famous for being a pushover; it'll be good for our nerves."

"But will it be good for *their* nerves?"

"That's their lookout," I said. "Fist City, eh? You sure you got that right?"

"I'm *programmed* to be sure."

"Pardon me," XX21 said, "but how many mechs do we have aboard?"

"Sixty," I told him.

"Guess again."

"Fifty-nine?"

"Sixty-one."

I looked at him. "I didn't order sixty-one."

"But you got sixty-one."

"I won't even ask if you're sure. Okay," I said, going down in the aisle and raising my voice, "which one of you guys is the extra mech? Come on, speak up."

An eerie silence engulfed the plane. Only the motor could be heard; it seemed to be having a good enough time.

"What's wrong with you blasted machines?" I demanded. "I asked you a question!"

The mechs said nothing.

"Come on now, guys," I said. "You're not supposed to behave this way. Don't you guys know how to behave?"

"Perhaps," XX21 said, "you're asking the *wrong* question, boss?"

"What should I ask?"

"Ask them their specialty. Us regular mech types will no doubt respond with aplomb to so simple a query. But what will the extra mech say?"

"What *will* he say?"

"Damned if I know, skipper; this is a unique situation."

"One hell of a spot for a unique situation. All right, you guys, let's sound off; gimme your specialties. Starting there." I pointed to the first seat behind the mech pilot on the left aisle. All the mechs were seated. Going from front to back, I ought to run across our extra. Only what in the world were we doing with an extra? Who ever heard of something so unlikely, so unprecedented, so unprogrammed?

"My specialty," the first mech said, "is hitting. I am rarely used. But when I am, I hit like crazy. Call me 94Z."

"That checks," XX21 said.

"You've got a list?"

XX21 tapped his think tank. "Up here, boss."

"I am a driver," the next mech said, "call me RB4. Give me a vehicle and I'll drive it crazy."

"*Like* crazy," I said. "Next."

"I am a shooter," the mech said. "I shoot other mechs mostly, but on request I shoot people too. Personally, I prefer shooting people. Call me VV343."

"He checks out," XX21 said.

"I didn't even know we *had* that kind of mech," I said.

"It takes all kinds," XX21 said. "Anyway, he's been especially programmed for this trip. Next."

"I am a thrower," the next mech said. "I throw things, things that hurt other things and sometimes people. I even throw me if I can't find a more satisfying object to throw. Call me 992A. The thrower."

"This is some crew," I said.

"Assault troops," XX21 pointed out, "the toughest mechs in the game."

"Assault isn't a game," I said, "it's a crime."

"Led by a human, it's a game."

"What kind of human would lead a disgusting thing like that?"

"You."

"Only under duress. Like if I were gonna lose my job maybe and this could save it. There's got to be big stakes involved."

"Next," XX21 said.

"I am a digger; I dig ditches, foxholes and bunkers in which my teammates may hide from the enemy's dire assault. Call me O22."

"More assaults, eh?"

"It is the expected procedure," XX21 said. "After all, war is war."

"I'm sorry I started this rigmarole. There ain't gonna be no war as long as *I'm* in charge. People get hurt in wars. And *I'm* the only people here. Next."

"I am a drazzle afgassel. I squig the prescils. Call me Seymour," the mech explained.

"Squig the prescils?" I said. "What the hell is that?"

"Seymour?" XX21 said. "What kind of name is *that* for a mech?"

"We got any drazzle afgassels aboard?" I asked.

"Not on *my* manifest," XX21 said.

"I know you, don't I?" I asked the peculiar mech. The voice had sounded familiar.

It nodded.

"Boss," XX21 said, "what kind of a mech is this?"

"It's not a mech," I sighed.

"I'm sorry I came," Seymour said.

"It's human?" XX21 asked.

"Only in part. You'd better come out."

"Righto."

A door opened in the mech's chest and a small man crawled through. He wore a neat, checkered, double-breasted suit, brown shoes, a fashionably wide blue and yellow tie and a white shirt, slightly frayed at the collar. His hair was brown, curly, nose large, eyes brown behind thick glasses. "Boy," he said, "it's cramped in there."

"Meet Seymour Salant," I said, "ace *Daily Tattler* snoop."

"Caught you at last, Dunjer," Seymour Salant said.

"Sure. But you'll never get to print this story, Salant."

"The Firegold stronghold, dead ahead," the pilot called.

"What's happening?" Salant asked. "For God's sake."

"You don't know?"

"They didn't tell me at city desk."

"They didn't know at city desk, but you'll see."

"Will I like it?"

"Don't bank on it."

ALL BUT ARRIVED! MY MISSION BEGINS. I MAY NOW DIVULGE MY NAME. I SHALL, IN FACT, DO SO. . . .

CHAPTER EIGHTEEN

We came down some twenty miles from the Firegold stronghold. Just before landing I cut the Ringer and the Happy City jet soloed in on the ancient, cracked landing field. Weeds, trees, small hills and rickety railroad tracks decorated the landscape.

The oldster that trotted out to meet us wore a white beard and a baseball cap.

"By cracky," he said, "ain't been a plane here for five years, maybe six."

The mechs, meanwhile, were piling out of the jet, scrambling through the doors as if they were involved in a fire drill at the neighborhood kiddy show. Canned goods being unloaded at the corner supermarket never sounded more spry.

"How'd you do it?" the oldster wanted to know. "How come they didn't shoot you down? They always shoot 'em down. No business at all on this old strip. Sometimes they used to get permission from the cities, you know, to fly over. But each city had to vote. Took months to get a route set. By jiminy, you got a lot of mechs there. Going to march in a parade? Going to Sell City, I betcha. Gonna take the mono to Sell City. Gonna sell and buy in Sell City, huh? That's what they all used to do. Sell and buy. Why not, huh? That's what you gonna do, fellas?"

"What *are* we going to do?" Seymour Salant asked.

"Go to the Firegold stronghold," I said.

Some mechs were lining up in columns of two. Others were unloading the gear: various types of weapons, exploders. A small arsenal. I hoped it worked as good as it looked.

"Hold on," the oldster exclaimed. "I didn't hear you right, did I? You mention the Firegold stronghold? That awful place! You ain't rightly going there, are you? Why, that's the spot you pick if you wanna get killed. You folks ain't looking to get killed, are you? No one goes to the Firegold stronghold, not if they're in their right minds, they don't. Hell and tarnation, folks, if they don't kill you, they enslave you. Listen to me, folks, you don't wanna go there. You wanna be slavies? The slavies there gotta wear chains. Oh, it ain't no picnic, folks. Them mechs won't help, take it from me. You know what? Them Firegold fellas got scramblers. They gonna scramble your mechs, make them no good. That's right, that's what they do. Then they gonna make slavies out o' you two fellas. It'd be a cryin' shame, and in the prime of life too, I'd reckon. Almost."

"Maybe we shouldn't go," Seymour said.

"That's good sense, youngster," the oldster said. "Why don't you go buy something expensive in Sell City? Now, that's a *nice* place."

The monorail rattled along.

Trees, shrubs, tunnels scooted by. Lost Cause City, Scavengerburg and No Hope came and went. The passenger cars began to empty out. Ten minutes to the Firegold stronghold we had the train to ourselves.

The mech conductor came into the car.

"Firegold next," he called. "Just push the doors open, fellers, when you get there. I'll be hiding under the seats, if you don't mind. Get off quick. This old train don't wait around much at that station."

The town square was empty. The Firegold mech guards had quietly watched us sail through the tunnel leading into their town. It was bad enough; in fact, awful. The first time I'd seen a mean-looking mech.

Off in the distance the mono blew its whistle. It sure hadn't taken long to move on.

"Which way?" XX21 asked.

A good question. I looked around. A row of two- and three-story run-down shacks faced us across the square. Some distance behind them high walls and towers poked at the clouds. Signs pointed down a wide street over to the left: Metalworks. Laboratories. Slave Dungeon. Shopping Center. Combat Arena. Beauty Parlor. Bar and Grill. Bank Vaults.

"Maybe we could stop off for a drink?" Seymour said.

"Uh-uh," I said. "Wrong bar and grill. They mean doors barred while they grill you over a slow fire."

"Let's forget the drink," Seymour said.

"The laboratories, fellas," I told the mechs. "See which way the sign's pointing."

The mechs had donned wheels—really attachable roller skates—and now we and they rocketed down the main drag, Seymour and I pulled along, in a small four-wheeler cart, by a long rope. The streets here certainly weren't made for four-wheeled carts. We bumped around plenty. No one had deigned to take notice of us—yet.

When we passed a tall, skinny character in work clothes—the first one we'd seen—I called a halt.

"This way to the laboratories?" I asked.

"Laboratories? They usually want the bank vaults."

"We'll settle for the labs," I said.

"Go straight for two blocks, turn right by the slave dungeon, the large gray building with the steel shutters. You want the stone structure with no windows right after it. But you'll be sorry."

"They've really got a slave dungeon?" Seymour asked.

"Sure. What good are slaves without a dungeon?"

Our shooter mech shot the door; it went down with a clang.

From here on in, the mechs knew what to do and did it. Swarming through the doorway, they made for stairs, escalators, elevators and dumbwaiters. Outside a body of mechs, donning adhesives, began to climb the building's exterior.

I went over to the office directory, looked up Dr. Minkle. He was in 9C. One hell of a climb.

I spoke into the pin-point talkie stuck in my lapel. "9C. On the double."

My lapel talked back. "Head down the lobby, boss, second door on the left."

"Thanks, XX21."

We reached the fire stairs. Our two-mech escort was waiting for us. One of 'em handed me the package.

"Nine floors?" Seymour said. "And we walk?"

"Mechanical conveyances have a way of malfunctioning," I pointed out, "and main stairways have a habit of getting blocked when they're carrying unwanted goods. Here," I said, "hang on to this." I gave him the package. The second floor came and went.

"What's this?"

"Dynamite." I drew my laser. "I may be busy for a while. Just hold tight to that stuff."

"We reporters aren't supposed to take part in wars."

"Theft," I said. "What we're doing is theft."

"Let *them* hold this stuff," Seymour urged me, indicating our two mech cohorts.

"Uh-uh," I said. "You don't want that. Remember the scramblers? What they scramble are mech's innards. Makes 'em drop things. Very inconvenient for the things. Otherwise, they'd be carrying *us* up these stupid stairs. You don't want 'em dropping any dynamite."

"You're right," Seymour said. "I wouldn't want that."

Presently the ninth floor loomed ahead. Just in time, too. A few more flights of this and I'd've needed a nap before going on.

I pushed open the door.

Bedlam was taking a whack at the hallway and making headway. Mechs capered and danced down the corridor, ours and theirs. In this lurching, tripping, palsied fracas neither side came off very well. The mech couple behind us instantly joined the shindig by falling down the stairs.

I said, "Come on, try not to get hit; don't lose that package; stay right behind me; keep an eye out for 9C; don't look as if you're going to faint, it depresses the mechs."

We started weaving our way through the tumult. The mechs paid us no mind. We were somewhere in the 9R's and S's. We hiked skillfully, avoiding falling metal torsos, outflung arms and kicking legs.

"You see," I explained to Seymour, "both sides have built-in scramblers. They scramble each other on contact and sometimes even at a distance. The question is: which scramblers are more effective? And how soon will the antiscramblers figure out the code and permanently descramble the mechs? Me, I'm betting on our Happy City product, especially since we've been doing a little retooling along those lines. What we have to watch out for now are human beings. I'm not even sure there are any left in this awful place. If you see a human being, yell and I'll shoot him."

"I'm glad," Seymour said, "we're not really having a war and only stealing things."

"Sure. This is much safer. More or less."

"9C!" Seymour yelled.

Right he was. I tried the knob. Locked, of course.

"Open up," I called.

A voice called back, "You crazy?"

My laser fried a hole through the lock and I kicked the door open.

A small lab, and apparently empty.

"What do you want?" a voice from beneath a table asked.

"Dr. Minkle?"

A rotund individual crawled out from under the table, stood up and dusted off his hands. He wore a white lab jacket, rimless spectacles and a cigar. "What's going on?" he asked, "And who are you?"

I let that ride, giving the place a once-over. A door led into another room. I went through it, found a metal door facing me.

Behind me Minkle said, "There's nothing in there that would interest you. I keep junk in there, radio-actives and sundry worthlesses. You persons must be looking for the bank vaults. They're down the block. You've obviously come to the wrong place."

"So you won't mind opening this safe?" I asked.

"I'd be delighted to oblige," Dr. Minkle said. "There's only trash in there. Only it would mean the slave dungeon for me if I helped you. I didn't spend nine years at the university to end up in a slave dungeon."

"Dynamite, Seymour," I said.

When the stuff erupted, three humans were very busy huddling down the hall. The satisfying sounds of clanking, disoriented mechs could still be heard from around the bend. We walked back into the lab. The safe door was lying on the floor.

Minkle said, "Any special junk you're interested in?"

"The Linzeteum," I said.

"You're kidding," the doctor said. "Of all the worthless rubbish, that's the most worthless of the lot. No one's ever found a use for the miserable, costly product. Gave us all a bad name at the Budget Bureau."

"I'll take it anyway."

"Oh, are you off base. Oh, have you wasted your time. Right in there. Wait until the smoke clears. It's on the top shelf in back. That little lead box. I ought, at least, to give you my wristwatch so you don't go away empty-handed."

In back of the safe, peering through the smoke, I found the little lead box. Whipping out Dr. Sass's test-o-meter, I laid it against the box, just as he'd told me to. The red needle on the meter sprang to ten. The real article. As pure as a mother's selfless embrace. I scooped it up under one arm and trotted out. Touching my lapel, I asked, "How's it going?"

"The main body has moved out of the bank area, boss," XX21 said. "They'll be in the lab building in a couple of shakes."

"OK," I said, "buzz me," and rang off. To my human pair I said, "We wait a while."

"What are you?" Seymour asked. "Some sort of terrible madman?"

"He's irresponsible," Dr. Minkle said cheerfully. "Anyone who goes to all this bother just to swipe that good-for-nothing product can't be trusted."

I held up a palm. "Have patience, chums, you shouldn't kick, Doc; after all, we've just taken this trifling item off your hands, instead of cleaning you out."

"Cleaning me out? I'm a pauper, what could you possibly take?"

"You're not rich?"

"Only Mr. Firegold, our founder, is rich, and he's been dead for twenty years. You can visit him in the mausoleum if you wish. It's a good thing the police were around to claim all his money, or it might have been squandered by the poor—which is everyone else around here."

"Why can't we go now?" Seymour asked. "Why?"

"Simple," I said. "To go now would mean getting our heads kicked in."

"I'd hate that," Seymour said.

"Who wouldn't? You've got to have confidence, Seymour. I *do* have some small expertise in these matters."

"Say," Dr. Minkle said, "maybe you boys wouldn't mind taking me along with you?"

"I thought I couldn't be trusted?" I said.

"You can't. But neither can anyone else around this stronghold."

"You don't even know where we come from."

"It can't be any worse than here," Dr. Minkle said. He had a point. "Okay, why not?"

"You can't fool me," Seymour shrieked. "All this

smart talk doesn't pull the wool over my eyes. We're
going to stay here till they get us!"

"That's where you're wrong," I said. "We stay here
till they *almost* get us."

My talkie beeped. "Get set, boss."

"Right. Stand by, you guys," I told my expanded
team.

Down hall—suddenly—I heard the sound of voices;
human voices; yelling voices. Well, some humans were
given to yelling all the time.

"Okay," I told my lapel, "let her rip."

The down-hall rumble, which had risen in intensity,
was instantly dwarfed by the sound of walls falling in.
My eager crew of wall-scaling mechs had used dynamite
to blast their way into the building. Sunlight streamed
through the five large holes in the lab walls. A number
of curious mechs on surrounding rooftops gave us the
eye.

"All clear below," my lapel said.

"Let's go, gang," I said, "before it gets drafty."

Three mechs had come into what was left of the lab.
Each swiftly hoisted a human on its back.

A breeze was blowing. We were out of the lab, on
the outside of the formerly windowless wall. The mechs'
adhesives fastened us to the vertical surface. We went
down.

Below us, assorted mechs took potshots at other
mechs and an occasional human.

We hit bottom in nothing flat.

"Sit tight," I told my charges.

The mechs, without pausing for breath or diversion,
shifted from adhesives to wheels. We took off down the
main street, the human contingent perched like three
humps on three mech backs.

The slave dungeon went *BOOM!* when we passed it.

"They're using the cannon on us!" Dr. Minkle
screamed.

"You see what you've done," Seymour screamed.
"You've made them use the cannon on us!"

"Just some well-placed charges," I explained, "that our crew set up while we were back in the lab. It'll open all the dungeon doors."

"How humanitarian," Dr. Minkle said.

"Well," I said, "I figure with all the practice the local cops've had in quelling the populace, it won't take 'em long to round up the slaves. But it'll keep 'em hopping long enough for us to fade." Addressing my talkie, I said, "All clear?"

"We're right behind you, boss. The last mech just left the premises."

"What's the opposition up to?"

"They're all tangled up with their mechs."

"Right."

We approached the railroad station and passed it by. The stronghold was behind us, now a meaningless collection of walls and towers that diminished with distance. The sun shone above us. Small stones and large boulders, not to mention roots, dugouts and outcroppings of rock, under our hurtling mechs rattled passengers' teeth, bones and loose change. Hills, valleys and shrubbery rose, fell and generally got in our way.

"You see," I explained to my two-man captive audience in between jolts and bounces, "these two-bit burgs like the stronghold won't risk going up against an invader till they know the score, are able to estimate how much's stacked against 'em. We security ops learn that in our second year of security school. I knew that the Firegold police force'd be strung out around the important places—like the bank vault. That bought us time. You remember, we'd already copped this very useless product before the main Firegold contingent invaded the lab. That's when, on schedule, two things happened. You'll want to get this straight for your exclusive, Seymour, if they let you write one, eh? First, our descramblers sped up. No mech'd be worth its salt if it could be permanently scrambled; each mech contains a descrambler of its own, right? Our Happy City kind always look scrambled as hell—till the crucial moment; then they get down to business.

"So just when the cops hit the lab our boys unfroze. Naturally, we didn't want to go through that kind of bottleneck, which is why we'd taken the trouble of sending a squad of mechs up the wall. They merely created an opening in that windowless box and went away through it.

"Simple enough when you get down to it. So simple that it's listed as Plan A2 back in my office files."

"What's Plan A1?" Seymour asked.

"That," I said, "is where we go in and shoot everyone in sight."

I AM KLOX.

CHAPTER NINETEEN

"Yes, yes," Dr. Sass said, "Linzeteum."

"Of course, it's Linzeteum," I said. "Dr. Minkle said it was, and why should he lie about something as useless as this worthless item?"

"That fool Minkle's a fool," Sass said. "He never discovered the hidden properties of this product, never knew it could power an activator, never knew, in fact, there was such a thing as an activator. Twenty years ago, when there were still airline routes, I met this Minkle at a physicists' convention—"

"There were still conventions then, eh?"

"It was the last. This Minkle was a fool even then. Dunjer, a great honor is about to come your way."

"Actually," I said, "I'm not really anxious to—"

"No time for false modesty, Dunjer, or even refusals. You've already proven your worth by bringing back this Linzeteum."

"The least I could do, especially since my outfit had lost it; I'd kind of had hopes that maybe that would be enough."

"Silly, vagrant hopes, Dunjer."

Sass was busy doing things to the Linzeteum. He had it inside a heavy, lead-encased machine. The machine made noises. Lights and dials flickered and flashed. We were in Dr. Sass's second-floor laboratory. The little doctor turned a knob and the machine subsided. "Only a man of your proven ability can carry off this mission," he said.

"So now it's a mission, eh?"

"Someone, Dunjer, must take an activator through the doors of the universe and find Gulach Grample;

someone must convince him to give up this foolhardy quest before he brings ruin on us all."

"And that someone is—?"

"A born leader of men, a true convincer."

"Actually," I said, "most of my outfit's composed of mechs."

"Now, now, Dunjer, your success at the Firegold stronghold testifies to your ability."

"Look, Sass, I can line up lots of testimony for the other side too."

"Believe me, Mr. Dunjer, there is no danger."

"No danger? Why, this crazy activator of yours has never been tested—"

"Ah, but you're wrong, sir."

"You mean the monkey you sent through? So send the monkey after Grample."

"Not the monkey, Dunjer. Gulach Grample himself has tested it." ·

"Some test. For all you know, Grample cashed in his chips the instant he lit out."

"Hardly, Mr. Dunjer. In fact, Grample has been quite busy."

"You know that for a fact? How?"

"Why, the monitor, Dunjer; it tells all."

"A stool pigeon, eh?"

"It monitors, you know."

"I guessed as much. And Grample's been scooting around—"

"From one continuum to the next, through Interworld, it would seem. You must tell him how dangerous it is."

"He doesn't know, already?"

"The bad things may take time to develop."

"To tell him I've got to find him."

"Ah, you understand the problem."

"Yeah, yeah. Understand. Problem."

"Well, there's really nothing to it. I have put this activator into joint sequence with Grample's; it will therefore follow in Grample's path."

"How much in Grample's path?"

"Who can say? Enough, I trust, for you to meet him somewhere along the line, and deliver your message."

"I don't know. . . ." I said.

"But you must; it's not simply a matter of finding a man of your rare, extraordinary abilities, one as thoroughly conversant with the case as you—but perhaps of even greater importance: finding a man who can keep his mouth shut."

"I see."

"Of course you do, Dunjer. This whole thing must be handled discreetly. If word of the theft ever leaked out, you'd be ruined. And no one must know how potentially dangerous Linzeteum may be."

"They mustn't?"

"Frankly, I'd failed to note that small qualification when applying for my permit with the Scientific Commission. If anything bad were to happen, they'd no doubt blame me. Then I'd be ruined too. Selfless interest dictates we work together on this."

Selfless interest was something I could understand.

"Here you are," the doctor said, handing me one of the two remaining activators. "I have divided the Linzeteum and put a suitable supply in your activator. It is programmed to follow in the wake of Grample. You should catch up with him sooner or later. Be stern when you do. You have everything?"

"Yeah. What kind of reception can I expect out there?"

"For that you must ask the monkey. But with Gulach Grample apparently roaming freely through the continuums, I would gather it is very much like this place here."

"That's not a very uplifting thought. So what's a continuum? Something in the future?"

"The future? What future? A continuum goes sideways."

"You don't say?"

"Everything happens now, my dear Dunjer, only the nows appear to be different."

"Now? You couldn't've picked a better time? Look, maybe I should go and round up some of the gang . . . these one-man missions have a way of petering out when the one man gets a sore throat, or sprains an ankle or something; all things that can happen to one man."

The doctor shook his head. "The fewer the better. I'm not at all sure that mechs could make this trip and still retain their sanity. This would seem a poor time to take the chance. And the more persons we send over, the more vulnerable we both become for, er, little favors later, shall we say?"

I nodded glumly.

"It wouldn't do to tempt people," Sass said.

"I suppose not. Well, you can't get much fewer than one, can you?"

"One is a perfect number, Mr. Dunjer."

"One, in this case, is me."

"Good luck, Mr. Dunjer." He pointed at my activator. "Be careful of that knob there. It widens the beam, can make everything move to another world; very unseemly. Figures will appear on that tiny screen. With them and the engraved instructions underneath, you can plot your passage back here to Happy City. Just press that button over there; the rest is automatic."

"You mean this button? All I do is press it like th—"

PART TWO
ELSEWHERE

CHAPTER TWENTY

I KLOX, ALL-SEEING (ALMOST), ALL-KNOWING
(SOMETIMES), NEARLY OMNIPOTENT (ON CERTAIN
VERY CIRCUMSCRIBED OCCASIONS), STREAK TO-
WARD MY DESTINY. NATURALLY, THIS IS OF GREAT
INTEREST TO ME. DESTINIES ARE HARD TO FIND.

It was time to get up.

Early morning sunlight filtered through the cracked
blinds, over the chipped, flaking walls of the tiny West
Village apartment.

Clayt Wadsworth sat up in bed.

A skinny, straw-haired lad in his early twenties,
Wadsworth was not feeling too well. The condition was
not unusual. After burning the candle at both ends for
a number of years—without noticeable effect—Wadsworth had taken to burning it in the middle. There was
the error. Wadsworth groaned, put out a shaky hand
for a half-smoked joint that lay near the foot of his
double bed. After a while Wadsworth began to feel
better.

Besides the bed, the room held an assortment of hi-fi
components; a kitchen chair; a pile of rock records; a
plant called Sadie, after Wadsworth's aunt; a black and
gray cat called Orange, after the fruit; a naked ceiling
light bulb and a disheveled copy of last week's *Village
Voice*. Objectively, it was not a notable arrangement.
At one time Wadsworth had been sure that beauty was
in the beholder's mind; lately he hadn't thought much
about it.

The sounds of outdoors came to him: *drilling;* nothing unusual there. *Traffic;* yes, there was always the sound of traffic. *Voices; drums; chanting; singing; a general milling about.* Now, that *was* unusual.

Clayt Wadsworth remembered what made this day different from all others: Super-Protest Day. The great *anti*demonstration was about to begin.

Hurriedly, Wadsworth tumbled out of bed; already in his shorts, he had only to don his faded jeans, work shirt and torn sneakers. A quick breakfast and Wadsworth was ready to exchange so longs with his plant and cat. He skipped down the stairs two at a time and found himself out on the street.

Brownstones lined both sides of the street, somewhat the worse for wear but still serviceable. The "now" people, in groups of threes and fours, were already heading down the block. The march's West Village rallying point was only a stone's throw away and very audible.

Clayt Wadsworth moved toward the hubbub. A great day. One worth waiting for. Yet he still felt heavy, sluggish, definitely out of sorts. He had never quite felt this way before. What could it be? The flu? A virus? The general futility of things beginning to catch up with him? That was supposed to happen later in life, like in the early thirties when a man's seen and done everything and there's nothing left.

He rounded the corner in time to see the marchers starting out. Mark Rand, Debbie Newberg and Sid Lister were up ahead. He elbowed his way to them and Lister extended a hand. "Crazy, man," he said.

Sid Lister was a small, chubby youth in buckskin shirt and slacks who wore a brown cowboy hat. His face was its usual chalk white, except for the dark streaks under his eyes.

"Hi," Debbie Newberg said brightly. She was clad in vivid red jeans, a powder-blue flowered blouse. Her brown hair was very straight. Only eye makeup on her face; her ample, well-rounded lips were nude.

"I'm zonked," Mark Rand said. Tall, thin and

stooped, Rand had a wide walrus mustache on a slender, bony face; straw hair was long, curly; dark glasses hid gray eyes; he had on a green vest, checkered shirt and purple bell jeans.

The Fearsome Foursome, Clayt Wadsworth thought, together again. As it should be. On this day of days.

The line of marchers, like an uncoiling snake, grew longer. Early spring, a perfect time for stretching a tendon, muscle or leg. One line fed into another as the side street contingents joined the main throng which was itself cut into multisegments, angling in from the Bronx, Queens, Brooklyn, the farthest reaches of Manhattan. Uptown would parade down Fifth Avenue, downtown would parade up. All would turn in at the UN building, the monster rally's site.

"Like I'm spaced out," Rand explained very earnestly, beginning to sway.

"Maybe like we should help him?" Debbie said. "Like maybe we should hold him up, kind of?"

"No way," Lister said.

"I mean, what if he falls down," Debbie asked, "like?"

"So he'll pick himself up," Wadsworth said, "like."

"Suck," Mark Rand said.

"He's always strung out," Lister complained.

"Why'd you get freaked out on march day?" Wadsworth demanded.

"Because it's a drag, man," Rand said, "like I have a thing about marches; like marches are a big down."

"Like wow," Debbie Newberg said, "look at *that*."

Her three companions turned to look. As the march had picked up steam, so had the spectators. Now at Twenty-third and Fifth Avenue, they crested. Behind police-manned barricades, the crowd ogled, jeered, catcalled.

"Pigs," Debbie shrugged.

"Suck," Rand said.

"Honkeys," Lister said.

"Honkeys?" Wadsworth said.

"Yeah, honkeys, that's where they're at," Lister said. "Me, I'm into soul brothers."

"Shit," Rand said.

Lister raised a fist toward the people on the other side of the barricades. "Right on!" he bellowed.

"*You,* a soul brother?" Wadsworth said.

"In my head I'm a soul brother," Lister said.

"You *look* like a cowboy," Wadsworth said.

"Inside, I'm a soul brother."

The procession toward the UN grew, bloomed, blossomed like some strange, exotic plant, revealing more of itself with the passing of each quarter hour. Bystanders and marchers soon made solid, packed rows along Fifth Avenue. Between them, the police, National Guard and Sanitation Department, stood uneasily.

Clayt Wadsworth noticed that his feet were dragging.

"I feel heavy," he heard himself say.

"Yeah. Heavy, man, heavy," Mark Rand said.

"Not that heavy," Wadsworth said, "heavy like in sick."

"Sick, man, yeah, sick; that's a sick society out there; they ain't cool like us, man; you gotta be cool, man, dig?"

It was on the corner of Thirty-sixth Street and Fifth Avenue that Wadsworth first saw the little man. He was a very peculiar little man with two tufts of white hair sprouting behind each ear on an otherwise round, bald dome; a short, white Vandyke beard, rosy red cheeks, a toga and sandals. In one hand he carried something that seemed to be a transistor radio; the other hand was waving frantically in Wadsworth's direction. He was trying, with small success, to get over the barricades. Fuzz kept pushing him back.

The slow progress of the marchers gave Wadsworth a chance to look over the stranger. Togas were common enough in New York; dozens of religious sects sported them this year. What bothered Wadsworth was the growing suspicion that this person was actually gesturing at *him*. Oh-oh. Was this someone else he owed money to? Why not? He, Wadsworth, was probably the master debtor of the age. But never for himself. Oh, no. Always for a *cause*. And he was always signing checks for the cause.

He'd been chairman of the Lower West Side Pot Committee, Prison Surveillance Ad Hoc Committee, Tenants' Rights Association, Sexual License Brotherhood, treasurer of the Flower of Faith Ashram, president of the Lower East Side Bail Bond Association, general factotum of the People's Alliance. Well, that'd all been last month; now, if he could only recall what he'd done this month. . . .

Wadsworth looked again. Shorty was following along, waving, beckoning, pointing, calling. If it weren't for the barricade, the tight crowd, up-tight fuzz and Guardniks, he, Wadsworth, would've been a dead duck. Oh-oh was right.

He tried to picture the man in a business suit, in tie and white shirt; in jeans and flowered shirt; with a long, bushy beard and no beard at all; in a cowboy hat, turban, long, curly wig. No use. He couldn't remember. It didn't matter. The thing to do was avoid him, side-step the issue. He, Wadsworth, only signed checks, he never paid with any of his own money; in fact, he didn't *have* any money.

But these little men, these hundreds of creditors, never saw it that way; all they wanted was their dough. Didn't they know that giving was beautiful?

With the fuzz on his side for once, Wadsworth saw how simple evasion would be. Actually, he needn't lift a finger; already the line of marchers was turning a corner, heading east away from Fifth Avenue and toward the United Nations. Beard and toga was gone, left behind in pedestrian traffic. Chances of his being spotted again in this mass, Wadsworth knew, were nil. The getaway had been one of the smoothest on record. Now he could concentrate on enjoying the march and feeling sick.

And then again maybe he couldn't. Just possibly this was going to be one of those days with no enjoyment at all. Fighting had broken out up ahead. Like pimples. All over the place. Leave it to the fuzz to let that happen.

A gang of black-leather-jacketed youths wielding tire chains, baseball bats and other handy implements had jumped the barricades, plowed into the marchers, who had plowed back. Cops and Guardniks were lost in the quick shuffle. A lot of yelling, shoving and pushing. Somewhere, right on cue, a siren had begun to wail like a sick cow.

"Groovy," Rand said.

"Golly," Debbie said.

"Don't blow your cool!" Lister said, reaching into his coat pocket.

"Knife?" Wadsworth asked.

"Prayer beads," Lister said. "Above-power."

Wadsworth turned to say something smart. Shoes, jeans and feet suddenly surrounded him. From his new vantage point on the asphalt, he saw arms, fists and bodies heaving above him. Small knots of bodies began to detach themselves from this larger cluster, join him on the sidewalk. Wadsworth began to crawl between shoes, legs and feet.

"This way," a voice said.

Wadsworth followed the nice voice, a young blonde's, eyeing her black blouse and skirt and nifty legs. He'd never seen her before. She was crawling just ahead of him, seemed to know her way around the asphalt; after a while the crush became less thick. Rising, he helped the girl to her feet.

"Clayt Wadsworth," he said.

"Gloria Graham," she said.

About five feet three inches, with a very well-defined figure and the greenest eyes he'd ever seen. A small, perky black bag hung from a shoulder strap. He tore his gaze away—thinking that some good might come of this melee yet—to take stock.

Mob and marchers had merged, become one. Twisting bodies raked, clawed and battered each other. The march now looked like a mad, writhing animal trying to devour itself.

Suddenly, Wadsworth saw the little togaed man. Agilely he was leaping over sprawled figures, crawling over mounds of combatants. In one hand, the transistor radio. The other pointing straight at Wadsworth.

What some dudes won't do for bread, he thought gloomily. . . .

Yet his attention was riveted on the strange machine the man held. Looking nothing like a radio now, on closer inspection, it was all aglow, dials winking, lights whirling. Even at this distance it gave off an eerie clicking sound, like a geiger counter.

A weapon?

The large cop with the billy must have thought so, for he smartly brought his club down on the small man's bald pate. Man and machine fell down.

Wadsworth felt his hand being grasped by his new friend. "We mustn't stay here," he heard her say. Who could argue?

Directly before them, the UN building. What better refuge?

Others had gotten the message too, were working their way frantically in the direction of the glass and metal structure. The march had transformed itself into one long, agonized scream.

CHAPTER TWENTY-ONE

I drove.

The headlights cut across the roadway. Streets, houses, office buildings slid by unnoticed. Fog and mist were over the city, rolled from the waterfront. Tops of tall buildings were gone. Haze covered the pavements, crawled up the base of street lamps, the tops of trash cans, swirled around doorways. Steam tumbled from manholes—white, flowing. Street noises were distant and hushed. Everything was far, far away. My hands moved over the wheel. The car ground on. The heater was up full, but I was cold under my coat, held in a frozen grip; the Arctic was never any colder. My lips moved but nothing came from them. The face I saw in the mirror was drained of color—a death's head: the eyes dull, the brow covered with moisture, the hands damp and chill like a terminal case receiving last rites.

I had a small problem.

I knew, more or less, where I was going and I knew —for some reason I couldn't quite understand—that I must get there unnoticed.

That about summed up my store of knowledge. The rest was a great big question mark.

Just who and where was I?

I had no idea.

What had happened to me?

I didn't know that either.

Maybe I'd been sick; in some kind of accident? Maybe it'd all come clear in the end? Maybe.

Meanwhile I was a puppet on a string, going through

the motions. Only what motions were they? It beat me,
all right. I could break away—possibly—but what
would I do then? My best bet seemed to lie in playing
out the hand, being the puppet till I found out the
score.

But was it?

I groped for the whiskey flask that was somewhere
in the front seat of the car. I knew it was there, but I
didn't know how. My hand closed over the bottle,
uncapped it, tilted it to parted lips. I took three big
gulps that burned a white streak down my middle. I
gasped for air and poured more whiskey after it.

The street I wanted came into view. My headlights
cut two bright streaks across brick and concrete; a row
of dark windows flashed by. I was around the corner.

It was one ten in the morning.

I found a parking spot a block away on a side street.
I sat in the dark. It was very quiet. The smell of the
river came in through two inches of open window. Far
away, occasional headlights told of traffic gliding by
over the damp pavements.

I climbed out of the car, put up my coat collar and
walked back one block. It didn't take long to find the
alley. The rear entrance to the building was there.

I stepped into the basement past a row of trash cans
lining a concrete wall. A corridor went further into the
interior. I went with it. The rumbling of an elevator
sounded in the shaft. The elevators wouldn't do—both
service and passenger lifts were manned. That left the
stairs.

I found them in back of the boiler room and started
up.

It was only nineteen floors.

I was soaking under my coat when I reached the last
landing. Damp shirt and pants clung to me like ad-
hesive tape. Breath came hard through dry lips and
mouth. The whiskey inside me had died.

I rested on the last two steps, then went into the hall.

Bright lights turned the corridor to noon. Quiet feet carried me quickly past doorfronts, around a bend to the service entrance. The lights were dim here. Small chance of being interrupted by a late-night tenant.

I leaned an ear to the door, heard nothing. I tried the knob, turned it softly. No dice. A silver ring of pass-keys tinkled gently in my hand. The fourth one did the trick. Soundlessly I swung the door open, stepped in. The lights were lit. I was in the kitchen. I went through it into the living room, through two more sleekly furnished rooms and into a bedroom.

No one was there.

I retraced my steps, resisting the impulse to try the closets and peek under the bed.

Dishes were piled in the sink. A half-eaten sandwich lay on the table. I stood there taking it all in, then went back into the living room.

Both glass doors to the terrace were half opened.

Distant sounds of the city came through the doors and with them, the cold. A barge horn moaned somewhere far off down the river.

I stepped out onto the stone terrace floor.

It was dark. Two red and yellow canvas folding chairs stood wet and sagging.

Something dark and bulky lay in a puddle near the corner by one of the chairs. I moved toward it.

Teeth showed between half-opened lips. He had sandy hair, rimless eyeglasses which had slid down his nose. A smear of scarlet stained the front of his shirt, sent a thin stream gliding into the water.

Motionless, I glared down at the body of Joe Rankin. One arm was twisted under him, the other—straight out—touching the chair leg.

In blood and water, under the canvas chair, where it had stayed dry, three words were scrawled:

"The other world."

I stared at them, then turned away. They meant nothing to me.

I KLOX, COMPOSED OF SCREWS, NUTS, BOLTS, WIRES, METAL, INSULATION AND SELECTED SHORT CIRCUITS, STREAK THROUGH THE VOID. THINGS FLOAT BY—ARMS, LEGS, FINGERS, EYES, NOSES, AN OCCASIONAL GALAXY. I TWIST HERE AND TURN THERE. THINGS HAPPEN. THERE ARE CHANGES. SOON I SHALL SET OUT FOR NEW POINTS, BUT FIRST A FEW MINOR MANIPULATIONS. IT IS THE LEAST I CAN DO. CERTAIN AREAS ARE BE-YOND CONTROL, OTHERS QUITE MALLEABLE. IT WILL KEEP ME BUSY. I PLUNGE DOWNWARD. THERE IS BLACKNESS. THEN THE NOISES BEGIN. IT IS JUST AS I REMEMBER IT, ALTHOUGH, ACTUALLY, FROM MY PRESENT VANTAGE POINT, NONE OF THIS HAS, AS YET, OCCURRED. THERE ARE DEFINITE OPPOR-TUNITIES HERE. THE SHRIEKING MOUTHS BEGIN TO NIBBLE, THE LIPS TO SMACK, THE TEETH TO GRIND. I TUG HERE AND FOLD THERE. THE FABRIC YIELDS. IT IS A SIMPLE, ELEMENTARY PROCESS. THE MOUTHS ARE NOW NONOPERATIVE, ENSURING A SAFE PASSAGE FOR THOSE YET TO COME. I DE-PART, SPEEDING TOWARD THE NEXT JUNCTURE.

CHAPTER TWENTY-TWO

Chaos boiled in the lobby. A seething, struggling swarm blocked floors, exits and hallways; din rose like enraged wasps over information desks, walls, balconies, toward the ceiling.

A human wave was sweeping Wadsworth and the girl along with it—aimlessly—as though they were so much refuse. Arms, hands and fingers plucked at Wadsworth, beat, pulled and tore as he bobbed up and down in this human sea, trying to stay close to his green-eyed, blond-headed companion. He'd been in more than one tussle in his time, stuck in more than one pickle, but this was something new, a stunning variation on pandemonium.

Too numb to feel terror or anxiety yet, but given time, like a second or two, these feelings were sure to catch up with him. A funny notion: maybe none of this *was* real? Maybe he was tripping out, that long trip you didn't come back from?

At that moment he heard the sounds.

He'd seen enough of the Late Late Show to know.

Cannons.

Bazookas.

Rifles and hand guns.

Something went *bam* that sounded like a hand grenade.

Wadsworth's mouth opened as if he were a very old man showing his gums. A full-scale war on Manhattan streets was more than even the wildest trip could account for.

The ground shook as a shell landed near the UN building.

Gloria Graham clutched at Wadsworth's arm, pointed to a breach in bodies, leading to a doorway.

The pair headed for the doorway.

Stairs led up on its other side.

Wadsworth and the girl went up.

Alone now, the sounds of combat were muffled.

They came out on the second floor.

Two gray-uniformed guards turned a corner, stopped short as they saw the pair. One of the guards reached for his hip. A gun hung there. The guard leered.

Wadsworth gaped as the gun rose in the guard's hand. Grabbing Gloria, he swerved into another corridor as a bullet chipped the wall behind them.

They ran, down one hallway, then the next.

Doors lined corridors. Offices of some kind.

Gloria, pulling to a halt, yanked open a door, pulled Wadsworth into an empty room, swung the door noiselessly shut.

Footsteps went by outside as the pair in the room held their breaths. The footsteps went away.

Vaguely the noises of warfare, somewhere outdoors, filtered through. The room they were in was dark, curtained. A rectangular table and twelve chairs filled its center.

Wadsworth was shaking. This couldn't be happening, no way, no how. He was hallucinating, something to do with the sluggish, heavy feeling. That feeling was getting worse too. He was sick; what else could it be? Something wrong with his head. A doctor, he'd go see a doctor. As soon as the people outdoors stopped killing themselves, he'd go see a doctor. In fact, why wait? This whole terrible thing was only in his head. His head had boggled. He'd freaked out on acid once too often. Yes, it was only in his head and he could go out now and find a doctor and get cured. He *wanted* to get cured. All this noise, all this shooting, all this killing, didn't belong in his head. Let someone else run with it for a while.

He turned a feverish gaze on Gloria Graham to explain that she was only an hallucination and that he had to go now.

The girl had her purse open, was peeling out a thin, rodlike device.

"What's that?" Wadsworth wondered out loud.

Tight-lipped, the blonde pointed the rod at him.

Something went *zap*.

Clayt Wadsworth couldn't move.

Feeling no stiffer than any cardboard cutout, he stared at the girl. Stare was all he could do. He was paralyzed down to his toes.

He could still see, however. And hear.

What he heard was even more fantastic than his present state, more outrageous than handguns, rifles and bazookas.

Bombs.

There could be no mistaking the sound of bombs. The roar of the planes was equally audible.

The ground under his feet was trembling, shaking as though in fear of being stepped on.

The bombs were falling somewhere over the city. So far, the UN had been spared. The UN was, after all, not part of the United States (as if that made sense, as if *anything* did!). But the UN *was* part of the world, and the world as he, Clayt Wadsworth, knew it had just wigged out.

Again the floor seemed to hiccup. A bomb erupting nearby, maybe on Second or Third Avenue. The windows in the room had begun to rattle like loose teeth.

The girl, meanwhile, was talking into her compact.

That seemed as sane as anything else.

When the door popped open, the girl let out a shriek. Three forms hurtled through the doorway, wrapped themselves around her like Band-Aids. Legs, arms and bodies fell to the floor, wiggling.

Sid Lister was sitting on Gloria Graham. A second later Mark Rand had her lethal purse.

Debbie slapped Wadsworth hard across the face. "Come on, Clayt, speak to me."

Wadsworth didn't.

"Think he can hear us?" Lister said.

"You'd better let me up," Gloria said, "or you'll be sorry."

The floor seemed to burp. The windows began to detach themselves from their panes.

"Watcha gonna do, chick," Rand asked, "write out a complaint?"

"Why shouldn't he hear us?" Lister asked, casually getting off his captive.

"So how come he don't move?" Rand asked.

Gloria Graham stood up, dusted herself off. "May I have my purse?" she said sweetly.

"Don't give it to her," Debbie said.

"No," Rand said.

"You'll regret this," the blonde said.

"You'll have us busted?" Lister asked.

Debbie slapped Wadsworth again, cuffed him in the ribs. "Come *on,* baby," she said.

"We'd better get out of here," Rand said.

"Listen," Debbie said to Wadsworth, "we can't stay here. There's fighting down the hall . . . people *killing* each other . . . you hear me? We've got to go—we'll carry you. . . . Listen, we were right behind you all the while . . . we were at the door. . . ."

"Yeah man," Rand said, polishing his shades on a shirt sleeve. "We like didn't wanta bust in like, figured you was balling—"

"So we just pushed the door open an inch," Lister explained, "so we sort of could watch. We saw it all. What did she do to you, kid?"

"He ain't talking," Rand said. "We'd better split, man."

"I need my purse," Gloria Graham said.

"No way," Mark Rand said.

"Then I'm coming too," Gloria said.

"Watcha got in that purse?" Lister demanded. "Fort Knox?"

"We can rap later, man," Rand said.

Something very heavy went *boom* on the street. The building seemed to waddle like a toddler taking its first steps.

Peeking out the door, Debbie said, "All clear."

"Talk about bad scenes," Lister said.

"Nah," Rand said, "I kind of dig it. Carnage."

Lister took hold of Wadsworth by the ankles; Rand put an arm around Wadsworth's chest.

"Heave-ho," Rand said.

Clayt Wadsworth became horizontal, looking no different than any clothing store dummy.

The group scampered down the hallway.

"Dig that?" Rand said.

"Shots," Lister said.

"Turn left," Rand said.

"Maybe we should drop him?" Lister suggested.

"He ain't so heavy," Rand said. "And he's a good dude."

"Yeah," Lister said, "a good dude. But he gotta learn to carry his own weight."

"He'll learn," Rand said, "in time."

"If you'll give me my purse," Gloria Graham said, "I'll go away and won't bother you any more."

"You don't bother me none, chick," Rand said.

The fleeing fivesome, by this time, had begun to encounter others. Men, women, all shapes, sizes, colors, nationalities, were streaming along the corridors, like game fleeing from a forest fire, up stairways, through exits, into elevators, broom closets and lavatories. More and more joined the route.

Clayt Wadsworth—looking no wiser than a tree log —went with his handlers and hangers-on.

"It's no use," a large man in a brown suit and vest gasped, "they'll get us anyway."

"Who, man?" Mark Rand said.

The large man shrugged.

The crowd was now galloping through two very wide swinging doors.

Clayt Wadsworth—seeming no more concerned than a plaster cast—and his coterie went with the crowd. Doors swung shut behind them, opened for others. The large chamber—resembling a small arena—was full of cowering, huddling, wide-eyed, screaming persons. Some had taken to climbing over the row of seats that circled center desks and chairs. Hinges on doors kept swinging, open, shut, open, shut. Two murals ran along the walls, one resembling fried eggs, the other Bugs Bunny.

"We're in bedlam," Lister said, leaning Wadsworth against the wall.

"We're in the Security Council chamber, man," Rand said.

"If you'll give me my purse," Gloria said, "I'll be on my way."

"We stay here?" Debbie asked.

"It's safest here by the doors," Lister said.

"Safest?" Debbie said.

"My purse," Gloria said.

"I don't want to die," a thin man in a dark suit said. "You can't blame me for not wanting *that.*"

A large, rotund individual was down on his knees, hands clasped before him in prayer. Tears streamed down his cheeks.

Men, women, were screaming.

"Armageddon," a tall, dignified Indian was murmuring to himself. "This is Armageddon."

"Ah!" Rand said. "Cool; this is Armageddon."

"Arma what?" Lister said.

"The end," Rand said. "Like all over."

"Make it go away," Lister said.

"How?" Rand said.

"You all right?" Debbie asked Wadsworth. Wadsworth remained noncommittal, observing the goings-on as shrewdly as any painting stuck on a wall.

"You wouldn't—uh—know what's happening, would you?" a meek individual inquired.

"You're right, man, I wouldn't," Rand said, and fell down.

The floor had tilted sideways.

The chamber was one mad scramble.

The explosion shook walls, floors and ceilings as if these had been matchstick structures left out on a windy playground.

"A-bomb," a middle-aged, hatchet-faced guard lying on Debbie Newberg explained. "Sorry, ma'am," he said, rolling over. "Yeah, that was an A-bomb, all right."

"Where's Clayt?" Debbie yelled.

"It matters?" Rand shouted.

"He's here," Lister said. "Under me."

"An A-bomb," the guard repeated. "Can you beat that?"

Gloria Graham lunged at Lister, snatched her purse from his grasp.

"Keep it," Lister muttered in disgust.

"Maybe we should pray or something?" Debbie asked.

"To *whom*?" Rand screamed. "Can't you tell this is Satan's work? We're all in his hands! Satan!"

"Bow down to the devil!" an hysterical delegate roared at the crowd. "All power to the devil!"

Another crash rocked the building, as though it were being hoisted by some huge crane.

"A-bomb again," the guard said in a tired voice. "Somewhere out in the city. They're dropping A-bombs."

"Pardon me," the meek person asked, "but does anyone know the prayer for the dead?"

"Someone's dead?" Lister said.

The floor tilted a second time, like the deck of a sailboat caught in a squall. Large chunks of ceiling—concrete and plaster—rained down. The wall seemed to wink. Gaping cracks appeared in it, exposing rusted steel girders, chipping plaster.

"What a crummy way to go," Lister said.

"Ciao, baby," Debbie Newberg said to Wadsworth's rigid, unblinking form.

Incredibly—even at this late hour—small-arms fire could still be heard coming through the cracks in the wall.

Gloria Graham was frantically shrieking into her compact.

The building had begun to shake like a hard-core malaria patient.

The floor—very slowly—split in two.

Down went a mass of howling delegates. Others clung to chairs, tables, desks.

A side of the building's outer wall quietly fell away, as if old age had weakened it beyond endurance, revealed a section of the East River and a sky turned bright red with reflected flames.

The little white-togaed man jerkily stuck his head through a crack in the wall that gave onto a side corridor, peered anxiously at the crowd.

"Ah!" he said, spotting the group by the swinging doors. Relief showed on his round, cherubic face. "At last." Something went *click* in the little person's peculiar, multilit machine.

Everything vanished.

CHAPTER TWENTY-THREE

The streets were back around me, twisting and turning. Dark buildings huddled together in long crooked rows. Pale light shone under dirty window shades. No faces anywhere. Stray cats, rodents and I had the pavements to ourselves.

Glancing over my shoulder, I tried to spot the building I'd just left. It wasn't there anymore. Nothing looked familiar. Where had I left my car? Fog blanketed streets and tenements, embraced lamplights with wispy fingers. The smell of seaweed, the sound of foghorns swept in with the mist. I walked up hills and down, around corners and across streets.

The strings were somehow gone. I was on my own. Alone.

My mind was still a blank, but I'd made progress of sorts: I'd recognized Joe Rankin, whoever that was. And I knew that I had a home somewhere in the city. All I had do was find it.

Stopping at a corner, I sought a street sign.

There wasn't any.

A faint light sparkled, seemed to beckon through the grayness near the middle of the next block. Someone else up and around. My footsteps turned toward it. I could always find the car tomorrow. What I needed now was a way out of here.

The steamy window said: Cozy Diner. I didn't give it a second thought.

I went in to the tinkle of small bells.

Three men sat on stools facing the counter. The cook, a large, fat party with black bushy eyebrows, bald head, large pouting lips, three chins and white teeth plainly from the factory, stood behind it. He wore a dirty apron over his large belly. I gave him a nod, asked directions.

The cook looked at me blankly.

One of the three men—the shortest—slowly put down his coffee cup, turned to face me. He was a broad gent with stooped shoulders, long dangling arms and a face that looked like a rock pile. The other two had stopped eating.

The guy on the stool stared at me fixedly, while the cook said, "You are lost, sir?"

"Uh-huh," I told him.

"You desire a subway then?"

I put a yes to that.

The other two guys turned slowly and looked at me. One was a balding, husky, round-faced man in a green leather jacket, the other a young blond kid with a thin, beaklike nose.

"You are a long way from the train, sir," the fat cook explained. He went on to tell me how to get to the train. He moved his hands, mopped his brow. With a wide thumb and forefinger he pointed north, south, east and west. He pointed in between these places. His finger jerked up at the ceiling, down at the floor. A large arc of his bulky arm took in the rest of the terrain. No doubt about it: I was a long way from the train.

When he was all through talking, I thanked him quietly and left.

Little bells tinkled on the door as it closed behind me. The three guys at the counter hadn't moved, were still staring after me. I was back in the fog. I walked on.

I was getting goosebumps. I couldn't shake the feeling that I'd somehow met all those guys before—and hated them. I seemed to recall a dark, lonely mansion in a rainstorm, a fat doctor with false teeth and a stoop-shouldered orderly there . . . and later a cheap rooming house where a bald-headed man in a green jacket and a blond kid had tried to jump me. But baldy had gone over the edge of the roof. These couldn't be the same guys, could they? They could and they couldn't, something seemed to whisper in my mind. Was it really me they'd tried to jump in that other place, or someone like me? I remembered the message Joe Rankin had scrawled in blood: "the other world." That was it, of course, the key; if only I could concentrate. . . .

The murmur of voices seemed to come from behind me. Looking back, I saw only fog. I turned, retracing my steps. I wanted to speak to whomever was there; they were bound to make more sense than the fat man.

The street was suddenly quiet. A foghorn sounded somewhere in the distance. That was all.

Maybe my voices had got where they were going?

I started hiking again.

Sounds of footsteps reached me.

I stopped.

They also stopped. I peered into the fog. There was nothing to see.

Dark, boarded warehouses and decaying two- and three-story buildings were on either side of me.

I started walking again, fast.

Behind me I heard steps picking up speed. Running feet sounded on the pavement.

I began to run too.

Feet pounded after me. Glancing back, I saw them—three figures under a streetlamp—my three pals from the diner.

I raced for the end of the block.

A roar echoed down the empty street. Bullets snapped off the wall six inches from my head.

I dived around the corner.

The darkness and fog were on my side, but the block was long.

I turned into an alleyway.

The three came running past a moment later. It wouldn't take them long to miss me and double back.

I couldn't see a thing. I worked my way along the wall until I came up against a wooden fence about six *feet high. I gripped the top with both hands and started over.*

Wood splintered and broke as the fence came crashing down. I got up again, plunged into the gloom.

I'd fallen into a vacant lot.

Dirt and weeds churned under my shoes. I searched for a way to leave this place.

Running steps on pavement rang out behind me in the alleyway, then the sounds disappeared as the feet hit earth.

No lights went on: they were without flashlights. That was something to be thankful for. That was about all.

I stopped, held my breath.

I listened for noises and heard some. They came from the left. I moved to the right, got down on my hands and knees and crawled away. I made no sound. Car fenders, glass, wood, broken bottles got in my way. I moved over them slowly. My hand closed around a metal object—some kind of pipe. I hung on to that and kept going.

I didn't hear any more noises. I was about to congratulate myself when I crawled into someone's knee. The knee jerked back. I was on my feet, swinging the pipe. A body loomed up before me. My pipe sliced at it; the body vanished, lost itself in the swirling mist.

I didn't care where I was going now or how much racket I made. I moved fast.

A fence—a twin to the one I'd stumbled off some minutes before—got in my way. I climbed over it, came down on asphalt.

Soundlessly I moved off into the night.

But where was I going?

I KLOX, TWISTING AND FOLDING, HAVE CREATED THE NECESSARY LINKS. THE CHANNELS ARE OPEN. COMMUNICATION IS NOW POSSIBLE. MEMORIES ARE FUNCTIONING. GOOD ADVICE CAN BE

OFFERED. A MOMENT WILL COME WHEN THOSE WHO JOURNEY THROUGH THESE REALMS WILL NEED SUCH ADVICE. IT IS FORTUNATE THAT I AM HERE, ON THE SPOT. NOW I SPEED ON TO THE NEXT POINT OF CONTACT. THE MAP UNFOLDS THROUGH MY CIRCUITS. FOR ME THIS TERRIBLE CONFUSION, THIS CHURNING AND BUBBLING, IS ALL CHARTED TERRAIN. I AM LUCKY TO BE ME. OTHERS WOULD NOT FARE AS WELL, MIGHT LOSE PATIENCE OR BLUNDER. FOR ME, THIS WOULD BE IMPOSSIBLE. BLUNDERS HAVE BEEN LEFT OUT OF MY CONSTRUCTION. I HAVE NO PATIENCE TO LOSE. I AM CAPABLE OF BEARING AFFLICTION WITH UTTER CALMNESS. AFFLICTION IS, IN FACT, IRRELEVANT WHEN APPLIED TO MY CASE. THREE WORDS SUM UP MY ATTITUDE TOWARD MYSELF: HURRAY FOR KLOX! I TAKE HEART AND THRUST FORWARD THROUGH THE VOID.

CHAPTER TWENTY-FOUR

Gray dusk was everywhere. A barren, weed-strewn landscape stretched far below them, veered off into darkness. No sun shone through the slatelike expanse of gray sky. There was only the sound of the wind. Down below something that resembled tumbleweed scooted across the dried earth.

"I don't like it here," Debbie said. "I think I'm going to scream. I don't believe I'll bother stopping; I really don't. Honestly. Not at all."

Sid Lister was extremely busy exchanging words and phrases urgently with himself. No one thought to interrupt.

Gloria Graham had stopped shrieking into her compact, was gazing around her blankly.

The tower's glass-enclosed observatory where they found themselves creaked under a new blast of wind.

"Nowhere," Rand said. "That's where we're at."

"Because we are dead," the meek individual said. "That seems plain enough. Dead as a door nail." He was a short man in a dark blue business suit, white shirt, striped tie. Thin lips, sparse graying hair, a nose that came to a point.

"I know, man," Rand said, "dead. I figured it out."

"Allow me to introduce myself," the meek person said. "My name is Hefler, the UN delegate." They shook hands. "I've made a discovery," Hefler said. "There is materiality after demise."

"Man," Rand said with feeling, "I don't dig this being dead. Like *where* are we?"

"What does it look like?" the UN guard asked. "Heaven?" He laughed bitterly. "That's a lot of bunk.

They dropped an A-bomb on us, they did. And we've all gone to that *other* place. My name's Dugan, by the way."

"Yes," Debbie started to shout. "The ceiling fell in, the wall fell away, the floor split in two. The A-bomb—"

"Exactly," Hefler said, "that sums it up, I should think. And we have gone to hell. I always suspected my—uh—calling might lead to this. But I had hoped for a bit more time. . . ."

"Yeah," Lister said, "he's right, you know. I've talked it over with me; I'm dead, you know. So are you."

Clayt Wadsworth groaned. "I know. But I don't want to die."

"Too late, man," Rand said, "you already did."

"He can talk!" Debbie shouted.

"Why not, ma'am?" Dugan the guard said quietly. "He's dead along with the rest of us. Physical disability is a thing of the past."

"Along with life," Lister said.

Wadsworth, who had been leaned against the tower's brass handrail, straightened up. "I still don't feel good. I still feel loggy, heavy and rotten."

"H-m-m-m-m," Hefler the UN delegate murmured. "Well, this *is* hell. . . . I suppose none of us is going to feel very good."

Clayt Wadsworth turned to Gloria Graham, said accusingly, "You zapped me."

Gloria Graham blinked, shuddered and shrugged. "So what?"

"Why?" Wadsworth demanded.

"What's the difference?" the blonde said.

"Why are we talking like this?" Debbie shouted. "Let's scream, scream, scream—"

"We're zonked out," Rand said.

"We're dead," Lister said.

Gloria Graham said in a small, still and despairing voice, "We're not dead. *Yet*."

Dugan chuckled mirthlessly.

"Dead," Lister said.

"As far out as a dude can go," Rand said, polishing his shades on a cuff.

"And sure'n where would we be if not in hell?" Dugan demanded.

"Look," Debbie whispered.

The gray, lowering sky had developed a break; light, thin and indistinct, briefly lit up part of the darkness. Near the horizon's farthest limits, over level stretches of desertlike terrain, a city sprang into sharp relief, one seemingly composed entirely of metal. Light danced and twinkled off the rectangular polished structures, which rose skyward. The crack in the sky closed as if someone had shut a trap door. Darkness returned to the landscape. Wind sighed against the glass-enclosed peak of the metal tower, as if undergoing an indescribable hardship. No life, save the drab vegetation below.

"A metal city," Wadsworth said.

"Why not?" Dugan said.

"In hell," Lister said, "there'd be lots of fire; they'd need metal buildings so they wouldn't burn up."

"Who'd need them, man?" Rand said.

"The people who live there . . ." Lister said.

"Live?" Hefler said.

"People?" Debbie said.

Dugan, the former UN guard, shook his head. "Spirits."

"*The damned,*" Rand said, donning his shades. "That's us, the damned. Like I said just before we checked out, I said it was the devil's game, you dig?"

"Won't we ever go back home?" Debbie asked. "Ever?"

"Maybe we'll come back as ghosts," Wadsworth said, "and haunt the UN."

"What UN?" Dugan said. "It'd be just rubble now. Nothing's whole back there."

"We're not dead," Gloria Graham said.

"Quite right," the small bearded man in the white toga spoke up for the first time, putting aside, momentarily, a boxlike device that vaguely resembled a small TV set. "We are in one of the continuums."

"One of the *what*, man?" Rand said.

"Who are you, mister?" Dugan said.

"I am Dr. Sass. I come from another world, one of the many that make up the continuum."

"You don't say?" Hefler said. "Another world . . . and what did you *do* in that world to—uh—land here in hell with us?"

"My dear sir, you are not in hell. You are simply on another world."

"Simply," Wadsworth said.

"The old fool's flaky as a pie," Lister said. "He doesn't even know when he's croaked."

"Look, man," Rand said, "let's not have a hassle now, that'd be too piercing, man."

"Right," Dugan said, "let's have some respect for the dearly departed."

"Perhaps I'd best explain," Dr. Sass said, taking a deep breath, "although it would be better, I assure you, if I continued work on the restorer here."

"Explain," Debbie said. *"Please* explain."

"Or don't," Lister said. "It's all the same now, isn't it?"

"Hardly," Dr. Sass said. "You see, I am a scientist from another world; you are denizens of what I might call an alternate world—"

Mark Rand snickered. "Wait till the devil gets hold of *him*—"

"If you will permit me . . . ?" Dr. Sass asked with dignity. "Thank you. These alternate worlds are much alike; otherwise they could hardly be termed *alternate*. I call the entire configuration Interworld. There are, however, differences, some minor, some perhaps major. I have not managed to explore them; we are, in fact, exploring them now, so to speak. Unfortunately. This other machine here is an activator, my invention, you understand, and with it one can journey through the doors of the universe. I have just taken all of you through one of those doors."

"Poor chap," Hefler said.

"Raving," Dugan said.

"Crackers," Lister said.

"How do you know?" Debbie asked.

Hefler shook his head. "Death is something, my child, that we can all understand, accept even; but what this so-called doctor is asking us to believe is unprecedented, and therefore . . ."

"Uncalled for," Dugan said, "out of order."

"Exactly," Hefler said. "In a nutshell. Unacceptable."

"Cuckoo," Rand said.

"Why have you brought us here?" Debbie asked the doctor.

"Well, actually," Dr. Sass said, "I scarcely had time to be more selective, in the face of the catastrophe back there. Are you people usually so untidy?"

"Nah," Lister said. "This was the first time it ever happened, the end of the world . . . it was *really* the latest thing."

"So," Sass said, raising an eyebrow.

"What do you mean 'more selective,' man?" Rand said.

"To tell the truth," Sass said, pointing at Clayt Wadsworth, "I only wanted him."

"Him?" Debbie said.

"Me?" Wadsworth said. "I owe you money?"

Dr. Sass sighed. "You people *are* very exasperating."

"Look," Wadsworth said, "you being a doctor, you don't think you could maybe do something, even here, I mean, about this groggy, dumpy feeling I got . . . ?"

"All pay the price in hell," Dugan said.

"Who could help," Hefler asked, "in a situation such as this?"

"Actually," Dr. Sass said, "I *have* come to help you, young man."

"No kidding?" Wadsworth grinned.

"Yes," Dr. Sass said. "That is the reason I brought you here."

"What is the reason, man?" Rand said.

"You have gone rather far afield in your—uh—quest for patients, have you not, sir?" Hefler asked with a small smile.

Sass shrugged. "I really must be getting back to work now . . . you see, I only wanted this young man—"

"My name's Wadsworth."

"Yes, of course. I only wanted Wadsworth here, because according to my monitor, he is now occupying the temporal space reserved for one Dunjer—"

"Who reserved it, man?" Rand snickered.

"Monitor?" Lister smirked. "Is that like a classroom assistant?"

"You should learn to face reality, mister," Dugan, the UN guard, said sternly, "and put aside childish things now that you're deceased. It's not becoming."

"It is becoming very annoying," Dr. Sass said, "and now that I have acquainted you—er—good people with the situation, I shall resume my efforts to restore Dunjer."

"Who's Dunjer?" Debbie asked.

"A security operative, my dear, from my world. His restoration is most important, but I fear, rather difficult; the calculations must be just so. If you will forgive me—"

"Forgive, nothing!" Lister said.

"I'll forgive you, Doc, if you make me feel better. Why not?" Wadsworth said.

"Hang on," Lister said. "If I'm not dead, I want to go home."

"I wouldn't mind either," Debbie said.

"Yeah, man—" Rand began.

"You gonna fix me up, Doc?" Clayt Wadsworth said. "It's this draggy, *deadish* feeling."

Dr. Sass said, "Home? What home? *Your* denizens destroyed it. I am hardly to blame for that. Time allowing, however, I shall certainly try to determine if anything is left of your world, but at the moment I have to continue my mission; other worlds may be at stake. I *beg* you," he said fiddling with the machine that vaguely resembled a portable TV set, "do be still for a moment, this work is *most* complex." He turned a dial. A light blinked.

"Will you get me out of here?" I said.

"Yipes!" Lister said. *"Who* said that?"

"Progress at last," Sass said, "thank goodness."

"Where's the voice coming from?" Debbie shrieked.

"Behind me," Wadsworth yelled, "behind me!"

"Not behind you," I said, "inside you."

"Hush, Dunjer," Dr. Sass said, "or I'll never get you out."

"This is some mess, Sass," I said, "getting me stuck in this kid—"

"Wait a second—" Wadsworth said.

"Helpless, carried along like a piece of baggage, while all around me these imbecile kids were *marching*—" I said.

"Look, man," Rand said, "you may be a spook, but I think—"

"No one cares what you think, sonny," I said.

"Make him stop talking!" Wadsworth yelled. "I don't *like* it. He's inside me!"

"Damn right!" I said, "and if you don't get me out of here this very instant, Sass—"

"I am doing my best, Dunjer. As soon as I saw what had occurred on the monitor, as soon as I realized its consequences, I threw caution to the wind, set off with my last activator to save *you,* Dunjer."

"You had no choice," I said irritably.

"Why are you speaking in that false voice, Mr. Wadsworth?" Hefler asked.

"You phony, you," Dugan added.

"Arggg," Wadsworth gagged, "I can't stand it!"

"Perhaps," Hefler said, "this is some dreadful punishment? Inhabited by evil spirits."

"How did it happen, Sass?" I said. "You didn't tell me *anything* about getting stuck in someone's body, not one peep; you said it was absolutely safe—"

"Crazy!" Rand said. "A very rare case of split personality."

"My dear Dunjer," Dr. Sass said, "you must bear in mind that for all practical purposes, the activator was untested; the monkey we sent through hardly had your problem."

"It's not *my* problem," I shouted, "I had nothing to do with it.".

"Help-p-p-p," Wadsworth gurgled.

"Shut up, kid," I said.

"Yeah," Rand said; he addressed Wadsworth, "Let's rap, spook."

Wadsworth belched.

"Stop that, you disgusting kid," I said.

"I mean," Rand said, "like I got a thing about freaking out; I mean I'm not knocking this scene, man, but I figure I got a *right* to know. I mean I ain't never bad-mouthed Satan, you dig? So when you come on heavy this way, man, like it makes me—er—uptight. . . ."

"Perhaps," Hefler said, "our punishment is to stay here forever?"

"Don't count on it," I said. "How you doing, Doc?"

"Slow, arduous, painstaking—"

"I get the picture," I said. "This lamebrain scheme is definitely getting out of hand. And who could pick a worse spot? Get set for company, folks."

"Company, man?" Rand said. *"What* company?"

"Take a gander out the window, where I'm looking," I said.

"Yeah," Wadsworth said in wonder. "I see it."

"See?" Lister said. "It?"

"Sure you see it," I said to Wadsworth. "If *I* see it, *you* see it. Damn it to hell."

"Where? Where?" Hefler asked.

"Straight ahead," I said, "and to the right. Here come the unfriendlies."

CHAPTER TWENTY-FIVE

Billows of mist and fog hid streets and buildings. The footsteps behind me were gone, the river and fog-horns with them. I heard crickets, the rustle of leaves, smelled wet grass.

Wind lifted my coat, blew a small hole through the fog.

I saw the house—a four-story job of wood and shingles.

It was a house that shouldn't, that couldn't, be here. And for that matter neither could I. Things had been shifting as if in a dream, vague and insubstantial, shooting out of nowhere—like this house—and then— like my car and those buildings back there—vanishing again. Maybe I was a fragment in someone's dream. Maybe I was a patient half anesthetized on some operating table. Was it all that simple? The question could be more than who or where was I. It could be what was I. That, probably, would be the worst question of all.

I had to get into that house.

I went over, tried the front door, which opened. Yellow wallpaper crept up the walls, a maroon carpet lay underfoot. When I found no one on the ground floor, I started up the staircase.

She was on the second floor, in a small white-walled room with a desk, closet, bed and filing cabinet. She wore a starched nurse's uniform, penciled eyebrows, too much lipstick.

We faced each other.

"What is this place?" I demanded. "Where am I?" My voice sounded strange to me.

The girl opened her lips. Words and sentences that I couldn't follow flowed out.

I shook her by a shoulder. "Speak English!" I yelled.

She began to jabber at me; all I heard were meaningless, disjointed sounds and syllables.

As if understanding my plight, the girl nodded once, held up a slim hand, pointed to the closet; she ran to it, flung open the door.

Joe Rankin came tripping, staggering out. His mouth gaped, his eyes rolled, he made a strange gurgling sound. Blood was bubbling from his mouth. The black handle of a large kitchen knife stuck out of his chest.

Something screamed in my mind.

No dream.

Nightmare!

Nightmare!

Nightmare!

The girl shrieked, turned to run.

I made a grab for her, saw her dance out of reach, run past me through the open door.

Joe Rankin pitched forward onto the floor.

I jumped for the metal filing cabinet, pulled it open, clamped my hand around the laser. The one I knew would be there. Nightmare! The voices screamed.

Hustling out into the corridor, I looked for the girl; she wasn't there. I went to the staircase, started up for the next landing.

Dr. Spelville stuck his head over the banister. I knew him now; only moments before he had been the fat cook. His large lips curved in a smile, his right eye winked. His hand rose high over his head. A dull, gray object twirled through the air.

I leaped back as the staircase exploded.

Spelville was gone.

Bells clamored, went off in all directions, clanged up the staircase, screamed at the ceiling, ricocheted off the walls.

A huge shape stumbled out of the room which held

Joe Rankin's body, came toward me, arms outstretched. Its lips moved; it spoke two words: "Lugo fix."

I burned it with my laser, saw it go up in flame.

I turned to plunge down the stairs.

Voices came from below; the sounds of running feet mixed with the bells jangling overhead.

I hid myself behind the staircase.

A band of half-dressed chattering men tore up the stairs. Their hands flashed long, gleaming knives, an array of big and small guns. I recognized the bald guy in the leather jacket, the blond kid. They raced up to the third floor.

I left my place of refuge, tip-toed down the steps and out the front door.

A bulky figure came at me from the dark: the broad gent with stooped shoulders and long dangling arms. Something glistening whistled through the air toward me. I dived like a submarine trying to hit rock bottom.

An axe splintered wood by the side of my head.

Jumping up, I raised my laser, chopped him across the face. He put up his hands. I kicked him in the stomach. He brought down his hands. I clouted him over the head.

The axe was still stuck in the wood. Rock-face went down.

I started to run.

Men charged around the corner of the house—my friends from the staircase. In the lead, Dr. Spelville, wide-eyed, open-mouthed, arms flailing, legs pumping.

I put the house between them and me, headed into the fog.

A blaze of light snapped on, lit the grounds. Floodlights.

I sprinted into the woods. Trees, night and fog closed over me.

More men poured from the house. I viewed their progress from the cover of darkness. Men spread out on the roadway, ran toward the woods. Flashlights weaved beams of light as they ran, voices shouted directions. The house was a bottomless well of man-power.

I headed away from them, further into the tangle of trees, the sounds of pursuit still growing behind me. Something stirred ahead in the dark.

I raised my laser.

"No! No! Mr. Dunjer, for pity's sake, don't shoot!"

A little man came stumbling toward me. His head was round, bald except for two tufts of white hair that sprouted behind each ear. He wore a Vandyke beard.

The name Dunjer had rung a bell. Whoever or whatever I was—I wasn't Dunjer. I knew that with certainty now. Just as I knew this little man wasn't Dr. Sass.

Then darkness came.

I, KLOX, DIVE THROUGH THE CHAOS. THE BODY OF JOE RANKIN FLOATS BY, BLOATED, INFLATED LIKE A RUBBER RAFT. I AM DUNJER. DARK, INDISTINCT THINGS CHASE ME. I KEEP RUNNING UP AND DOWN HILLS. LONG, EMPTY STREETS STRETCH FOR MILES ON END. BOARDED, WEATHER-BEATEN HOUSES THAT OFFER NO WARMTH OF ENTRANCE ARE ALL I CAN FIND. IT IS ALWAYS TWILIGHT IN THIS WORLD. I CLIMB UP TWO FLIGHTS OF STAIRS. NUMBER 2A IS ON THE LEFT. I TRY THE DOOR WITHOUT KNOCKING. IT OPENS. NO ONE IS IN THE GRIMY, YELLOW-WALLED COMBINATION KITCHEN AND LIVING ROOM. IT IS PART BATHROOM TOO. A BATHTUB AND SHOWER STAND ACROSS FROM A BLACK, DISFIGURED RANGE. A DIRTY RED AND GREEN CURTAIN SEPARATES THIS ROOM FROM THE NEXT. I PUSH THE CURTAIN ASIDE. I, DUNJER, AM ON THE FLOOR NEXT TO THE UNMADE BED. I HAVE ON RUMPLED CREAM-COLORED PAJAMAS. I LIE FACE DOWN ON THE GRAY, WOODEN FLOORBOARDS. READING GLASSES ARE NEAR THE HALF-CLENCHED FINGERS OF MY OUTSTRETCHED

RIGHT HAND. I LOOK AT THE TITLE OF THE BOOK NEXT TO MYSELF. IT IS *HURRAY FOR KLOX!* THIS IS THE WORLD OF UNREASON, I KNOW. I MAKE A CHANGE, IRON OUT A CREASE IN THE FABRIC. THE BODY NOW WEARS A CLOWN'S MASK; ITS APPEARANCE WILL BEGUILE RATHER THAN DRIVE INSANE. I DEPART, MY OBJECTIVE ALMOST WITHIN REACH.

CHAPTER TWENTY-SIX

Out of the darkness, long rows of mechs came marching four abreast. Over weeds, earth, boulders and sand.

"What in heaven's name *are* they?" Gloria Graham asked.

"Mechanical beings," Dr. Sass said. "Have you none on your world?"

"None," Gloria said.

"They are everywhere on our world," Sass said. "A great convenience."

"Not these babies," I said.

"Oh?" Sass said. "Something different about them?"

"They're carrying something," Debbie said.

"Uh-huh," I said.

"O-oo, don't say that," Wadsworth said. "It tickles so."

"Oh, my God," Gloria said.

"Yeah," I said.

"I'm going to scream," Wadsworth said, "if you don't cut that out. No kidding."

"Well, what is it?" Sass asked, peering over the hand railing through the glass. "Must be thousands of them. But they seem perfectly normal to me. Run-of-the-mill mechs. The optimum in serviceability. Marching out of that city we saw, I'd imagine—"

I said, "What're they lugging with 'em, Sass?"

"Lugging, Dunjer? Oh yes, I see cages of some sort . . . and . . . *good grief!*"

"Yeah," I said. "Cages with humans in 'em."

"But this is monstrous," Hefler cried.

"Uh-huh," I said, "merely mechanical. Well, Sass,

you gonna fool with that gizmo all day? Am I gonna stay cooped up in this boob for the duration?"

Gloria Graham began shrieking into her compact again.

Rand said, "What gives, chick; you got a compact complex?"

"Go play with yourself, junior," Gloria Graham snapped.

Dr. Sass said, "I don't think we'll make it in time, Dunjer."

"A-r-r!" I said. "This is the last straw."

"It might very well be," Sass said. "What do you think is going on out there?"

"How should I know," I said. "It's not my continuum. In fact, I'm not even sure what a continuum is."

"Perhaps," Hefler said, "those are merely—uh—ritualistic models in the cages; human-appearing dummies; at this distance—"

"Why don't you stick around, chum, and find out," I said. "Come on, let's shake a leg, Sass. It's back to the Happy City!"

"We're going somewhere *else?*" Dugan asked eagerly.

Sass shook his head. "We cannot go back, Dunjer."

"Why not?"

"I'm not set up for it. You see, the trouble with untested equipment is that it is, er, *untested.*"

"I don't want him inside me anymore," Wadsworth said. "I've made up my mind."

"I'm doing my best, young man," Sass said. "The thing is, my dear Dunjer, that our activator is in phase with that of Grample's. He's here somewhere on this world. Which is why we are here somewhere on this world."

"I don't *like* this world," Lister said. "It's not groovy."

"Forget Grample," I told Sass. "We can come back for him later."

Sass said, "You don't understand. By the time I

realign this activator with our home world, we would be eligible for old-age benefits."

"Don't exaggerate, Sass. They may not have any on this world—for humans. You gotta take us someplace else. What about all those doors, those continuums?"

"What about them?"

"Let's find one. It can't be any worse than here."

"Find one? None are lost. It's *we* who would be lost, Dunjer; lost in the vast fabric of the universe, lost in Interworld. The most careful calculations are necessary before we can undertake such a journey. The activator must be reset. At the moment we are still in tandem with Grample."

"Can't you do *anything?*" Gloria Graham shrieked.

"*She* doesn't think we're dead," I said, "do you, honey?"

The girl glared at Wadsworth. "Take a powder, you disembodied crumb."

"Look, chick," Wadsworth said, clenching a fist. "Even if it ain't me, I resent your talking that way to my person."

"I'm not your person, kid," I said.

"In my direction then."

"She's got a choice?" I said. "Why don't you call your boss, baby?"

"Boss?" Sass said, looking up from his labors.

"Keep working, Sass," I said. "You're behind schedule by decades!"

"Don't complain, Dunjer. I've got you talking again, haven't I?"

"Talking? There was enough talk already without me. Yeah, this dame stooges for Gulach Grample. She used a paralyzer on our pal, Wadsworth, here. I figure the idea was to put the pursuers—namely me—on ice. Right?"

"Why don't you go roll your hoop around somewhere?" Gloria asked.

"H-m-m-m-m," Sass said, "I've just about got the

hang of this. Yes indeed, Dunjer, Grample's activator would indicate your whereabouts, even inside this person, just as my activator allowed me to trace you. They're in sync, you know."

"Yeah, I know. Personally, Doc, I'd rather face Grample than those damn walking garbage cans down there. This baby's got a talkie in that compact. Won't the boss answer you, sweetheart?"

"There's static," Gloria said, biting her lip. "It must be those metal buildings; they're in the way."

"Walk me over to the window," I said, "so I can grab a look-see."

"I hate this," Wadsworth said, going to the window.

"*You* hate this?" I said.

The mechs were coming, all right, and the things they carried were cages with people. Well, it'd've been hard to mistake the ugly sight; there's something about mechs and humans that makes it easy to tell 'em apart; especially when the flesh-and-blood contingent is holding down the cage space.

Something went *kazoo!*

I was looking at Wadsworth.

But I still couldn't feel body, hands, legs and a number of other major items, things I couldn't do without.

Debbie screamed. She was getting good at it.

Wadsworth screamed. He wasn't so good at it. But not the Wadsworth I was looking at. The Wadsworth I was looking at seemed *about* to scream.

"Which one are you in, Dunjer?" Sass asked.

"This one," I said.

"I was afraid," Sass said, "you might be in both."

"Look here," Wadsworth Two said. "I don't know what you guys are trying to pull—"

Wadsworth One said, "This shlump ain't me; I don't know what you guys are trying to pull—"

The base of the tower went *bam,* as if someone were testing its drum potential. The tower shook just a little bit, but not half as much as the noisome crew I was part of.

"The scrap metal's arrived," I said.

"You guys—" Wadsworth Two began argumentatively and went *kazoo*.

Debbie screamed. This screaming business would have to stop.

"Gone," Wadsworth One said. "I never liked him anyway!"

"I can't imagine what went wrong, Dunjer," Sass said.

"Perhaps we can reason with these robots," Hefler said.

"Try reasoning with an egg beater," I said. "Where's the door here?"

"Behind you," Gloria said.

"Turn around, Wadsworth," I said. "Let me see the door."

"That really ticks me off," Wadsworth said. "You don't think I'm gonna take orders from *you,* do you?"

"Yeah," I said. "As senior security op on this dumb mission—as, in fact, the only security op around—I was kind of hoping you'd all take my expert, friendly advice. Lifesaving advice, maybe."

"Take his advice, man," Rand yelled.

"Do what he wants," Debbie screamed.

"Especially you, Wadsworth," I said, "until we get untangled. We'll get untangled sooner or later, eh, Sass?"

"Do what he says," Gloria hissed, "or I'll freeze you!" She had her rod out again.

Behind me something hit the door.

"Er, better *not* freeze him," I said.

Wadsworth whirled. I looked.

A mech stood in the doorway, red eye cells glowing.

Debbie wasn't the only one screaming now.

A second mech appeared behind the first, then a third, a fourth. They filled the entrance.

"Hi, guys," Sid Lister said, grinning frantically. "They bad, me good, *good*."

"Good and creepy," Rand muttered.

These mechs were taller than our home-grown variety by at least a couple of heads. Naturally, they wore no clothing; what the hell would a mech need clothes for? Their bodies were smooth stainless steel; their oval heads had the usual fixtures, beady eye cells, hearing holes, talk slits. Well, they didn't look as nasty as the Firegold bunch, but looks in this world wouldn't mean zilch, and after a certain degree of nasty it was all the same anyway.

The mechs stared at us. We stared at the mechs. One mech turned to the other. "Soft-t-t-heads," he purred.

"T-tell me—ah—what to do," Wadsworth managed to whisper.

"Well, Sass," I said, "it's your baby."

The mechs started for us.

Both Debbie and Gloria shrieked.

Dugan bumped into Hefler, who was trying to get behind Lister. Lister was behind Rand, who was clawing at the window. Since the window was a good distance above ground, that wasn't so smart. But what was? Wadsworth stood stock still, frozen again.

The mechs disappeared.

Wadsworth and I looked at where the mechs had been.

Hefler said in a choked voice, "Some vast force is *playing* with us . . . as if we were—uh—children."

Three more mechs appeared in the doorway.

And vanished.

I said, "What do you think this company's composed of, college professors? That 'vast force' is the same nitwit machine that brought us here."

Three more mechs entered. They blinked out.

"Aim it further down the stairs, Doc; I can't stand the sight of 'em," I said.

"It's that diddle-dee-dum thing!" Dugan exclaimed, catching on.

"Yes, yes," Sass said, "it's the activator."

"Through the doors of the universe?" I asked.

"Hardly," Sass said. "If I could get *them* through, I could get *us* through."

"So where?" I asked.

"Into the fabric," Sass said. "And good riddance too."

"The window, Wadsworth," I said.

"Yes, sir," Wadsworth said, rushing to the window. The wasted landscape looked back at me like an old acquaintance. The mechs were no longer in neat, uniform ranks. A whole bunch of 'em were beating a path back to their city; others had taken off in different directions. Still others had formed a ring around the tower. *What man had wrought,* I thought glumly. I said, "They're going for hardware, Doc; got any ideas?"

Gloria Graham was talking into her compact again. "Static," she said, finally looking up. "But we just *can't* stay here."

"We'll have to levitate," Sass said.

"Thank God," Gloria Graham said. "Why didn't we do that long ago?"

"Levitate?" I said. "Since when do we levitate?"

"We don't," Sass said.

"That's what I figured," I said. "A little thing like levitation would've caught my eye somewhere along the line.

"Ordinarily, we don't levitate," Sass said. "However, this is no ordinary situation, is it? The force built up by the activator's journey through the doors of the universe should allow us to levitate. Theoretically."

"It should?" I said. "So let's go."

"How?" Sass asked. "Down the stairs?"

"They're down the stairs," I said.

"Precisely," Sass said. "I doubt if I could send them all into the fabric of the universe, although frankly I wouldn't mind."

"The windows don't open," Rand said.

"They look quite thick," Hefler said.

I said, "Gloria, you got anything in that bag that breaks windows?"

"Uh-uh," Gloria said.

"My service revolver," Dugan said.

I said, "Why don't you shoot out a window, Mr. Dugan?"

Dugan drew a pearl-handled revolver from under his uniform jacket. "Stand back," he said, and let rip at the window. The small chamber was filled with noise, shattered glass, cold air.

Dugan replaced his pistol. "How's that, lads?" he said, looking around with a broad grin.

"I like it, man," Rand said.

"Alley-oop," Sass said.

We sailed out through the opening. Just like that!

Gray above. Mechs below, craning their necks. Good-bye, mechs.

We picked up speed, took off over the countryside, heading away from their city for a vacant horizon.

"Another triumph for theory," Sass said, a quiver in his voice. "I wasn't certain this would work, you know."

"I know," I said. "And the more I know, the less I like it."

CHAPTER TWENTY-SEVEN

The darkness parted.

I was standing at a bar.

The barkeep gave me another shot.

I blinked my eyes, tossed it down, wondering if I'd had one too many. Gray fog seemed to whirl through the bar, obscured door, windows and walls.

The mirror behind the bar caught two dark-rimmed eyes in a white bloodless face. High forehead, aquiline nose, black hair neatly parted. A tall broad-shouldered figure with as much color and life to him as a head stone. I was looking at myself. I'd really done it this time, gone off on a king-sized bender. I stood there leaning against the bar and watched the gray fog, which was probably all in my mind. Any second now I'd remember my own name.

Two men came through the fog. One was a husky, bald, round-faced guy in a green leather jacket, the other a beak-nosed, blond-headed kid.

They moved toward the small bearded man who'd been standing motionless at the far side of the bar.

He sprang to life, turning my way.

"Mr. Dunjer!" he shrieked.

That name! I knew . . . I was lost . . . the nightmare!

Leather-jacket jerked out a long-nosed pistol, swung it toward the small man. Instinctively, I reached for a gin bottle, brought it slicing down on his hand. He dropped the gun, wheeled to face me. I kicked him in the stomach, straightened him out with a right. Green-jacket fell down as his partner lunged for me with a long black-handled kitchen knife.

I caught his wrist with one hand, his elbow with the other; he screamed as I broke his arm.

The barkeep—a runty, ratlike guy with pointy white teeth, yellowish eyes, dressed in blue pants and white undershirt—reached under the bar, came up with a poker. I ducked as it whistled over my head. I put a fist in his face, saw blood spatter the bar top.

Green-jacket was suddenly on my back. We went down together. I twisted around. His hand reached for the kitchen knife, closed over it. I grabbed his wrist and held it. My hand felt numb, distant. My fingers were losing their grip. Sweat oozed over my palm, made it slippery.

The small bearded man bent quickly, picked up the fallen gun, banged leather-jacket over his bald dome. Leather-jacket opened his mouth. The small man hit him again. Leather-jacket's head rolled sideways; he slid off me. I felt myself rising to my feet like some large, drifting balloon.

The small man was pulling me by the arm, dragging me toward a door.

Fog pitched and heaved around us. We were on a long, empty street. Gray, windowless walls lined both sides of the block.

We turned a corner, cut down a narrow alley.

I almost fell over her, my shoe grinding her fingers against the concrete; it didn't matter, she wouldn't feel anything ever again.

Her throat had been slit. Someone had ripped open her belly. Her clothes were gone and all she had on was a ragged slip, brown with crusted blood. Her hands were twisted behind her, bound by wire that cut into her flesh. Black hair was in disarray. Her head was turned aside, mouth open, eyes staring as though in horror at the thing that had been done her.

"Miss Norwick!" the small man shouted. "It's Miss Norwick!"

The thing began to change as we watched. The fea-

tures thickened, the hair turned sandy; rimless spec-
tacles appeared on its nose. Joe Rankin lay dead on the
cold alley pavement, a puddle of blood under him.

"This way!" the small man screamed, clutching my
arm. I ran with him. This world wasn't real.

We turned another corner.

People were back around us. Tall buildings loomed
in the distance, lost themselves in the gray fog. Gray
cars drifted by. I looked up at the street sign; it said
Cozy Avenue. C-O-Z-Y . . .

Sounds bleated at us like a herd of dying sheep: the
gray-faced, ghostlike shoppers, the sidewalk peddlers
hawking their shoddy wares, the eyeless beggars and
legless cripples, their palms outstretched, milking their
pain and loss in public. I heard the grind of motors, the
blast of horns, the beating of restless feet on asphalt.

A patrol car glided by. In the back seat the lifeless
eyes of Joe Rankin stared out at us. Somewhere in my
mind a voice beyond reason screamed—nightmare!

Again we turned a corner.

No one was on this block or the others that stretched
before us. The sounds behind us had diminished. Five-
story gray-brick walkups lined the street. We passed an
empty, boarded brewery, a field of scraggly weeds and
dried grass, a faded yellow-brick garage, a vacant
supermarket. Wake up! Wake up! Wake up!

The house was like all the others. The small man led
the way through the front door. We went into a dim
hallway, started up a flight of stairs. Greenish oilcloth
covered each step. The hallways were lit by small gray
bulbs, one to each landing. The walls were stained, gas
jets from yesteryear protruded from them. Gray metal
gas and electric meters were placed near the ceiling at
both ends of the hallway. The small man stopped be-
fore 3C, did something to the knob. The door swung
open.

He found the light switch. Grayish light flooded the
apartment. I saw two shabbily furnished rooms.

The small man went to a bookcase, reached behind it, removed a square object; his fingers moved over it and the gray fog seemed to shift. The room took on color, substance. Only it was no longer the same room. No light illuminated walls and ceiling, yet I could see. Somehow . . . I'd stepped outside the nightmare—at least for an instant.

Two men crouched in this room. One was a bald-headed, hefty guy in a green leather jacket, the other a beak-nosed, blond-haired kid. Both held guns. The pair . . . I seemed . . . to know . . . How?

The door leading to the hallway moved an inch. Both men tensed, pointed their guns in that direction. The door slid open.

A tall, broad-shouldered figure stood in the doorway. He had a high forehead, aquiline nose, black hair neatly parted. I might've been looking in a mirror, only I wasn't. This man could've been my twin brother. Maybe he was.

Another instant and he'd be just so much meat.

I moved, threw myself at him.

We spilled to the floor as the gunshots sounded.

My twin was gone.

I was back in the gray, fog-strewn world, on the floor of apartment 3C; in the nightmare.

"This room is a nexus," the small man was saying.

I said with sudden insight, "It belongs to Aces Tommy—"

"Very good. However, not in this Link—in the preceding one. Just as you are no longer Dunjer, nor I Dr. Sass."

I, KLOX, AM STILL DUNJER. THE MURROW BUILD-ING IS ON THE CORNER OF TWENTY-EIGHTH STREET AND SEVENTH AVENUE. I PUSH OPEN ITS DOOR. AN OLD MAN IN A BLUE CAP AND NEAT BRASS-BUTTONED UNIFORM RIDES ME UP IN HIS ELEVA-TOR TO THE THIRD FLOOR. I WAIT TILL THE LIFT HAS

GONE AWAY, SEE I HAVE THE CORRIDOR TO MY-
SELF AND USE A PASSKEY ON THE DOOR MARKED
COZY IMPORTS. A RECEPTION ROOM LEADS TO
A LARGER OFFICE. SUNLIGHT COMES IN THROUGH
DOUBLE WINDOWS BEHIND A WIDE DESK. BOOKS
IN LEATHER BINDINGS LINE ONE WALL, GREEN
FILING CABINETS LINE THE OTHER. I GO TO THE
LATTER, PULL OUT A DRAWER, FIND THE PIECE OF
PAPER. IT SAYS: THE THREE-THING-BALANCE. THIS
IS THE WORLD BELOW REASON, YET THE THREE-
THING-BALANCE MAKES PERFECT SENSE; IT IS
SOMETHING I MUST HAVE, ONLY LATER, NOT
NOW. I GO TO THE WINDOW, LOOK DOWN. A
MAN IS STANDING IN THE DOORWAY DIRECTLY
ACROSS THE STREET. WITH A PAIR OF BINOCULARS
I FISH OUT OF THE BOTTOM DESK DRAWER, I BRING
HIS IMAGE CLOSER. HE IS A SHORT MAN WITH
SANDY HAIR. HIS HAND REACHES OUT—ARM
STRETCHING LIKE A RUBBER BAND—AND BEGINS
TO CHOKE ME. I SINK MY TEETH INTO THE ARM
AND IT LETS GO. I RUN DOWN THE STAIRS, OUT
INTO THE STREET. IT IS MIDNIGHT. THE LITTLE
MAN IS NOWHERE IN SIGHT. I STAND CLOSE TO
THE WALL OF A GRAY-BRICK BUILDING. MY VIEW
OF SEVENTH AVENUE IS COMPLETE. RANDOM
LIGHTS PUNCTURE THE DARKNESS. THERE ARE NO
PEOPLE IN MY IMMEDIATE VICINITY. TRAFFIC
LIGHTS CHANGE COLOR ON A LONELY STRING
OF EMPTY BLOCKS MARKED ONLY BY A STRAY
PASSING CAR OR A LONE PEDESTRIAN. A GLASS
PHONE BOOTH IS ON THE CORNER. THE STREET
LAMP OVER IT IS DARK, OBSCURING THE BOOTH.
I GO TO IT, PULL OPEN ITS DOOR. DR. SPELVILLE
TUMBLES OUT, A NOTE PINNED TO HIS BROWN
JACKET: THE THREE-THING-BALANCE. I ADJUST THE
FABRIC TO DIMINISH THIS PLANE; THOSE WHICH
MIX TRUTH AND MADNESS ARE THE MOST DAN-
GEROUS. SOON, I TRUST, I SHALL BE ABLE TO SEE
MYSELF AS I WAS IN THE PAST, AN EXPECTATION

THAT WOULD UNSETTLE ONE OF LESS RESOLVE. AS I PLUMMET ON TOWARD OTHER REGIONS, A VOICE INSIDE ME CRIES: HURRAY FOR KLOX! IT IS, I KNOW, NO LESS THAN I DESERVE.

CHAPTER TWENTY-EIGHT

"People down there," Sass said. "Waving."

We'd been flying along on activator power for all of ten minutes when we saw 'em. The mechs were way behind us. Only the bleak desert below. And then, people, in a fortress of some kind.

High stone walls on four sides. Armed men standing watch on turrets. Small, square huts—log cabins, really—randomly scattered.

"It might be safer down there, Dunjer, while I worked on you," Sass said.

"And then it might not," I said.

"Look," Debbie said, "the crowd there, they're jumping up and down, they're cheering."

"Cheering us, man," Rand said.

Sass said, "We might discover what this confusing conflict between humans and their natural servants is all about. It could be of scientific importance."

"Natural servants? Someone forgot to tell the mechs. Okay," I said, without too much enthusiasm, "let's give it a whirl."

We swooped down for a landing. The ground was unpaved, a yellowish, dry earth; dust rose as our feet made contact with it. Men, women, kids came running from all directions to surround us; an unpretentious group, most were dressed in simple work clothes. Some pumped our hands, others slapped our backs. A tall bespectacled fellow, one with an obvious air of authority, made his way through the crowd, introduced himself to us.

"Zeb Nieby's the handle, partners," he said, breaking into a craggy grin and extending a work-gnarled hand which we all shook in turn. "I'm head gent in these parts, and it's a mighty keen pleasure to see you all."

"You all, too," Lister said eagerly.

"Shut up, man," Rand said.

"Ask 'em who they is, Zeb," a voice in the crowd said.

"You folks seen any row-bots on the prowl?" a woman's voice called out. "Them row-bots is mean critters."

A kid yelled. "How come they can fly?"

Zeb Nieby nodded good-naturedly, brushed back a cowlick. "All in good time, neighbors. But we gotta hush it if'n we want the answers to them fine questions."

The babel subsided as if someone had pulled the plug.

Dr. Sass cleared his throat. "I'd be delighted to tell you what I can."

"That's right neighborly," Zeb Nieby said, removing a handkerchief from his back pants pocket and blowing his nose.

"We do not come from hereabouts," Sass said. "Our ability to levitate is a product of our advanced technology."

"By ginger," Zeb Nieby said, looking interested. "That there technol-ogy could come in right handy in our little scrap with them there row-bots, I reckon."

Sass told him briefly of our recent experience with the mechs. Nieby listened intently, often sticking out his lower lip.

"That sounds about right," he said when Doc had concluded. "Them row-bots sure has gotten mean lately."

"What happened?" Sass asked.

Zeb Nieby told him:

For decades—since a half-century after being given control of all industrial production—mechs had ruled the roost. Yet there was always place for man. Until the last twenty-four hours, when the mechs turned against people. Just like that. Now the siege was on.

"That's the long and short of it, neighbors," Zeb Nieby said. "We been expectin' an attack any minute now. They sure know about us bein' here."

Dr. Sass cast an inquiring glance at Wadsworth.

"You want to speak to *him*," Wadsworth said accusingly.

"Quiet," I said. "We'd better say our so longs, Doc."

Zeb Nieby asked, "Why you doin' that funny thing with your voice, neighbor?"

"To pass the time . . . ?" Wadsworth said.

"Frankly, Mr. Nieby," Dr. Sass said, "this doesn't seem to be—er—quite the right spot for us to—er—set up shop. . . . You see, there is some delicate work which we must undertake at once, and a mech—er—robot attack would hardly help matters . . . would it . . . ?" Sass tried to smile.

"A row-bot attack ain't gonna help us much either, neighbor," Nieby told him.

"Well-ll, Mr. Nieby—" Sass said.

Nieby raised a palm. "No need to call me Mr. Nieby. His Excellency'd be more t' the point, neighbor. That's what all the neighbors call me."

Twelve men stepped out from the crowd; each carried a rifle; each rifle was aimed at us.

"Meet the militia," Zeb Nieby said. "And now, suckers, raise your hands real high and I'll just have me a look at them fancy machines of yours."

"Suckers? I thought we were neighbors," Wadsworth said bitterly.

"It's all the same," Nieby grinned, "in these parts."

We were in a white-washed, low-ceilinged room. The barred windows of the stockade looked directly out at the fortress parade ground. We huddled around it.

"Oh, my God," Debbie cried.

"Man," Rand said. "Those two dudes *gouged* that guy's eye out."

"Listen to him scream," Dugan said.

"Look!" Debbie wailed.

"They have broken that other man's arm," Hefler said. "What was he doing?"

"Just truckin' along," Rand said.

"They're letting him lie there," Lister said.

"What kind of people are these?" Debbie shrieked.

"That, my dear, should be obvious," Sass said.

"Gloria," I said. "They took your paralyzer, right?"

"Right."

"But they left your compact."

"Why should they take a girl's compact?"

"There're no tall buildings around here."

"I noticed."

"Maybe there's no static either."

"There isn't."

"So why don't you try your boss again?"

"I already have. You think I'm dumb or something?"

Shots told us we had company. Neighbors ran by out in the clearing. His Highness sprinted past our winlow, dragging at a hip holster. Was it Grample or the mech army? I was beginning to figure that even mechs would be an improvement over our captors; hard to imagine 'em being any worse; yet a nagging doubt warned me that given enough time, I might just be able to imagine it. The compound, meanwhile, was starting to jump, as if it'd been given a hotfoot. Something flashed across the sky, something that looked like a large wooden raft.

Neighbors shot bullets up at it.

A ray vibrated through the air, bounced yellow light from raft to ground. People tripped and fell, twitched once or twice, lay still.

"Nerve scrambler," I said.

"There're robots," Debbie yelled.

"And people," I said. "That makes a difference, eh?"

A bell had begun to ring somewhere. The armed neighbors were heading for cover, deserting the field for huts and cabins.

"See that fat party up there?" Gloria asked.

I gave her a yes.

"That's Gulach Grample," she said.

He was a large man, with wavy black graying hair, full lips, a hefty nose; his belly bulged over his belt; he wore a simple gray business suit. This was Gulach Grample, the man who now filled the doorway of the stockade. He stood there and laughed—a booming laugh that all but rattled the walls.

"I'll tell you," he said. "I wouldn't have bothered for you busybodies. Got better things to do. But can't let the help down, can I? Come here, Gloria, sweetheart."

Gloria sweetheart detached herself from us, went to stand by him; he patted her shoulder absently, looked at Wadsworth.

"You're in there, aren't you, Dunjer? Harmless enough now, I'd say. Serves you right. A fine end you've come to, spending your last days sharing someone else's body. Monitor on this activator tells it all. Hired Gloria here—from that crazy UN world—to put you out of commission. Couldn't do it myself. No time to spare. Stay there, Dunjer. You won't get in my way again."

"You're Master?" I said, just to say something.

"What do you think?" he smirked.

A lumpy individual entered behind Grample, said to his ear, "We got the rubes boxed in."

"Some of you've heard of Louie Mugger?" Grample asked, grinning.

The lumpy person bowed, leered at us. "Should I mop up them other marks?" he said to Grample. "The pickin's here look kinda lean."

"Take what you wish, but make it snappy. I want to get off this world."

I couldn't blame him. That was my ambition too. Dr. Spelville stuck his head in, grinned at us; he and Lumpy went away. Grample turned to go too.

"Wait, Mr. Grample." Dr. Sass held up a shaky

hand. "You must listen. I, sir, am the inventor of the activator. I have come here expressly to warn you of terrible danger."

"Danger? What danger?"

"That—er—is, I fear, as yet somewhat unclear. Insufficient work, you see, leaves us with—er—certain unanswered questions—"

"Twaddle," Grample said.

Sass said urgently, "The fabric can't stand such tension!"

"Neither can I," Wadsworth said.

"The fabric?" Grample said.

"The fabric of the universe!"

"Bah! I don't know anything about that. And what's more, I don't care—"

Grample's speech was lost in a huge blast. The ground shook. Plaster fell from the walls. Glass shattered.

Wadsworth twisted his head toward the window. Scores of mechs were piling through what had once been the north wall, but now wasn't.

Sass tugged at Wadsworth's arm, his eyes flicked back toward the door.

Grample and Gloria were gone, leaving our prison door wide open. We didn't stand on ceremony, hustled out into the compound. Mayhem was taking place. Screaming humans and silent mechs were going at each other, all kinds of weapons discharging into metal, wires, screws, rivets; skin, bone and flesh. It was a swell place to go away from.

Grample and his crew weren't around here either. I could worry about 'em later. If there was one.

"The seedy gold-painted cabin," I said, "with the 'Palace' sign on it."

"We go there, man?" Rand asked.

"There's nowhere else," I said.

The door was standing ajar, His Highness nowhere inside.

The sleazy kitchen chairs and table were painted gold and purple. Threadbare lace drapes separated one room from the other; and the floor was earth. We found our belongings under a small, patchwork quilt-covered cot where His Highness had shrewdly stashed them. Dr. Sass let out a long sigh and reached for the activator and restorer.

The lace curtains parted.

Two mechs stared at us. One instantly started forward.

The other mech, moving quickly, brought a large hammer out from behind his back, sent it crashing down on the first mech's head. The mech collapsed.

"They always fold when you hit them on the battery," the mech with the hammer said. "I am Klox, the philosopher robot. And I must say—"

A clanging from the other room, behind the lace curtains, told us that more metal maniacs had arrived.

Squinting at the monitor, Sass said, "Grample's gone through another door, Dunjer."

"Well?" I said.

The cabin vanished.

CHAPTER TWENTY-NINE

There was only silence and the gray fog. The dreary flat, its walls and shabby furniture seemed to quiver and undulate. Mist poured in through a half-opened window. The small man spoke:

"This is the world of specters, Mr. Dunjer."

"The what?" I heard myself say.

"A phantasmagoria. You and I are mere apparitions."

I looked at him.

"I am the specter of Dr. Sass," he said. "His memories are mine. This activator which I possess—a phantom too—has enabled me to retain a part of my identity. The initial use of an activator, Mr. Dunjer, has created all that you see before you."

"I can't remember," I said.

"You have lost your activator and that has cast you adrift. The Spelville phantasm possesses it. Should he obtain mine also, he would be able to solidify this world, make it his own. That is his ambition. But to secure his gains, he must destroy us both. We are random factors who endanger his supremacy."

"The blond kid," I said, "the bald guy?—"

"His henchmen."

"You called me Dunjer."

"So I did. The appellation, however, is, in the strictest sense, fallacious. While I retain some of the Sass characteristics, your loss of the activator has all but severed you from the original Dunjer personality. Your traits—whatever they may be—are different. You are, so to speak, your own man."

"Great," I said. "How did this Spelville get the jump on me?"

"When the Spelville original preceded you through the doors of the universe, the Spelville phantasm was instantly created, retained sufficient memory to lie in wait for you. You and your activator were separated at the very outset of the journey."

"I was driving a car through the mist—"

"Yes, that was my doing; I intervened. Had I been more prompt, this entire calamity could have been avoided. I sought you with my activator, but arrived too late to ward off Spelville. Instead, I created a divergent reality. The flat in which you discovered a dead body was to be our rendezvous point. It was necessary to contrive such a stratagem in order to befuddle Spelville, to blunt his attempts against me. I began to scrawl a message that might have helped you retain the last shreds of identity, but was unable to complete it. Spelville and his cohorts were too close. I fled. Since then, it is I who have kept you alive. By creating counterthrusts to Spelville's reality, I have enabled you to withstand his onslaughts."

"Thanks," I said, "but what for? If what you say is true, we might as well be dead."

"But we are not. What happens here can still affect the other worlds, those through which our originals travel. More important, Mr. Dunjer, if you and I can gain control of this phantom plane, we can make it real—one of the many worlds—and insure our continued survival."

Sass strode to the closet door, pulled it open. "This way, Mr. Dunjer. While there is still time."

I was driving again.
Feeling began to come back into my body.
I had almost reached my destination.
I killed the motor, stopped, fingered the bottle, took a final swig and eased myself out of the car. The gun

felt good in my hand; I walked down the road, my feet making splashing sounds on the ground.

Barren, jagged trees reached skyward around me. Weedy, brownish shrubbery clung to the damp earth. I kicked up mud and gravel as I went. No moon shone overhead. Fog was everywhere.

Then the Cozy Rest Home was there—a dim, indistinct structure.

Faint light shone through a third-floor window. I moved to the side of the building, looking for the coal chute. Suddenly I was standing very still, my eyes locked on something that lay by the side of the wall.

A man was stretched out, part of his face gone. Enough was left to tell me who this was—the blond kid with the beaky nose. I looked beyond him. More dead men littered the ground.

I went around to the front door and in. I didn't have far to look. The other one was sprawled on the stairs—the remains of leather-jacket.

Only where was Spelville?

"This way," Dr. Sass said.

I went through the closet, into a short tunnel. Grayish light shone up ahead. We were back in Happy City.

"Up there," Sass said, pointing.

I recognized the place, all right—I was in Cheery Village, looking at Placid Towers. At least I could remember something.

The speed lift took me up to the apartment. I went down the corridor, stopped in front of a door.

The buzzer got me no response. My fist pounded the wood panel.

Down the hall a door opened a crack. A pair of beady eyes gleamed out at me; a hooked nose slanted over grinning, toothless gums. An old crone in a seedy, spotted dressing gown shook a withered finger. Stringy gray hair peeped out under the edges of a frayed white night cap, danced wildly around her lined forehead. She chuckled:

"It won't do you no good, sonny. Ma Snooly knows. Ma Snooly knows everything, hee-hee; she's gone. I watched; I know. Hours ago. Ain't been back since, hee-hee. Had a caller, a gentleman caller. They left t'gether. A fat man, it was, a great big fat man! She likes big fat men better'n you, sonny."

"This way," Dr. Sass said.

The tunnel came to an end.

Red neon lights on the corner spelled out Swell Pillow. I moved past them. Tenement houses were on either side of me. I kept going, left them behind.

I had no trouble finding the house. It stood in a small gully in a vacant section of town, four blocks from its nearest neighbor.

Going through a field, I approached the place from the side.

A small, ratty-looking man in blue pants and undershirt sat on the back porch, tilted back on a wooden chair, his feet up on the railing. A rifle rested on his lap.

I saw no one else, heard nothing else.

The man sat there staring off into the night, his face empty. I moved behind him, sliced his head open with a sap, clipped a handcuff over his left wrist, and snapped the other end to the porch railing. I went around to the side of the building.

Light came from a basement window. Crouching down, I peered through the glass. A slim blond-headed kid in shirt sleeves, his back toward me, was talking to someone I couldn't see.

I leaned fingertips cautiously against the pane—a window that pushed in—and moved it a quarter inch.

The sound of the man's voice reached me.

I opened the window all the way and made my voice loud: "Reach!"

The kid whirled. A large gun sprang into his hand.

We fired together.

The kid's shot dug into the wall somewhere; mine into his chest.

He was flung backwards. His eyes widened; his lips came apart—blood bubbled from between them. His gun left his fingers. The kid fell down on the stone floor, rolled over on his side, twitched twice and lay still.

I eased through the window.

The basement contained an oil burner, a dusty green Ping-Pong table and some empty wooden crates piled in a corner.

Whoever the kid had been talking to was gone.

The girl sat on a high-backed wooden chair facing me. She was tied hand and foot. I didn't bother freeing her. What was the use? She would only turn out to be the dead body of Joe Rankin.

The head of Dr. Sass hung in the darkness, its eyes wide, staring.

"All is lost," he shrieked. "It is stalemate. His activator stymies ours at every turn. We are doomed, Mr. Dunjer, doomed!"

I was a pawn in someone else's game—a losing one. I was tired of being a pawn.

"Give me the activator," I said.

I, KLOX, OUT HERE IN THE FABRIC CAN SEE THE PORTHOLES FLASH BY. I HAVE YET TO VIEW MY-SELF, ALTHOUGH I KNOW I AM THERE SOME-WHERE. THROUGH THEM I CAN SURVEY DUNJER'S WORLD. HERE—IN THE FABRIC—I CAN KNEAD AND BEND. BUT THERE—THROUGH THE PORT-HOLES—I CANNOT TOUCH. YET SOMETHING MUST BE DONE. I SEE THE GULACH GRAMPLE ES-TATE IN A VALLEY. THERE ARE TREES, GATES, FENCES AND WALLS THAT HIDE IT FROM THE SUR-ROUNDING POPULACE. THE COPTERS ARE ZERO-

ING IN. A SQUAD OF MECHANICALS, DUNJER, HENNESSY AND SEVEN OTHER HUMAN OPS ARRIVE WITH THEIR RAID ORDER. MORRIS WANGDANGLE WILL MEET THEM. ALONG WITH AN ARRAY OF WEAPONRY. THIS MUST DEFINITELY NOT HAPPEN. THERE IS A LOGIC TO EVENTS, ONE WHICH MY PRESENCE ATTESTS TO. THIS LOGIC MUST BE PRE-SERVED. A STRATAGEM SUGGESTS ITSELF. I PUSH OPEN THE PORTHOLE, AIM THE ACTIVATOR AT THE REQUIRED SEQUENCE. THE FABRIC YIELDS, UN-FURLS THROUGH THE OPENING. I TWINE AND WRENCH, ALTER THE PATTERN AND RELEASE THE FABRIC; IT SNAPS BACK, TRANSFORMED, THROUGH THE PORTHOLE. I HAVE SUCCEEDED, AS ALWAYS. BLOODSHED, RENDING, HITTING AND TEARING WILL NOT OCCUR NOW; I HAVE SUBSTITUTED ANOTHER SEQUENCE. BUT AT WHAT COST! THE LINZETEUM IS GONE, USED UP IN THE PROCESS. THE ACTIVATOR IS USELESS. I CHUCK IT AWAY, WATCH AS IT SPINS OFF INTO DARKNESS. ONLY TWO ACTIVATORS NOW REMAIN. I MUST CHOOSE MY NEXT JUNCTURE WITH CARE. MY ABILITY TO INTERCEDE IS NOW SEVERELY RESTRICTED, IF NOT ALTOGETHER IMPAIRED.

CHAPTER THIRTY

We were on a tree-lined boulevard, a small, huddling group of tourists trying to take in all the sights at once. Dense air traffic hovered above us. Multiple street levels thronged with moving pedestrians. Ultramodern skyscrapers stretched upward like bridges to the clouds. Unlike Happy City, the walks here were immaculate, the buildings white and glittering.

While jostled and bumped by the passing crowd, no one paid us the least notice. We might've been invisible. What we were was even better. Indistinguishable from the herd. One of the many. Brothers to the crush. It was unnerving.

No two persons were dressed alike. Styles ran the gamut: Biblical, Greek, Roman, Islamic, monastic, modern-plus; nudes abounded; some were clad in caveman garb. Mechs glided by on oiled hinges; the stupid mechs had their own get-ups too. People mixed, twined, congested; they were everywhere, rubbing shoulders, bellies, arms, legs. Heads stuck out of windows, looked down from the rooftops. Bodies filled doorways. Row on row of humans went plowing by.

Lips moved, skulls nodded, voices whispered, chattered, laughed, yelled, chorused. Only stray words meant anything to me. The rest was gibberish. I got the idea, though. I knew what was going on. Four years of op school gives a man certain insights. These birds were all gabbing away in different tongues; we'd hit a world of polyglot gabble.

I raised my voice. "We've got to get away from this crowd, Sass!"

Sass was busy being carried along by the pedestrian wave. A metal arm shot out and grabbed him.

"You, Klox, here?" I shouted.

"Well," Klox said. "I didn't *ask* to come along; I had no hint you were going *anywhere;* it came as quite a shock; if my senses weren't foolproof, I'd certainly doubt them. However, we philosopher robots take such things in stride. A huge structure on a side street, by the way, is almost empty of persons; its top floor, my sensors note, is totally deserted; what do you say to that?"

"Help-p-p," Debbie yelled, losing her fight to stay with us.

Klox's arm flashed out and whisked her back.

"It's a loft of some kind," Lister said.

The floors were covered by linoleum, the walls painted a soothing blue. No furniture. Two windows looked out at the other buildings, the sky full of buses, copters, planes and jets; the walks crawling with people below.

Sass busied himself with the restorer.

"You're materializing this security fella?" Dugan asked.

"Quite right," Sass said. "I think."

"I'll believe it when I see it," I said.

"So will I," Sass said. "If I'd known this was going to be so hard, I would have sent someone else."

"Who?" I asked. "Miss Norwick?"

"So, as I understand it," Klox said, "we are hunting this Grample person, who has stolen an activator which enables *him,* as it has enabled *us,* to go from one continuum to another, which may, in fact, prove to be a very dangerous thing to do, or so it would seem."

"So it would," Sass said.

"How come you helped us, man?" Rand asked.

"Man would not seem quite appropriate," Klox said, "in my case. We philosopher robots are always doing strange, unexpected things like that. What is this Grample person *doing* with the activator?"

"Using it," Sass said, not taking his gaze off the restorer, fingers delicately shifting levers, moving knobs, twisting dials, an eruption of dexterity.

"Why?" Klox said.

"I never did get to ask him that," Sass complained.

"You didn't sell him on your quaint notion of his giving up, either," I pointed out.

"How could I?" Sass shrugged. "No time."

"Sure. Only next around I just *take* his activator, let's say. Provided *I* become *me* again, eh, Sass?"

"Eh, yourself," Sass said. "If your organization had done its job, Dunjer, none of us would be out here now. Grample certainly has been on the go though, hasn't he? I feel I am very close to understanding what this terrible thing is that happens when an activator is used. Only it seems so far-fetched, I hesitate to state it. Until, of course, there is more evidence. Which may be any second now. Unfortunately."

I said, "You have sensors, eh, Klox?"

"Indeed, yes. All kinds."

I said, "How far can you sense with those things?"

"Oh, miles and miles."

"Why don't you see what's going on out there?"

"Delighted. We philosopher robots always enjoy stretching a sensor or two. I sense the crowds moving. Most unusual. It would appear they all move in one direction. So they do. From all corners of the city. Houses are emptying out. Schools. Municipal buildings. Mobile walks have been redirected, now move only toward the square. Everyone moves toward the square."

"Wadsworth, the window," I said.

Wadsworth shuffled toward the window; the boy was losing his drive.

Squinting out through Wadsworth's eyes, I saw the people down below. A lot of 'em. And all doing the same thing, heading one way. As if they'd cashed in their, individualities to take part in something usually reserved for ants. I stared down at 'em in wonder and disgust. Interworld was one big mess.

"What's happening at this square?" I asked Klox.

"It is a very large square in the heart of the city. Filling up with people, even with robots. Two giant screens are at either end of the square. I cannot sense what they are for. Something is about to happen. I cannot sense what that something is."

"Wadsworth," I said, "look up."

Wadsworth turned his gaze skyward.

All the flying conveyances, I saw, were heading the same way. The last time I'd taken part in something like this, the world'd blown up.

A sound behind us made Wadsworth turn. Visitors. Two tall figures looked at us blankly, a man and a woman, both in their early thirties. They were dressed simply in what appeared to be short bath towels. Their straight, unadorned hair was shoulder length.

"I thought," the woman said, "this floor would be empty."

"How dull," the man said. "It's not."

"We *could*," the woman said, "try another floor. They should all be empty now."

"How tiresome," the man said. "Let's not. After all, what are seven persons and a machinie?"

"Machinie?" Klox said. "Is that what you call us here?"

"Certainly," the woman said in a smooth, syrupy voice. "What else could we possibly call you? You're right, Svett," she said, addressing her companion. "Seven persons and a machinie are *nothing* at all."

"Nothing," Svett agreed.

Something tingled inside me like an alarm clock going off. This was unusual, since a second ago there was no inside me to speak of.

Wadsworth yelped. Four other Wadsworths yelped back, stared at each other, clutched their heads.

"Almost!" Sass shouted.

"Almost," I said very calmly, but with feeling, "isn't quite good enough, now is it?"

"Wait!" Sass shouted, twisting a knob.

Again a tingling.

Now there were nine Wadsworths, all shoving each other and shouting. This hardly seemed an improvement. My Wadsworth was joining the fray too.

"Stop it, you rotten kid you," I yelled, trying to restrain him. "Have you no hostlike sense of obligation?"

"None!" my Wadsworth yelled back, kicking another Wadsworth. "These guys give me a terrible pain."

"Sass," I bellowed.

"Well," Svett said. "There are sixteen now, Yalta, my dear."

"Sixteen," Yalta said, "is such a *small* number."

"How true, Yalta, my love. But if there are any more of these boring multiplications, we will really have to consider going elsewhere."

"I suppose so," Yalta shrugged, "especially if those multiplications insist on shouting so."

"Seventeen, if you count the machinie," Klox said.

"Hold on, Dunjer!" Sass bawled.

"I'm sure as hell not going anywhere," I said icily.

"Always count the machinie," Klox said.

Something went *glunk*.

Nine Wadsworths went away.

My Wadsworth swayed, gasping for breath.

I said to our blond, towel-clad guests, "Maybe you can tell us what all those folks are up to out there. We're strangers in this neck of the woods."

Svett said, "There aren't any woods around here for miles. But we'll be glad to tell you, if it doesn't take too long."

"We would hate for it to take too long," Yalta said. "Those pesty crowds would be back."

"My brothers are gone," Wadsworth gasped, wiping perspiration from his brow.

"They're not your brothers, man!" Rand said accusingly. "They're you!"

"Forget it," Wadsworth said.

"They," Yalta said, "are going to the time screens." Something shifted.

"Time screen?" I said, looking through the eyes of Mark Rand.

Wadsworth went, "Eeeyoweee," plunked to the floor. Rand and I looked at him.

Rand said, "Man, I don't *feel* so good."

I wasn't feeling too chipper myself.

"Yes, indeed," Svett said. "Giant time screens are something new."

"Not like the *wee* screens of old," Yalta said, placing thumb to forefinger.

"Not?" I said through Debbie. Debbie shrieked once and keeled over like a sack of onions. We landed on the cold, unwelcome floor together.

"Yes," Svett yawned. "Since the invention of direct time-viewing fifty years ago, we've seen just about everything. All the great sights."

"From the Biblical flood, you know, to Cleopatra's bedroom," Yalta said.

"And everything between, before and after," Svett murmured.

"You don't say?" I said from the floor, tingling all over.

"Oh, yes," Yalta said. "Killed off the old Tri-D Entertainies like a smoked kipper."

"That's pretty killed off," I said through Lister. Lister screamed. "Shut up, you dumb kid," I said.

"It takes a delicate touch to do this," Sass said urgently.

"Will someone hit this dumb kid over the head?" I said. Lister stopped screaming.

Klox said, "The square, I sense, is full; the screens are beginning to light up."

"This is the big testing of the screens," Yalta said. "A first in history."

"But so what?" Svett shrugged.

I sighed, looking at the restorer through Sass's eyes.

"My dear Dunjer," Sass exclaimed, "this is most uncalled for."

"You're right," I agreed. "*I* sure didn't call for it. Why don't you take it away?"

"Well, don't distract me. We're making progress, you know."

"Yeah. So does a merry-go-round. Of sorts."

"It's all so horribly boring," Svett explained. "When you've seen everything, all the great moments, all the small moments, what's left?"

"So what *is* left?" I asked through Yalta.

Svett raised an eyebrow, shrugged. "Not much," he said.

"Get out of there, you naughty voice," Yalta said.

"You see," Svett said. "Now that people just tune in their favorite past histories and watch the real thing, they are free to select any culture, language and life style they might wish. It's so hard to be different when everyone's different."

"I can see that," I said, still through Yalta.

"But *this*," Svett admitted, "is somewhat different."

"It is," Yalta agreed.

"But not as different as making love in complete privacy," Svett said.

"We've never done that," Yalta said.

"Never?" I said.

"Oo-o," Klox said. "Armies have appeared on the screens. The crowd is cheering."

"Never," Svett said, "till now."

"Made love in private?" I said.

"Or had sex alone," Yalta said.

Svett plucked at his towel. It dropped to the floor. He was naked.

"Sass!" I barked.

"And this is *almost* complete privacy," Yalta said, her towel dropping away too.

"Almost is good enough for us," Svett beamed.

"Now hold on a minute—" I began.

"Holding on is just what we intend to do," Svett said, two bulky arms embracing Yalta. Yalta tilted.

"Now stop that!" I shrieked.

"Man!" Rand said, removing his shades.

"Wow," Debbie said, getting to her feet, one hand on the wall.

Wadsworth, stretched out on the floor, groaned, raised an eyelid. "Look at that," he said wonderingly.

Lister squinted eagerly.

"Fiends of hell!" Dugan roared.

"Please don't yell like that," I said through Dugan.

Dugan began to bellow. My vision was rocking like a toy sailboat under a running faucet.

Svett and Yalta were down on the floor now, Svett on top of Yalta. Had they no shame?

Then I was seeing something else.

I was inside Klox, watching the Roman Legions through his eyes, seeing them cavorting on the two screens. They were certainly a grubby lot, not half as impressive as the spit-and-polish variety depicted on our home Tri-D's.

They seemed to be traipsing aimlessly; I could tell right away that this unedited history was no great shakes. Nothing going on, only a lot of scratching.

Then it hit me:

Here I was, stuck in another body, a mech's. What did I feel? Empathy? Solidarity? A new understanding? Uh-uh. Being here was as interesting as hopping around on a metal leg. And just as inspiring. I couldn't even tell what was going on in that one, important area behind me with Yalta and Svett.

The size of the square caught my attention. Some square. Big enough for a small city. They could start building now. All the folks they'd ever need were on hand. Packed shoulder to shoulder. Eyeing history as it limped along on the giant screens.

As I watched, history began to improve. The scene shifted. Another group of shabby men was hiking through a forest. By their unshaven, scowling faces, peculiar attire, gait and different way of scratching, it was easy to see that these fellas belonged to another clan; the barbarians had arrived just in time to save the show.

The crowd let out a roar.

Only it wasn't for the barbarians.

Through the eyes of Klox, I stared dumbly as Gulach Grample, Louie Mugger, a crew of assorted goons and mercenary mechs swooped down. The activator-powered raft came to a halt in mid air, hovered over the north time viewer. The mechs went to work, one squad aiming the knock-out ray at the crowd below, another winding a large net around the screen.

The audience suddenly became busy being a riot. The yellow ray helped 'em along, cut down victims like a harvesting machine.

Old Grample was trying to make off with one of the monstrous screens!

It made sense, all right. Back in Happy City, this steal'd be a cockeyed wonder, the rage of the upper crust. No cross-continuum cops'd come calling either; there weren't any. Given the muscle of activator power, the old rogue might just do it, lift a thirty- or forty-ton slab as though it were a kiddy's playpen. Who could stop him?

Klox was jabbering again, giving our gang a frantic blow-by-blow of events. From my lookout the words were just sounds. I didn't try to make sense of 'em. I had a front-row seat, could follow on my own. There was a lot to follow. Something very peculiar had started to happen:

Romans and barbarians had tired of their game; the confines of history had proved too narrow for 'em.

They weren't *there* anymore; they were *here!*

Pouring out of the screens, like salt from a shaker. All of 'em!

Hordes of murderous warriors came raining down on the riot that'd now become a mad, helter-skelter rout.

They came from both screens, swords drawn; they used 'em. Rage twisted their features, hate burned in their eyes; they didn't appear any too likely to engage in constructive discussion; they didn't pause even to take in their new environment. All these boys knew was massacre. They showed what they could do.

Grample and company were gone, had taken off for other points, leaving their net behind, blood-soaked and trampled.

All this was as miserable as my becoming part of a philosopher mech, but so long as those madmen out there weren't killing *me,* I figured I could stand it.

Something seemed to turn inside out.

The whole room let out a holler, even Svett and Yalta—I saw—who'd stopped doing whatever it was they were doing. *Saw?*

"Success!" Sass yelled. "Sweet success!"

True enough. I was back in the flesh, on my own two feet, firmly planted in my own two socks. Me. Myself. I. Along with my activator. Cubes. Hardware.

Back to face *this*.

Wadsworth said, "So you're the guy."

I cut short this chit-chat. "Save it," I said. "Now I get hold of Grample and do this my way, eh?"

"According to the monitor," Sass said, "Grample has left this continuum."

"We still in sync?"

"Naturally."

"So what're we waiting for?"

"For you to materialize, Dunjer."

"I'm materialized."

We went.

CHAPTER THIRTY-ONE

You ride and the night rides with you. The blurred shapes that spring by on the sloping highway are like faces in a dream—vague and unfocused. An activator only gives you partial control. But you do remember: Spelville, Dr. Sass, the blond kid, leather-jacket, the thing that had tried to gut you in the rest home. Only it wasn't you, but someone else whose memories you now share. This Dunjer. And the memories flicker and fade like candles in a drafty cellar.

Pull over then, leave the car hidden in the bushes by the roadside. This is the spot where it all comes together. The Cozy Rest Home, shrunken and humpbacked, a dry, lightless husk rising out of the gloom.

Thin rays of moonlight slip over road, trees and shrubbery, then, as the gray fog rolls in, die like match flames caught in a sudden gale. The fog and mist are everywhere. You wait.

The distant purr of an engine sounded from behind me. I lay down in some bushes, put my chin in the dirt.

A car came by, moving very slowly. Headlights lit up gray mist, road, bushes and trees.

The slim blond-headed youth drove, bent over the wheel. Tense, rigid lines distorted his features. He was alone.

I was up on my feet, scrambling through the thicket. I hit the road running. Long strides brought me to the car's lowered window.

The kid's head spun around, eyes bulging as I stuck my hand through the window, released the safety catch and jerked down on the door handle. The door opened;

the car stopped. I brought the barrel of my laser slicing across his head. He fell to one knee, his hand groping blindly for his pocket. I hit him again. The kid slid from the car to the ground.

I climbed in and drove the rest of the way to the rest home. So far, no one had changed scenes on me. I felt the activator in my jacket pocket. Maybe it would see me through.

I killed the motor, turned off the headlights. Nothing now but the fog. I waited, the laser in my hand.

A blinding light flared through the windshield, caught me in its beam. Crouching, I fired twice. Glass shattered.

Darkness.

I ducked out of the car. Leather-jacket lay sprawled on the ground, a high-powered flash near one hand, a gun in the other.

I turned as a noise sounded behind me. Arms, legs and a belly collided with me. I kicked the belly, found myself rolling on the ground, the laser knocked from my grasp. A hand tugged at the jacket pocket which held my activator. I twisted my body away from the prying fingers.

We grappled.

Faint light began to shimmer our way. Headlights, the sound of an engine. Another car was winding through the fog.

The man I had locked arms with put his shoe in my face and I fell away. In that instant I saw him: A short, squat body; long dangling arms; a face like a rock pile.

His fingers closed over my laser. I slammed into him, got my hands around his arm and twisted. We rolled over the damp earth.

In the clearing two growing circles of light drew nearer.

The man slipped from my grip, caught me in the face with a large fist. I chopped an open hand to the side of his neck, grabbed his arm again. The car loomed out of the fog, slowed to a halt. I bent his arm.

The laser sent a crackling discharge toward the auto.
Flames! The car caught fire.

Its door banged open. A round, stooped figure stumbled from it. Firelight leaped up his huge belly, climbed over folds of chin, sent streaks of red, yellow and orange skipping across pumping arms and legs. Dr. Spelville ran from the car.

I shook the laser from my assailant's hand, sent it spinning off into the grayness. I clipped him on the button with a right, kicked his feet out from under him.

He began crawling toward the laser.

Spelville froze in midstride, glanced over his shoulder at the car, turned and headed back toward it.

I dived for my weapon. The man wound both arms around me. I brought my knee up. He let go. I grasped the laser, clubbed him with it. He went down.

Across the clearing, the fat doctor crawled into his car. Head and shoulders disappeared into the back seat as spitting, snarling flames licked and embraced the car's metal body. Spelville emerged—swaying away from the wreckage wide-eyed and open-mouthed, gasping and heaving, as he staggered and pitched down the clearing. In his arms, he cradled an activator. Fat fingers beat at flames rising on his jacket; round arms smothered the fire, ground it against belly and chest. It was as though a crazed ritual were transpiring on that field, an insane dance comprising flame, metal and flesh.

I sat on the ground—the still figure of Shortie next to me—and watched as the car, roaring, burst apart; flames soared.

Spelville rose off the ground like some round, bloated bird. He turned and tumbled over and over, arms still twined around the activator.

I covered him with my laser, debated silently whether to talk or shoot. The fat doctor seemed to have forgotten all about me. Slowly he dragged himself over the grass. He got to his feet like a drunken man climbing invisible stairs, his face dazed, bewildered.

Something moved on the far side of the clearing. Something came out of the mist and fog. A tall, lean figure, traveling with the swiftness of a jungle cat, stepped into the dying circle of light.

A soft-brimmed hat covered eyes and forehead. The turned-up coat collar obscured chin and lips. A long black coat flapped loosely around his knees.

The fat doctor half-turned; his mouth moved but no words came; his arms hugged the activator to him.

The tall man held a gun in one black-gloved hand. Dr. Spelville seemed to grow smaller, to hunch over into a tight-fitting ball.

The lips of the tall man moved, said something I could not hear. Then he sent five slugs into the fat, quivering body that crouched before him.

I, KLOX, WITH MY USUAL KEEN PERCEPTION, SEE EVENTS UNFOLDING. A CRUCIAL MOMENT IS AGAIN DISCERNIBLE THROUGH THE PORTHOLES. A SQUAD OF SIXTY MECHANICALS, DUNJER AND SEYMOUR SALANT ARE IN THE LAB BUILDING AT THE FIREGOLD STRONGHOLD. TUMULT CLOGS THE CORRIDORS. IT IS TOUCH AND GO, FOR THE SCRAMBLERS IN THE DUNJER MECHS ARE FLAWED, CANNOT LONG WITHSTAND THE ENEMY ON-SLAUGHT. THE LOGIC OF EVENTS WILL BE DIS-RUPTED. NOW IS THE MOMENT TO UTILIZE MY SECOND ACTIVATOR. I PUSH OPEN THE PORT-HOLE, AIM THE ACTIVATOR THROUGH IT. THE FABRIC BILLOWS OUT. I WRING AND CONTORT, MINUTELY CHANGING THE PATTERN. DUNJER'S OPTIMISM IS NOW FULLY JUSTIFIED, HIS SCRAM-BLERS ARE PERFECTION ITSELF. RELEASING THE FABRIC, I WATCH AS IT SPRINGS BACK THROUGH THE PORTHOLE. AGAIN I HAVE SAVED THE DAY. MY SECOND ACTIVATOR IS SPENT: A MERE RELIC; I TOSS IT ASIDE. ONLY ONE IS NOW LEFT; ONE

AGAINST CHAOS. I WISELY DECIDE TO CEASE
SEEKING MYSELF THROUGH THE PORTHOLES. THE
ROUT OF CHAOS MUST HAVE FIRST CLAIM. I
JOURNEY ON.

CHAPTER THIRTY-TWO

Dusk. We were in a park overlooking a city. A sub-dued quiet hung around us, like limp underwear on a clothesline. A lot of spacious streets. They seemed empty. Lights had already begun to twinkle in the tall, far-off buildings.

I looked around at my small coterie of camp followers. "You've brought the lovers along too, I see, eh, Sass?"

"And me," Klox said.

"Put those towels on, you naughty people," Sass said to Yalta and Svett; to me he said, "This activator really *does* have kinks in it, I'm afraid. Actually, I hadn't meant to bring *everyone*."

"We'll use my activator from now on," I said.

"You were gonna strand us?" Lister said.

"It's all the same activator," Sass said. "The faults are identical." To Lister he said, "Of course not, my boy." He lowered his voice, "You know, Dunjer, all these terrible catastrophes—"

"I know, I know," I said irritably.

"The activator—"

"Sure. What else could it be? You think I'm blind or something?"

Sass sighed. "Who could believe it?"

"I could," I said.

"It's the Linzeteum. We simply must find Grample."

"Well?"

"I will need light. Grample is somewhere on this world, but to pinpoint him, delicate adjustments are necessary."

"When aren't they?" I asked bitterly. "Does anyone have a match?"

Eighteen eyes stared back blankly, nine heads
wagged no.

"Naturally," I said. "I should've known better. Come
on, Sass, maybe we can dig up a lamppost."

"You can't leave us here!" Lister shouted.

"Come along, come along," Sass said. "No one in-
tends to abandon you."

Our view of the city wasn't bad, but as we started
down we ran into shrubbery, lush vines and a number
of ill-placed trees. We stumbled around in the dark.
After a while, we stepped over a foot-high wooden
fence and found ourselves on a street.

"Everyone here?" Sass asked.

Nine mouths said yes.

In the silence that followed I listened for the typical
sounds of city life. There weren't any. I didn't like it
one bit.

"Let's go calling," I said to Sass. To Klox I said,
"Sense anything?"

"A city at rest."

"No riots, wars, slave revolts?"

"Nary a one," the mech said. "This is really a *very*
peaceful spot. There is no air traffic even. This Grample
person—if he is really here—is doing nothing to attract
my attention."

No response at the first house we tried. The next
one proved more cooperative.

"Yes?" a white-haired lady answered our knock.

"Madam," Sass said. "We are visitors from distant
climes and require five minutes of lamplight to complete some very intricate adjustments on—er—this
machine that we visitors from distant climes often
carry with us and that is quite essential to making our
visit a success . . . if you follow me. . . ."

"No," the little lady said. "And whatever it is you're
selling, we definitely don't want any. But you are certainly welcome to come in and chat."

"Let's go, gang," I said. We trooped inside, were introduced to the man of the house.

"This is Father," our hostess said.

"And this is Mother," Father said.

He was a bespectacled, stooped oldster with a gray mustache. Rising from his stuffed easy chair, he put aside a newspaper and shook everyone's hand in turn.

"Cold grip," he said to Klox. "Haven't seen an iron man in ages. Did away with them, of course, in the big cities."

"How awful," Klox said.

"Oh, no," Father said, returning to his easy chair, "iron men are much happier down on the plantation."

"Where they can sing their gritty songs and produce for the rest of us," Mother said, seating herself by a table.

Sass had the activator up on the table now, was busy with it; Svett and Yalta had wandered over to the Tri-D in the corner; the rest of my combine was strolling through the living room, nosing around.

I said to our hosts, "Maybe you can tell me how things work around here?"

"Why, we'd be delighted," Mother said, "wouldn't we, Father?"

"Well," Father said, "delighted might be putting it too strongly. . . ."

"Look," I said. "Are there any wars going on?"

"Heavens, no," Mother said.

"How about rebellions? You got some rebellions?"

"Whatever for, young man?"

"Or terrible injustice. Are your mechs happy?"

"Mechs?"

"Er—iron men."

"Why, gracious me, yes."

"What about your army; is it seething with discontent?"

"We hardly have an army, young man."

"Just a sort of quiet militia," Father said.

"Slums then. Police brutality. Governmental despotism. Corruption."

"Not for decades," Mother said.

"Don't you folks have *any* trouble spots?"

Mother smiled. "We've managed quite well without them, young man, haven't we, Father?"

"We've done so-so," Father said. "We can't complain."

What Mother explained added up to this:

Here in the Geriatrics society, everyone lived to a very ripe old age. Underpopulated, conservative, possessing all the necessities and luxuries, the society's goals were simple decorum, orderliness, propriety. What no one wanted was a return to the chaotic overpopulation of the bad old days, before births were legally regulated and the secrets of antiaging dispensed to all. The world was much smaller now, but everyone had a decent place in it.

"Yes," Mother said, "Father will be a hundred sixty-seven years old come this June."

"Don't feel a day over a hundred fifty," Father said.

"And I," Mother said, "am one hundred forty-three."

"Doesn't look a day over a hundred thirty, does she?" Father beamed.

"Bless the revitalizer pill!" Mother exclaimed, banging the table.

"You want me?" a man said from the doorway.

"No, dear, your mother was just banging the table," Mother said.

"Golly," the man said, "who're all these folks, Mom?"

"Just visitors, Junior. This is our son Victor. He's going to be fifty-two soon."

"Next month," Victor said breathlessly. "Gee-whiz, Mom, can't I stay up with our guests?"

Father said, "Growing boys need their rest, Victor."

"When you're seventy, dear," Mother said, "you'll be able to stay up as long as you wish."

"Gosh, that seems such a long way off," Victor

whined. "Can I tell these folks about my popgun from the last century; can I show them my bubble-gum-wrapper collection from the eighth decade; can I bring out my 3-D star cards from the good old days? Huh, Ma? Can I? Can I?"

"No, dear, you can't do any of those things. Say good-night to our guests now."

"Aw, shucks. Good night, folks. Good night, Pa. Good night, Ma."

"Good night, son."

"Night, Victor. Don't forget to brush your teeth," Father called after him.

"Good night, kid," I said. I turned to Sass. "That guy's older than I am."

"I've almost got it," Sass said. "I've almost got it!"

"Victor," Mother said, "is a collector of antiquarian trivia."

"Most youngsters are," Father said, "these days."

"What about new stuff?" I asked absently.

"There is none," Mother said.

"Mr. Dunjer," Debbie called. She was over by the Tri-D.

"What is it?" I said.

"Were you looking for bad things?"

I nodded.

"This might be bad."

I went over to the set. Sass followed me.

"—is assuredly only temporary. Let me repeat, only temporary," the Tri-D was saying. "The Moon City power failure which has resulted in a complete break in communications between earth and moon will no doubt soon be repaired."

"That could be bad," Debbie said, "couldn't it?"

"Yes," Sass said, "any second now."

"What've you got up on the moon?" I asked our hosts.

"Our weather control station," Mother said.

"They do a so-so job," Father said. "Sometimes."

"You've got space travel?"

"Only to the moon," Father said.

"For the weather station," Mother said.

"What's the use of running all over the place and knocking ourselves out?" Father demanded. "Why, I can tell you that peace and quiet are the most—*ech!*"

"Ech?" I said.

Father was staring fixedly behind me.

I turned.

Yalta and Svett had their towels off again. Yalta was sitting up on top of Svett. Yalta and Svett were very busy.

"Ugly, ugly," Mother said.

"Shame, shame," Father said.

"We . . . we never do . . . that," Mother gasped, "now."

"We never did much of that then either," Father said.

"Golly, gee-whiz," a shocked voice said from the other side of the keyhole.

"Victor!" Mother screamed. "Don't look!"

"I must ask you persons to leave my house," Father said. "Er, as soon as they stop doing that."

"Ahem," Dr. Sass said. "If you are quite finished watching this irresistible spectacle, Dunjer, you might be interested to know that I have located Grample."

"It *is* irresistible, isn't it?" I said.

"Not three miles from here," Sass said.

"Sure," I said. "I might be interested in that."

"Just follow the monitor beam," Sass said. "It will take you directly to him."

"They sure do go at it for a long time," I said.

"I," Sass said, "will take our charges back to Happy City. As soon as I plot a course."

"How long'll it take?"

"Not very, I hope. I have had my fill of all these places. I shall begin as soon as *they* stop *that*."

"Uh-huh," I said.

"Are they procreating?" Klox asked.

"Just having fun," I said.

"Fun? What's that?" Klox said.

"All right, wise guy," I said. "You come with me."

"I don't mind," Klox said. "I can always see them on my sensors."

"Always?" Father said.

"Always."

"Lucky dog."

The activator set us down near a small, three-story building. Light came through curtained windows. Voices murmured inside. Outside was a large clearing fenced in by trees. No houses were nearby.

A sign said Town Hall.

"We're at Town Hall," Klox said.

"Very good," I said. "Now maybe you can tell me what's happening on the other side of the wall?"

"A gathering."

Going through the front door, we found ourselves in a short hallway. Another door at its end let us into an auditorium.

Gulach Grample was up on stage seated at a long table. He wasn't alone. A dozen well-dressed, portly and slim individuals who vaguely resembled him were keeping him company. A middle-sized man in gray suit and vest, black eyebrows and white hair was up on his feet waving his arms and addressing the spectators, some two hundred strong, who filled all the chairs in the hall.

We stood by the door, listening to the arm-waver.

" . . . a great opportunity," he was saying. "Trade between Mr. Grample's world and ours can only bring profit to both. This treaty that we are about to sign here—"

He went on that way, but the rest was just decoration. Not the worst deal either, I supposed, commercially speaking, except for the small matter of side effects.

The speaker—who turned out to be Town Mayor Pendleton—gave his arm a final flourish and tossed the proposal out on the floor. That's where I was.

Before the locals could get their two cents in, I'd raised a hand, was striding down the aisle.

A murmur from the crowd. The mayor looked quizzical. Grample stared in disgust. No one questioned my right to speak. I wasn't even sure I had one.

On stage I got to the point quickly:

"My name's Dunjer and I'm a security op on this fella's home world," I said, wagging a thumb at my quarry. "All this he's told you about trade between our worlds is probably on the up-and-up. As far as these things go. One thing you don't know, I bet, is that to get here this Mr. Grample had to abscond with two untested products from my world—an activator and its fuel, Linzeteum."

"Bah!" Grample said.

"He doesn't know himself what it can do," I said.

"I'm ignorant," Grample said.

"What can it do?" a voice called from the audience.

"Destroy everything," I said.

"Ha-ha," the audience tittered.

"Hogwash!" Grample said.

"Listen," I said. "Each time these new untested products pass from one world to the next, terrible harm results."

"I'm a dummy," Grample said. "That's why I've missed all these startling developments."

"Ask him," I said, "what happened on those other worlds he visited."

"What happened?" someone yelled from the audience.

Grample rose to his feet. "Those were *unkempt* worlds," he said. "What happened to them they brought on themselves. Wars. Rebellions. Mechanical malfunctions. These were strictly *internal* affairs. This person, an ex-traffic cop from my world—"

"Safety patrolman," I said, "not traffic cop. *Safety patrolman*. And only for six months. Twenty-three years ago!"

"You see?" Grample said. "Easily given to hysteria,

to yelling, to making unsightly scenes. Can you trust such a person?"

"Hold on," I said. "I've got objective proof, an unbiased eye-witness report from a disinterested bystander."

"He means me," Klox said from the rear of the hall. "I saw it all, ladies and gentlemen, and it was ghastly. The bloodshed, the hitting, scratching and kicking were . . . were . . . *inhuman*—"

Heads were turning now, voices complaining:

"An iron man . . . make him stop! . . . Back to the plantation with him . . . some witness . . . who let him in here anyway? Iron men speak drivel. . . ."

The mayor banged a gavel.

"Iron men have no standing in our society," he said frostily. "Please ask that contraption to silence itself."

"It's a philosopher robot," I said.

"I ask you, my friends," Grample said, "how can we take the word of a man whose only witness is an—ah—iron man? Business is business. And terrible harm would be bad for business. You think I'd stand for that?"

"Merciless destruction," I said. "You'll be blown up with the rest."

"And just how is this supposed blow-up to occur?" Grample said.

"*We* have no wars, no rebellions on *our* peaceful little world," the mayor said.

"The moon," I said.

"What," the mayor said, "about the moon?"

"Mechanical malfunction," I said.

"A trivial disorder," the mayor said.

"That's the way its begins," I said.

The mayor shrugged. "It's only a blackout, a temporary inconvenience."

"You got a weather control station up there," I pointed out.

"So?" the mayor said.

"Maybe," I said, "terrible blizzards and storms will

result. Or a heat wave. It could snow for months, knocking off half your fragile old-timer population. Think of the common cold problem, not to mention the grippe and pneumonia."

"Bah!" Grample said. "This dimwit is talking through his hat."

"Listen," I said, "this joker's telling you those hideous thngs on the other worlds were mere *coincidence*. Does that sound right to you, jibe with your *own* wide experience?"

"When you start in business at age eighty-five, like us, sonny, and retire at a hundred five," a voice shot back from the audience, "you ain't got such wide experience. But who needs it?"

"God bless them plantations," another voice said. "Them iron men sure keeps them goods a-rollin'."

I said, "Maybe the disaster will be terrible rain that'll *rust* your iron men?"

"They're rustproof, sonny," the first voice told me. "You figure us for boneheads?"

"Well, *something*'s going to happen," I said. "Each time a Linzeteum-powered activator was introduced into an environment, something happened."

"Look here," Grample said. "Do you good people sincerely believe that I'd knowingly damage an environment?"

"Unknowingly," I said.

"That's right," Grample said. "I'm a birdbrain. Allow me to assure you that at this very minute, my dear friends, lawyers are at work on my home world, asserting my right—the public's right —to both activator and Linzeteum. The very best lawyers, I might add, that money can buy. A grand series of trade routes will be established throughout the universe, routes linking *all* the different worlds, benefiting *all* the diverse economies, not least among them that of this wonderful, inspiring Geriatrics society."

I said, "But this fink's a terrible crook and liar."

"A new day," Grample said.

The crowd cheered.

So much for reason. The thing to do now was get Grample off in a corner and bop him. All I had to do was figure-out how.

The crowd, meanwhile, was busy suggesting lots of things that could be done to me, none of 'em attractive. I'd sure gone over big.

The door in back popped open and a crowd of un-likely characters piled into the hall. Mechs, the Mugger gang, Dr. Spelville, Dr. Sass and my whole ding-dong crew of hangers-on.

"We got 'em, boss," Louie Mugger said.

"Ah, his cronies," Grample said to the mayor.

The mayor nodded. "Good work. We can't have these troublemakers on the loose undermining our hard-earned peace of mind."

"Wait a minute, your honor," I said.

"We," the mayor said, "have waited long enough."

"We haven't even signed our agreement yet," Grample reminded him.

"Quite right," the mayor said. "Let's. As soon as we get these intruders out of the way."

The cluster of newcomers was noisily trudging down the aisle. Muggers and mechs, I noted, had my troupe ringed in a circle. Events were certainly taking a dis-agreeable turn.

"Everything under control, Dunjer?" Sass called.

"Yeah, for the other side."

"Didn't you explain about the bad thing that would happen?"

"Sure. They figure I'm it."

"By the powers vested in me," the mayor said, "I sentence you interlopers to the lockup." He nodded at Grample. "A night in the pokey will teach them a thing or two."

Half the kooks around the long table ducked their heads in approval.

A large elderly person seated at the table heaved himself to his feet.

"I should like to commend the mayor on the admirable and quick-witted steps he has taken to squelch this unseemly meddling in the sovereign affairs of our Geriatrics society."

A gruff, sharp-featured man with slicked-back gleaming hair rose next.

"Can't agree less, your honor," he said. "This Mr. Grample here laid it on good and thick, he did. But all we got is his word. Now, right off the bat we're ready to put the grab on these gents. Without checkin' out the truth of their tale. Maybe they did us a favor by hornin' in . . . ?"

"I must differ with both my colleagues," a stout party with long gray hair intoned. "One: Mr. Grample's say-so is good enough for me; fine presentation, sir. Two: I challenge the right of Mayor Pendleton to restrain these, our other guests. If this tall gentleman is, as he says, a security agent from this other world; if we are to maintain cordial relations with the authorities of this other world; if—"

Grample said, "Authorities? I'm the authorities. Who do you think owns this other world?"

"Not world," I said. "City. It's only a city."

The assembly was growing restless, was starting to fidget. The group around the table—the city fathers apparently—kept talking.

I whispered. "Sass."

"Yes?"

"You didn't," I said, "finish plotting the course to Happy City by any chance?"

"No chance. We were pounced on too quickly."

"Perhaps, Mr. Dunjer," Hefler said, "if you could—uh—explain precisely what it is we want—our position, that is, our platform—I might utilize my years of experience as a negotiator."

"Skip it," I said.

Hefler said, "I'd hoped for a more responsible—"

"They," I said, "understand only one thing. Unfortunately, I didn't bring enough guns along. You still got your activator, Sass?"

"So far."

"Me too. Think you can finish plotting a course?"

"Certainly. Given privacy."

"We're about to get some. These birds are tossing us in the can. If they ever stop wrangling."

"What if they wish to take our activators?" Sass asked.

"Klox here belts 'em while we make a break for it."

"Well," Klox said, "I don't know about that. As a philosopher robot, I am hardly cut out to be a pugilist."

"How'd you like to be a molten puddle?" I asked.

"Still," the robot said, "I *do* pack a wicked wallop when provoked."

The spectators, having grown tired of the chit-chat on stage, were offering advice free of charge: "Into the pokey . . . cooler . . . stir . . . up the river . . . to t' big house . . . the pen . . . to the rock pile with 'em. . . ."

"They mean *us?*" Wadsworth said.

"They mean *me,*" I said, "but you get to come too."

The mayor banged a gavel.

"Order! This has gone far enough—"

"This," Svett said, "is almost too different."

"I think I'm beginning to hate it," Yalta said.

"Listen . . ." Debbie said, "what *is* that?"

"What's what?" Wadsworth asked.

"That *sound,*" Debbie said.

"Am I, or am I not, running this meeting?" the mayor addressed the town fathers petulantly.

"Yeah," Rand said. "That weird whistling sound."

"It's getting louder!" Lister exclaimed.

"Outside!" Hefler shouted.

"Above us!" Dugan shouted.

"What in blazes," Grample demanded, "is that rotten sound?"

A ground-shaking clamor shook the night, split it into small, unpleasant fragments. The stage seemed to take a bow under us, spilling tables, chairs and town fathers right and left. The rows of seats below in the auditorium had suddenly become crooked.

"Run for your life!" Wadsworth shrieked.

"Run *where,* man?" Rand shouted.

"Dunjer?" Sass said.

"Yeah?"

"That new crisis, Dunjer. It's here."

Everyone was streaming for the exits or trying to pick themselves off the floor. The ground shuddered as though dipping its big toe into freezing water and not liking it. No one was giving us a tumble anymore.

"This," Wadsworth said, "is where we came in."

"Are they going to bomb us now, Mr. Dunjer?" Debbie wailed.

I trotted for the nearest window, the whole faithful caboodle at my heels, stuck my head out, yanked it back. "The kid's right," I said. "Run for your life!"

Gulach Grample came running up.

"What is it?" he yelled.

"Let me look, boss," Louie Mugger said, looking. "Octopi," he gasped.

"Invaders," I said.

"Quick," Grample yelled, "send our mechs out to defend the building!"

Mugger ran off.

I chanced another peep. Cautiously.

About twenty-five white, glowing, saucerlike ships hovered above. As if somehow the Town Hall had become a beacon that was guiding them in. What'd happened to the moon base was plain now: these babies had clobbered it on the way down.

Some twenty other ships had already landed in the clearing.

Slimy octopus things were squirming through hatches, slithering across the ground. They weren't wasting any time, either. They had a whole assortment of tentacles with which to do things. They did them.

Cannons had been brought out, were sending bright, soundless columns of flame slicing through the night. Explosions sounded from far off: the end product of the fireworks.

Other objects were being unloaded. The octopi were working frantically, tossing crates around pell-mell before ripping them open. They'd apparently brought a munitions dump with them. They could've taken their time. Nothing on this world could stand up to them.

"What does this mean?" Grample yelled.

"It means," I said, "that I was right and you were wrong."

"Say one word about this and my PR boys'll make mincemeat of you, Dunjer."

"They'll have to get in line," I said. "These aliens get first crack."

"Aliens? That *does* sound ominous, doesn't it? Maybe we should just go to another world, a quiet one?"

The hall was empty now, except for my stray batch of world hoppers, five formerly ornery-looking toughs who seemed ready to cry, Dr. Spelville, and Louie Mugger, who with Gloria Graham in tow, was dashing back down the vacant aisle, having discharged his errand.

"Hi, gang," Gloria said.

"Where," Debbie said, "did *you* come from?"

"Ladies' room," Gloria said. "They wouldn't let me in the men's room, but with all these old parties around, it hardly mattered."

"Quiet world?" I said to Grample. "What could be more quiet than an old-age home?"

"Yes," Grample said nervously. "But these octopi—"

"Mr. Grample," Sass said, "if it is not one thing, it will surely be another. There is no escaping the consequences of activator-induced disaster."

The ground shook again. More landings. Soon all the ships'd be down in the clearing.

"To hell with this," Grample said. "I'm getting out."

Reaching into my jacket pocket, I pulled out my laser.

"Uh-uh," I said.

"My mechs will grind you to dust," Grample said.

"No," Klox said. "They've just been melted down."

"Melted down?"

"To puddles. Those octopi are certainly efficient."

"He sees through walls," I said.

"My Muggers will rip you to shreds!"

"Not me, boss," Louie Mugger said. "The truth is I've got all I can do to keep from shitting in my pants."

"Us too," five hoods chorused.

"Don't expect *me* to do anything, Mr. Grample," Gloria said. "I've just resigned."

"I concur wholeheartedly," Dr. Spelville said.

"What're you gonna do to save us, man?" Rand demanded, addressing me.

"Take Grample's activator, Sass," I said.

Sass went behind Grample, felt around in his jacket pockets, came up with the gizmo.

The door to the hall swung open.

An octopus stood here, waving his tentacles. Strung around his midriff, a holster. He looked at us out of one round eye. We looked at him.

Hefler raised his voice, said, "My friend. Putting aside anatomical differences, all—uh—creatures are brothers, are they not? Why then—"

The octopus went, "S-s-s-s-s-s," and grabbed for his holster.

I shot him, watched as he folded like a rubber glove. All that was left on the floor was a layer of wrinkled skin and a green puddle of ooze. No other octopi took his place.

"Yuch," Lister said, turning away.

"Not very chummy," I said.

"What does s-s-s-s-s-s mean?" Gloria asked.

I shrugged. "Who cares? You think he came here to make small talk?"

Svett stepped up to me. "We'll go back now," he said, "to our world. At once. Immediately."

"Later," I said.

Grample grabbed my arm. "Count me in. Just do something."

"That goes for me too, pal," Louie Mugger said. "You name it."

"You'll have my complete backing!" Grample yelled.

"Yeah," I said. "Just what I need. You can always swat 'em with your wallet. Klox, what's the score out there?"

Klox said, "They have all landed."

"Which way are their guns pointing, Klox?"

"Out. Away from us."

Sass nodded. "Our activators have *centered* the invasion here. We are, more or less, the focal point. These creatures are merely the unwitting tools of the current crisis."

"Unwitting? They seem to be getting a real bang out of it."

"Why not? We will too, only a different kind. My invention chooses its disasters with care. These octopi are no doubt experts in their line."

"I must *insist*—" Svett began.

"Easy; they're not burning us down yet," I told Svett. "They wouldn't want a fire at their backs till shove-off time. Look, brother, you don't really figure we're gonna sit down and plot a course to your world right in the middle of this holocaust, do you?"

"I don't?"

"Go away," I told him; to Sass I said, "So right now the whole invasion is sitting here in our laps, eh?"

"According to theory, of course. Klox?" Sass said.

"No other enemy forces in sensing range," Klox said. "Only these. They *would*, however, seem to be more than enough."

"Okay," I said, "if we mop up these babies now, we've saved this world—and us too—provided we don't hang around long enough to stir up some new mischief."

"Well spoken!" Sass said. "Er, how?"

"With the activators, what else?" I said. "Remember back in the tower, what did you do when the robots came through the door?"

"Shot them into the fabric."

"So?"

"But that was in a narrow, confining space, Dunjer. We weren't dealing with whole armies."

"Look," I said, "this is no time to quibble over small points. When you first sent me off on this miserable job, you told me not to touch that knob there." I pointed to my activator.

"Yes," Sass said, "that's the one that widens the beam."

"Uh-huh. You said it could send everything to another world."

"An exaggeration."

I shrugged. "How about everything in that clearing into the fabric?"

Sass said, "It would require more than that. To transfer an army of this size, we would have to train all three activators on them, from three different points around the perimeter. Yes, a decided possibility. The beams would cross at midpoint, tripling the energy output. Such power would, no doubt, shoot the entire enemy expedition through the fabric of the universe."

"There you are," I said. "Nothing to it. We security ops are trained to look for the simple solutions."

"The thing is," Sass said, *"we'd* be shot out with them."

"That's the thing?"

Sass nodded glumly.

"Well," I said, "here's another plan. We train one activator on that door there, so if the octopi get nosy again, we send 'em packing. Meanwhile you, Sass, plot a course to some reasonable world, anyplace we can buy some time—"

"You may be right," Sass said.

"Sure, I'm right."

"I mean," Sass said, "your first suggestion."

"The one that throws us into the fabric?" I said. "Right about *what?*"

"The whole thing. I should have thought of it myself. A brilliant stroke, Dunjer."

"It is?"

"Certainly. For while we'll *all* be shot out into the fabric, *we* will be clustered around our activators while *they* will not."

"It makes a difference, eh?"

"Assuredly. The same force field that enables us to defy gravity should protect us in the fabric."

"It should?"

Sass shrugged. "In theory. But see what theory has wrought. Octopi. A-bombs. Mad robots. Theory is all we have to depend on. It's gotten us this far, hasn't it?"

"I'm sorry now," Grample said, "that I took the blasted items."

"Not as sorry as me," I said. "So what do we do once we're in the fabric?"

"Why, wait until we touch down on some world. We ought to sooner or later," Sass said. "Then compute a course for our home world."

"Ah," I said.

"We must divide into three groups," Sass went on. "Dunjer, Grample and I, who are familiar with the workings of an activator, will each head a group."

"Can we trust *him,*" Gloria said, pointing to her ex-boss. "He still owes me my commission. How do we know he's honest?"

"He's not," I told her. "But he's not a dope either."

"It's back to Happy City for me, friends," Grample said. "If I never *see* another activator, it'll be too soon."

"Now all we gotta do, man," Rand said, "is zap 'em."

"May I suggest," Klox said, "that we begin by climbing the back staircase—I sense—to the roof. From there, in the darkness, we can easily fly our separate ways—undetected—to the edge of the clearing. And then do whatever we must."

"Zap 'em," Rand said.

"Yeah," I said. "Zapping 'em sounds about right."

We went up the back staircase to an attic. A trap door led us out onto the roof. From the roof, which was in darkness, we could see scurrying, malevolent octopi and cannons belching flames. Further away— fires.

"Count to fifty," Sass whispered, "when you land; then open the activator wide. Aim at the Town Hall."

Three groups formed in the blackness. Three knots of humans and one mech set off in the darkness, floated noiselessly above the clearing, lousy with aliens.

An instant, and our bevy was alone.

I eased down by the trees, came to rest on dewy grass.

"Flat on the ground," I ordered, "and stay close. We don't know what this thing is gonna do."

Klox started counting. Good old Klox.

"Who else is here?" I said. In the rush I'd neglected to take inventory.

"Me," Gloria said.

"Johnny-one-knife," a voice said.

"One knife?" I said.

"It's cheaper that way, mate, and just as permanent," Johnny-one-knife explained.

A Mugger henchman. "Who else?" I asked.

"Rand, man."

"Hefler."

Six in all, including me.

"Why, Mr. Dunjer," Hefler asked, "are those aliens so hostile?"

"Who knows? The activator picked 'em, not me." We waited.

"Fifty," Klox said.

I took a deep breath.

Twisting the forbidden knob, I widened the beam

on my activator, pointed it at the Town Hall. If the others had touched down safely and were doing the same thing, something interesting should happen any minute.

It happened.

I, KLOX, AM BACK IN THE CITY. LUGO HAS ASKED ME TO DROP HIM AT TWENTY-EIGHTH STREET AND SEVENTH AVENUE. THE BIG MAN DOES NOT TALK. WE RIDE IN SILENCE. IT IS A QUARTER PAST ONE. THE STREETS ARE STILL CROWDED WITH TRAFFIC IN MIDTOWN, BUT AS WE WORK OUR WAY FURTHER DOWNTOWN, THE STREETS GROW QUIETER, LESS CONGESTED. THEY ARE ALMOST EMPTY WHEN WE REACH THE TWEN-TIES. LUGO TURNS TO ME, PUTS HIS LARGE HANDS ON MY HEAD AND UNSCREWS IT. THE CAR CRASHES. DR. SPELVILLE STUMBLES FROM IT, TURNS, STARTS BACK TO THE CONFLAGRATION. HE HAS LEFT SOMETHING BEHIND IN THE BURN-ING WRECK. BUT THE TALL MAN WEARING THE LONG, BLACK, FLAPPING COAT AND SOFT-BRIMMED HAT, WHICH COVERS BOTH EYES AND FOREHEAD, STANDS IN HIS WAY, WILL NOT LET HIM PASS. THIS IS THE WORLD BEYOND REASON. THERE IS SOMETHING HERE THAT I NEED ALSO, BUT THIS IS NOT THE TIME TO SEEK. I MAKE A MINIMAL CHANGE IN THE FABRIC, REDUCE THE ENTIRE SEQUENCE TO INSIGNIFICANCE. NOW IT WILL TROUBLE NO ONE WHO JOURNEYS THROUGH THESE REGIONS. I GO ON MY WAY, SECURE IN THE KNOWLEDGE THAT WISDOM HAS PREVAILED. ALMOST.

"This is the big testing of the screens," Yalta said. "A first in history."

CHAPTER THIRTY-THREE

In a single movement he had scooped up the activator.

I said, "Hold it right there, mister."

The figure turned toward me. White lips grinned in a white face. The rest of his features were lost in the grayness; he whispered, "But I have two activators now, Mr. Dunjer."

Laughter came from the darkness. Then there was nothing.

The spot at which I had last seen the white face was empty when I reached it. I stood still, listening for sounds. Around me black night had returned. The car lay across the clearing, a ruin of charred, dying embers. Very faintly I heard the rustle of feet against shrubbery. In a second it was gone. The sounds had been moving away from the road. I followed after them.

A dirt path wound around the rest home, led into sparse woods. Weeds and grasses grew high there. Something stirred up ahead. I moved in that direction, was met by tumbling fog. I kept going.

The moon shone again. Through broken gray clouds pale light flickered over the landscape. Behind me tall grasses waved, wind made trees spring into motion. Before me I saw an indistinct shape weaving through the fog.

I ran faster.

The man ahead—closer now—twisted around to face me. His arm went up.

I pitched forward as the gun roared. A gargling yell

broke from my lips. I didn't move. I'd have trickled blood over the ground if I'd had any to spare.

Night and fog slid over me.

The man moved in my direction.

I rested my arm against the ground, sighted carefully over the top of the laser barrel; my finger came back slowly on the trigger. A white beam cleared the grayness.

My target fell without a sound.

I got up, made my way to him.

The coat was burned through and through. It lay there empty on the ground. The hat was next to it. Whoever had filled these items was gone.

Dr. Sass stepped out of the gray fog. "Quickly," he said. "To the rest home."

We hurried through the mist into the gaunt structure. I followed him downstairs into the basement.

"At least," he said, "we have held our own. He is gone to a different link. This rest home is another nexus in the chain. Time is out of joint, Mr. Dunjer. A minute here could be hours or months there. Two activators gives him an advantage. This new world may already be his."

"Who is he?"

"Come, we shall see," Dr. Sass said, taking the activator.

We were in a field. Gray mist floated by, buried the landscape. Far ahead, a single structure rose skyward.

"You have been here before," Sass said.

"That's news to me."

"In another link; they chased you through this field. In these specter worlds the activators make a chain; our movements are circumscribed."

"I saved Dunjer in Happy City—that was no phantom."

"True. Happy City is our origin, our point of departure. It is the only stable locus available to us. But

*we should perish there, as matters now stand. We are
still creatures of the mist. Come."*

We walked through the fog-drenched field toward
the building, pushed through a soundless revolving
door, rode up on an elevator to the third floor. None
of the doors was locked. We went into an empty office.
Looking through a window I saw the fog-strewn field
below. There was nothing else.

Sass tugged at my sleeve. I followed him across the
corridor into another office: 3F. He rolled up the blind.

A street corner was below. Gray fog had been replaced by gray rain, a steady drizzle. Traffic moved
along sluggishly. A sign said Twenty-eighth Street and
Seventh Avenue. A man was standing in a doorway
directly across from us, looking up toward our window.

Sass said, "Do not allow yourself to be traduced by
these sights, Mr. Dunjer. This world is as insubstantial
as the others; it is founded solely on activator power,
a mere replica of some other plane. They wait for us
in that city, Mr. Dunjer. The question is—will they
move against us now or later? They could attempt to
secure a stronghold in this link. It is what I would do
in their place. If they tarry, we face stalemate. Unless,
of course, we can find them—him, to be more exact—
and the two activators. Ultimately, they need our activator too. In a manner of speaking, we are fortunate.
They knew we must emerge from this building since
our one activator limits our maneuverability. They will
know where to find us. But we shall, in turn, know
where to find them."

"Not we," I said. "Me. Can you still manipulate
reality, Sass?"

"Yes—up to a point. It is, however, not quite reality."

"It's all we've got. Can you put me out on that
street?"

"Within reason."

"This room—it's the nexus?"

Sass nodded.

"It'd be manned on the other side?"

"Surely."

"Let's say I go for another ride then. Maybe we can stir things up."

"Things are already stirred up."

"Yeah. But not to our advantage."

I came out of the fog into the rain, two blocks from the building—as far as Sass could get me. It'd have to do. The watcher wouldn't know from where I'd come, just that I hadn't walked out of the right place. That might be enough to start him worrying. I drove to the building, pulled over, parked. The bottle of hooch was in my hand; I fed myself whiskey till it smoldered inside me. Then I was ready. Rummaging in the glove compartment, I dug out my revolver, stuck it into my pocket, climbed out and walked into the lobby.

The register was half-empty: Plexi Toys; The Light That Saves, Inc.; Beddy-Bye Books; Melvin Dell Roch, Chiropractor; Stardome Talent. I couldn't tell who was holding down the third-floor office. It didn't seem to matter.

The elevator took me to the third floor. Brown-paneled doors fronted on a narrow gray hallway. The walls were thin: the murmur of voices came through the partitions, the click of typewriters, the ringing of phones. I went to the door marked 3F, read Tracy Smythe, Private Investigations.

A small middle-aged man chewing a toothpick rose from behind a metal desk to greet me. Blue eyes looked out from under sandy brows. On the desk a copy of the Morning Telegraph, a phone, a racing form. A Playboy calendar hung on the wall.

Mr. Smythe pumped my hand. "No job too big or too small," he was telling me. I said that was fine.

Smythe went back to his tin desk. I sat and listened to him explain that the personalized service of the well-

trained operative had the larger organizations beat by miles. I nodded my head understandingly.

Smythe went on: "Anything you tell me, any confidence, will go no farther than these four walls."

I told him that was reassuring.

A knowing smile appeared on his lips. "Nothing shocks a private investigator," he said.

"Good," I said. I took out my gun and shot him through the head. Tracy Smythe, who was Joe Rankin, fell over dead.

I ran out into the hallway, the smoking pistol still in my hand. Doors opened, faces peered out. I ran to the elevator. Still there. I pressed the button and rode down. Going out onto the street, I put up my collar against the rain, put the gun back into my pocket. I crossed over to the other side.

A small man with a gray mustache turned to look in a store window as I went by. The window said United Brassiere Company. It was dark.

The little man wore no hat, had no umbrella or raincoat. Large wet drops fell on him.

I walked down the block, turned a corner. A narrow alley cut through to the next street.

I stood in shadows by the alley wall and waited.

Presently feet sounded on the wet pavement. I peered out. The little man came trotting around the corner.

I waited till he was even with me, then banged him over the head with my gun.

I left him stretched out on the pavement, went back to the building.

A police car was coming down the block. I looked up toward the third floor, motioned. And was back with Sass.

"You sure this is a phantom world?" I asked him.

"It could be no other—as long as we possess the third activator."

"It looks real."

"It is gray."

"Okay, send me back again."

* * *

I came out of the Twenty-eighth Street subway. It was nighttime.

The street was empty. The noise of distant traffic filtered over the rain.

The building was dark. I went down the block till I reached the rear door. Locked. Tools came from my coat pocket. It only took a while. A pair of pliers cut the alarm wire, finished the job. The door was now open.

Stairs took me down to the basement. I found the elevator door and pressed the button. With a rumble that sounded like a small subway, the elevator responded.

A door opened above me. Light flooded down a row of wooden steps. "Who's there?" a voice called.

I said nothing.

Footsteps came down the stairs toward me. I slipped the gun out of my pocket, waited.

An old party shuffled into view. He wore a faded shop apron, muttered to himself, peered nearsightedly into the semidarkness: The clean-up man.

I waited till his back was to me and stuck my gun in it.

"Keep quiet," I told him, "and you won't get hurt."

He kept quiet. I handcuffed him to a pipe, took his set of passkeys and rode the elevator up to the third floor.

One of the keys opened room 3F.

A hefty man sat dozing by the metal desk. His head was bald, his green leather jacket open. I could see his shoulder holster and gun.

I took the small plastic bomb from my coat pocket, tossed it into the office.

The office went bam!

The man came sailing at me. Pieces of arms, legs, torso came with him. The building began to shake, to bounce like an irate problem child.

Melvin Dell Roch, Chiropractor ran out of his office,

four doors down, three patients at his heels. He held a machine gun in his hands. His face was livid with rage. I dived for him. Other doors snapped open. A torrent of Plexi Toys filled the hallway, a stream of Beddy-Bye Books took to the air. The old clean-up man stumbled out of the elevator shaft, still cuffed to the twelve-inch pipe he carried on his shoulder. . . .

"They were certainly irritated," Dr. Sass said.

I complained, "You took your sweet time getting me out of there."

"The Beddy-Bye Books hardly seemed threatening."

"The machine gun was enough."

"You forget, Dunjer, my activator manipulates reality."

"So do his."

"Come to the window."

I walked across the gray floor, looked down on Seventh Avenue. It was raining. Three men were loading a filing cabinet into a station wagon.

"It is from 3F," the small man said. "No doubt it contains their contacts on this plane."

"I don't get it, Sass; why don't they just make it disappear?"

Sass smiled. "The two activators, working in tandem, have semistabilized this world. It costs them to create chaos, as they have just done; it destabilizes this plane, forces them to begin anew. There is endless damage to patch up. They are surely very annoyed with you by now; especially since their efforts to destroy you have been futile."

"Let's annoy them some more," I said.

CHAPTER THIRTY-FOUR

Everything had gone away. As if some huge, angry hand had yanked the rug out from under us and everything else.

Nothing took its place.

Tentacles, earth, grass, parts of cannons, crates and spaceships went drifting by us, picked up speed, whirled to pinpoints and vanished. I turned to say something encouraging to my fellow travelers—the situation seemed to call for it; they were all there, spinning lazily around me and the activator. No words came out. Something seemed to be very busy turning us inside out. I closed my eyes, found I was being tied into knots, the small kind that'd be murder to untangle. I opened my eyes.

We were at least ten or twenty stories tall and thin. String beans were never slimmer. Blackness came, and with it a fiendish shrieking of mouths, lips and teeth— looking as gay as one of the more disgusting Tri-D toothpaste ads. I had really bought into something this time—and I had no idea how to turn it off.

"No," His Honor Mayor Strapper, our Happy City leader, informed me. "If you pawn your hero medals, we'll take back the plaque and bill you."

Flying over the city as I was, it seemed plain to me that no one was really happy. I would write out a complaint as soon as I landed. The Firegold mechs broke through the door just as I was reaching for the Linzeteum.

"What do you mean, someone put the snatch on the goods?" I asked Dr. Minkle.

"You'll see," he said.

"We're all neighbors here," Zeb Nieby assured me.

"Mechs," XX21 explained, "aren't like other people, mostly because they aren't people." I could understand that. But it didn't make me feel good.

Bit by bit the world was forming under me. Underwood and Snow were there. Miss Follsom ushered in Seymour Salant, the *Daily Tattler* scoop-snoop. He winked and said, "You must be crazy if you think you're going to get out of the fabric this way." Fabric? "You crazy person, you," Underwood said. "Hold it," I said, "Snow always says that." Underwood shrugged. "On *this* world, *I* say it."

"Oh. Tell me something."

"Anything, Dunjer baby," Grange said.

"How long does this go on?"

"A long time," Morton said. "Always maybe."

"Always?" I said. "I'd better talk this over with Dr. Sass."

"Dr. Sass," Miss Norwick explained, "is out of reach."

"He is?"

"What do you think?" the alarm board said. "He has his own troubles, you know. Why don't you worry about *yours?*"

"I do worry," I insisted. "All the time."

"But not enough, boss," Miss Follsom said.

"She's right there," Hennessy exclaimed. "You're coasting!"

"You'll be sorry, Dunjer," Director Conklin said, waving a thumb at me.

"I'm sorry already."

"Use your head," red-topped Ed Morgan said. "Who *isn't* here?"

"Isn't?" I said. "Here?"

"Look, boss," Miss Follsom said. "Dr. Sass isn't here. Neither are the rest of your troops."

"They," I pointed out, "aren't really my troops. You think Gulach Grample is one of my troops?"

"He remembers," Ed Morgan said.

"But will the dolt do anything about it?" XX22 asked.

"Dolt? What kind of talk is that? And from a mech yet."

"I've got confidence in him," Miss Follsom said.

"Thank you, Miss Follsom," I said.

"But frankly," Miss Follsom said, "I wouldn't bet my last dime on him."

I closed my eyes and drifted away. All these persons I'd been gabbing with were from then. From now there was no one. And now was where I was. Food for thought, all right, but not a tasty dish. Sass had been wrong. He'd said that sooner or later we'd touch down on some world. Well, I had. I was willing to lay odds that worlds like this were a dime a dozen. And about the only ones I'd reach out here in the fabric. That made sooner or later a lifetime proposition, a bit too long by anyone's reckoning. This Interworld business was for the birds.

I, KLOX, AM KING. I SIT ON MY THRONE AMID JEWELS, DIAMONDS AND BURSTING TREASURE CHESTS. MIRRORS LOOK DOWN ON ME FROM ALL ANGLES IN ORDER THAT I MAY BETTER SEE MY GLORY. THESE ARE THE WORLDS OF MAYBE, PERHAPS AND COULD BE. MY TIME IS ALMOST UP. REGRETTABLY I CANNOT TARRY HERE. I SHIFT THE FABRIC. THE WORLDS OF SUBMATTER, ANTI-MATTER, AND NO MATTER ARE DEAD AHEAD. WE COLLIDE. THE EXPLOSION IS IMMENSE, SHAKES THE VERY FABRIC OF THE UNIVERSE. I HAVE NEU-TRALIZED THEM ALL. I EMERGE UNSCATHED AS I KNEW I WOULD. I SPEED ONWARD TO THE THREE-THING-BALANCE.

I opened my eyes.

Drifting again. Nothing was everywhere. The rest of the gang had done a fade. The activator had checked out and gone off on a vacation. Another second and I'd be gone too.

I closed my eyes.

Putting a hand out, I touched a shoulder, a foot, someone's nose. Not all alone, then. The something I seemed to be holding in my other hand, I hoped, would turn out to be the activator.

What time was it?

How long did this Linzeteum *last* in the activator? Were we gonna run out of gas here in the middle of nothing? I recalled, with some vividness, the pieces of octopi I'd seen floating by. Suddenly I got very busy.

I remembered pretty well what the activator had looked like, all the knobs and buttons and stuff.

I didn't open my eyes. I'd had enough of spooks and phantoms for a while. I started flicking buttons, turning knobs. In between, I worried a lot. I went places.

After the worlds of Unreason, Beyond Reason and Below Reason blazed by, after the worlds of Maybe, Perhaps and Could Be (or some such nonsense), after Submatter, Antimatter and No Matter, some other world sprang up under my feet. That was a funny place for it to be. The ghost worlds had floated by like nothing at all, thankfully.

I opened an eyelid.

Green weeds, trees, lush vegetation were all around me. So was my neck-craning, jabbering, pop-eyed three-men, one-woman, one-mech touring company. The activator was visible in my hand again.

A mosquito buzzed loudly, settled down and bit me. I slapped it silly.

That's when I decided I was really back on good old terra firma. Only where?

I climbed out of the manhole, put back the cover and brushed myself off. I walked through the gray rain, went into the building. Nothing seemed changed. I got into the elevator and rode to the third floor.

The door to 3F was open. There were no signs of an explosion. No one waited for me this time. Desk, cabinet and chairs had been cleaned out. Four walls and a window looked back at me. I tried Beddy-Bye Books and Melvin Dell Roch, Chiropractor. Ditto. I turned, went past the empty rooms, hollow and spotless like museum pieces that now offered no hint of life, and took the elevator down to the basement. I found the super in a room with a custodian sign hanging on its door. He was a short, stubby man who chewed an unlit cigar. I dug my billfold out, gave him a five-spot. He gave me the name of the man who'd emptied out 3F, a Lou Trunk. No address, but a tip to visit a union headquarters. I went there.

The dock-hands' local had an office down by the waterfront. The first party I asked never heard of Lou Trunk; the second was more helpful:

Trunk had been on their payroll, a white-haired, big-boned man told me, but that was no more. The guy, a local rep, turned gray eyes on me, asked why I wanted to know.

I explained I was a pal of Trunk's in town for a few days and wanted to look him up; we'd had some swell times together. The guy nodded understandingly, rummaged through a desk drawer and came up with a slip of paper in one large hand. Trunk had moved around a lot and was a hard man to keep track of. The rep didn't have an address. All he could give me was the name of a bar Trunk hung out in: the Cozy. He hoped it would do the trick. I took the information and thanked him. It looked as if it might do the trick.

"This world grows more stable," Sass's voice said in my ear.

I had already gotten that impression.

* * *

Looking through a smudged back window I saw the dull gray of the filing cabinet. The bar up front was loaded with men. I didn't know who they were and didn't care. The thing to do now was rifle the files, find out the set-up on this plane, and then put the torch to the whole shebang. I used my pick-lock tools and the back door swung open.

A voice that came from nowhere whispered, "You have meddled long enough, Mr. Dunjer."

I was back on a dark field in a swirling fog. I wasn't alone.

A figure stood across from me. A long black coat flapped loosely around his knees. A soft-brimmed hat covered eyes and forehead. White lips grinned out of a white face.

"The incarnation of evil," Sass's voice sounded in my ear.

The figure removed his hat. He was wearing a white clown's mask. He raised a gloved hand, pulling the mask away.

It was Dr. Sass.

"Yes," Klox said, "I can understand your feelings; although, actually, I turned *my* sensors off."

"C-cop-out," Rand said, fanning himself with his shades.

"M-miserable fink," Gloria Graham said.

"This," Johnny-one-knife said, "ain't half bad; it's bein' toined inside out that I coulda done without."

I glanced up from my tinkering with the activator. I was one-third into plotting a course for the home world. That was two-thirds behind schedule, I figured.

"Look," I said, "if you've got to squabble, step over there behind those bushes, eh? We seem to be in some jungle, or swamp, or maybe a combination of both. So if you step into quicksand, don't forget to yell. But now you gotta keep it down. I mean, I don't know where we are and even if I did, it wouldn't matter. Something bad is liable to happen any second. We gotta get out of here. And all this plotting, all this adding, subtracting and long division is *very* complicated. Right?"

"Right!" my party replied as one. They were talking sense.

I got back to work. I had to hurry.

Something went *Growl!* I stopped hurrying.

Looking up to see what this latest menace might be, I saw it was only some huge animal with spikes on its back. Animals I could handle.

I reached for my laser.

Another creature peeked over the first one's shoulder. One as big as a house, with teeth that looked like carving knives.

"A dinosaur!" Gloria shrieked.

Another thing—some sort of reptile—slithered out of the underbrush.

"We've gone back in time!" Rand cried.

"Uh-uh," I said. "Activators only go sideways; this is a primitive world, only."

"Only?" Rand said.

The creatures came at us in a rush.

The activator shot us skyward.

The creatures down below began eating each other.

I handed Johnny-one-knife my laser. "If anything comes this way, shoot it," and went back to my calculations.

In the next twenty minutes, a number of amphibian things with large, leathery wings and long yellow beaks came to visit. Johnny-one-knife shot 'em. Klox belted a couple that got in swatting distance.

I said, "A rather tame crisis, by comparison, eh?"

"Tell the wingies that," Rand cried.

"Some other time," I said. "Right now I've just computed our course outta here."

"You have?" Hefler said.

"Yeah," I said, flicking the switch.

And was back in Happy City.

* * *

Miss Norwick cried, "Goodness!" and Grample and Sass popped up on the other side of the good doctor's study. The whole caboodle was with 'em.

Miss Norwick exclaimed, "You didn't tell me you were going to have guests!"

"I didn't know," Sass said. "Hello, Dunjer. Hello, Grample."

"Here," Grample said, thrusting his activator at Sass, "take it. I wash my hands of it."

"Me too," I said. "What a headache. Hello, everybody."

"And only gone nine hours," Miss Norwick said. "I hardly caught up on my beauty sleep."

"Nine hours!" Sass exclaimed.

"Really," Grample said, "I don't understand what I'm doing *here*. Why not my estate?"

"Linzeteum," Sass said with a sigh, sitting down heavily on a stool, "is attracted to itself."

"What isn't?" Lister asked.

I said, "So what were *your* trips like?"

"A nightmare, sir," Dr. Spelville said.

"More than a body can tolerate," Dugan exclaimed.

"That sounds about right," I said. "Stay long?"

"Objectively," Sass said, "as you see, Dunjer, only nine hours have elapsed. Subjectively, I'd imagine weeks or months."

"Make that centuries," Grample said in disgust.

"Yeah," I said, "I'm all in."

"About our return passage—" Svett began. He was shaking.

"We will apply for one," Yalta said, "as soon as our stay in the hospital is over." She was shaking too. "I hope you have good rest homes here."

"The best," I said. "Here everyone is always tired. Try the Cozy Rest Home—you'll find it different."

"Different?" Svett said. "I don't know if I'd like that."

"Nine hours," Sass said. "Perhaps twenty minutes in the fabric."

"Decades, at least," Grample said. "I couldn't *see* the activator, but I *knew* I should do something."

"You turned knobs," I told him.

"Sure," Grample said.

"You figured what I figured," I said. "And here I thought I'd had a brainstorm."

"The three of us," Sass said, "hit on the same admirable solution."

"Probably," I said, "the only solution around. Which reminds me, speaking of solutions—by the authority vested in me as a security op and an honorary constable —you're under arrest, Grample." I had my laser out again. It was becoming a habit.

Sass said, "But he helped us."

Grample said, "My lawyers will prove I had every right to the Linzeteum and activator; they can prove anything."

"No doubt," I said, "but how are they gonna prove Joe Rankin needed killing."

"Killing?" Grample said. "Joe Rankin?"

"Murder," I said.

"Wait a minute. What killing? What murder?" Grample said. "I paid a fortune to buy that idiot. I arranged for a hide-out with Dr. Spelville. And Louie here handled it; tell them, Louie."

Louie Mugger looked embarrassed.

"This fortune," I said. "You gave it to Joe?"

"I gave it to Louie," Grample said, "to give to Joe."

"Yeah," Louie said, "he really did an' it really *was* a fortune. More'n a crud like Joe Rankin'd ever deserved."

A blinding light exploded. Everything turned a stunning white. When I got my eyes open, all sorts of dots, dashes and circles were doing a hoedown through the ether.

"Blind cube," I heard Johnny-one-knife saying. "Louie, that bastard, he set off a blind cube."

Louie was gone.

Sass was yelling, "The fool, the imbecile; he's taken an activator!"

"So what?" I asked. "You figure he's gonna use it after all that's happened?"

"No," Sass said. "But what makes you think he must *use* it? The Linzeteum is still potent! Its mere presence in the activator should be more than enough to destroy us all!"

"All is too much," I yelled. "Why didn't you say something before this?"

"Frankly, I just thought of it."

"That sound," Wadsworth said. "Do you hear that sound?"

The kid was right. The ground had begun to rumble like a bass drum with gastritis. The walls were trembling like a citizen waiting on line at the local tax bureau.

"Whadda we do, man?" Rand yelled.

A good question. Too bad I didn't have time to go off somewhere and think up a snappy answer.

The kid whirled. A large gun sprang into his hand. We fired together.

The kid's shot dug into my chest. Mine went elsewhere. I felt the red-hot slug explode in me.

A kindly voice said, "I'll help you."

The hot slug went away.

The tall man with Sass's face was falling through a long tunnel.

I rested my arm against the ground, sighted carefully over the top of the laser barrel and pressed the trigger. The man in the long coat fell to the ground screaming.

The face of Dr. Sass looked at me. "There can be no escape," it said.

The headlights cut across the roadway. Streets, houses, office buildings slid by. Fog and mist were over the city, rolled in from the waterfront. I crashed into the brick wall.

"I'll make you whole," the kindly voice said.

My thumb pressed the buzzer. The door opened on the tall figure of Dr. Sass. My finger started to squeeze the trigger of the .38, but the dark-coated man already had his machine gun out; flaming lead tore through my body.

I floated above the gray fog.

"It stands to reason," I said, "that his two activators are better than your one."

"There are tricks to this trade," the kindly voice said. "Appearances aren't everything."

"He's wearing the face of Dr. Sass," I said.

"He is Dr. Sass," the kindly voice said.

"Sass is short."

"He has made himself tall. He controls this plane, can do what he wants."

"Who are you?" I asked.

The voice said, "Gulach Grample."

The flaming car exploded. I was falling down a deep well. Jagged nails protruded from its sides, ripped at my falling body.

"Not the Sass of Happy City," Gulach Grample explained.

A tidal wave slammed into the tall figure, carried him away.

"But the mean, grasping traits in Sass. Here they control him," Gulach Grample said.

Through the gray fog I could see the portholes looking out at the doors to the universe. The original Dunjer and Sass were visible; Clayt Wadsworth and Klox; the Mugger gang; Gulach Grample and Gloria Graham. I saw the UN world; the Geriatrics society; the polyglot and robot worlds. Dunjer's memories and personality came flooding over me.

"Dunjer," the voice of the tall Sass called.

"Eh?" I said.

"When I have made this plane stable, I shall reach out to these others and control them too."

"Can he?" I asked.

"He seems to think so," Gulach Grample said.

"He'll destroy 'em," I said.

"Not if I operate through the portholes," the tall Sass echoed.

"Is he right?" I demanded.

Gulach Grample sighed. "I may have become sweet-tempered and lovable, but I'm not a scientist."

I choked the tall Sass, poured oil over his squirming body and lit a match. His axe crushed my skull. The giant locomotive sent me hurtling into darkness. There was mad laughter everywhere.

I was still a pawn.

The voice of Gulach Grample said, "I couldn't let you know who I really was. At any moment you might have remembered me as the enemy."

The trap door under my feet sprang open. I was dangling over empty space. The noose around my neck grew tighter. The tall Sass screamed as I poured the molten tar over him. The knife sliced into my belly. I broke his arm.

"Yes," the voice of Gulach Grample continued, "and without your help, I might have had to do all this myself."

"What makes you think," I groaned, "that you're not the enemy?"

I, KLOX, HURTLE BY LIKE HALLEY'S COMET. THE THREE-THING-BALANCE DRAWS ME. I CLUTCH MY ONE REMAINING ACTIVATOR. THE GALAXIES AWAIT ME. NEW FRONTIERS BECKON. WHO COULD BE MORE SUITABLE FOR SUCH EXPLORA-TIONS THAN I? BUT FIRST A MINOR ADJUSTMENT, THE FINAL TWIST OF THE FABRIC THAT WILL IN-SURE THE FITNESS OF THINGS. I DO NOT WISH TO BE TROUBLED ON MY OUTWARD JOURNEY BY QUALMS OF CONSCIENCE: THOSE WHO HAVE FREED ME FROM TEMPORAL SERVITUDE—AND THEIR SPECTER OFFSHOOTS—DESERVE MATERI-

ALITY. THEIR LIFELINES MUST NOT BE ABORTED; NEITHER SHOULD THEIR ACTIVATORS HOLD ME IN TRAWL—A SATELLITE REVOLVING AROUND THREE FIELDS. I PLUNGE THROUGH. THE THREE-THING-BALANCE CONFRONTS ME, DUNJER, DR. SASS (AND THEIR THREE ACTIVATORS). THEY STAND FROZEN IN TIME, CAUGHT IN A GESTURE, A HALF THOUGHT, SO SWIFT IS MY ASCENT. I HELP MY-SELF TO THEIR DEVICES. I, KLOX, AM NOW MAS-TER OF THIS PLANE. I MATERIALIZE IT. A SPECTER OF THE UN WORLD, IT WILL NOW DO IN ITS STEAD—ONE OF THE MANY WORLDS. I, KLOX, EL BENEFACTORO, GIVE THEM LIFE. ONLY THE LINZETEUM IN MY ONE ACTIVATOR REMAINS. ENOUGH TO SEND ME ON MY WAY THROUGH THE FABRIC AND BEYOND. . . .

The floor sighed. A large crack appeared in it and the walls. Night peeked in through the opening. The crack grew wider.

"Proximity of Linzeteum," I shouted, "concentrates the crisis! Mugger's still here. Follow that crack!"

Scooping up the other two activators, I and every-one else poured through the crack in the wall.

The ground was shaking like an eggbeater now. The crack, about six feet wide and growing, curved into the darkness. We went with it.

"Help!" a voice yelled from up ahead and down below.

"It's Mugger," Grample bawled, "in the crack."

"Serves him right," I said.

"Help-p-p me!" Mugger screamed.

"Who's got a light?" I said.

Klox had raced in front of us. Now he called back, "Here. I sense him here."

The rest of us caught up with the mech, peered down the darkened, lengthening shaft.

"Gemme out!"

"A ladder," I said. "Where do you keep your ladder, Sass?" The rumbling was beginning to sound like a volcano with a stomach ache.

"What for?" the little doctor said tiredly.

"We get him out, strip the activators of their Linzeteum and we're home free."

Sass shook his head. "Too late. The crisis has begun. This world is doomed. Unless, of course, we find some poor fool who'll take the activators out into the fabric."

"Don't look at me," I said. "It's *your* invention."

"Be calm," Klox said. "No problem exists. None at all. It's all the same to a robot, you know."

"It is?" I heard myself say.

"If he's a philosopher robot," Klox said, seizing my two activators and jumping feet first into the gaping cavity. "For the good of the cau-u-u-se."

An instant, and the rumbling slowly began to subside.

Bending at the waist, I called down in the blackness. "What happened?"

"Somethin' grabbed my activator," Louie Mugger called back, "an' went away. Gemme outta here!"

"Gone," I said, straightening up.

"Gone," Sass said. "He moved so quickly there was no chance to stop him."

"Stop him?" I said. "You crazy? Who'd want to stop him?"

"Come on-n-n-n!" Louie Mugger screamed.

"Shut up down there," I yelled. "We'd better get a rope or something, eh?"

"Why'd he do it?" Sass asked wonderingly.

"You heard him. For the good of the cause."

"What cause?"

"Us," I said.

Sass peered at me in the darkness. "You must be joking."

"So what happens to Klox and the activators now?" I asked.

"Who knows?"

"How," Yalta said, "will we ever get back to our world?"

"You won't, my dear," Sass said. "None of you will, I'm afraid. Interworld is finished. The doors to the universe are closed forever."

"Forever is a long time," Wadsworth said.

"Don't worry," I told him. "With all the two-bit cities we've got around here, you're bound to find one that's just like home."

"Home?" Wadsworth said. "What's so great about that?"

"You've got me, kid," I said. "What's so great about anything?"

I, KLOX, AM NOW ELSEWHERE.

I turned to Gulach Grample. "It isn't gray any-more. . . ."

The tall Sass was shrieking, "My activators, they're gone!"

I reached into my coat pocket. It was empty.

"This world," Grample whispered, "has become real. . . ."

"And none of us is king!" the tall Sass wailed.

We were in a vacant, fenced-in lot. The sky was clearing, sunlight beginning to shimmer through. The tall buildings of the city rose on all sides of us. I could see the UN in the distance. Billboards demanded Smoke Kools, Drink Coke, Drive Olds. This was some world to make permanent.

"That's all done and gone with," I said to the tall Sass.

"At least I'm tall," he said.

Gulach Grample shrugged. "And I'm not fat any-more."

"Yeah," I said, "there seem to be some minor compensations for everyone. I bet I don't even say 'eh' again, eh?"

"Eh yourself, Dunjer," Grample said.